CHANTRESS

ALSO BY
AMY BUTLER GREENFIELD

Chantress Alchemy

Chantress Fury

A Perfect Red

Virginia Bound

CHANTRESS

A **CHANTRESS** NOVEL

AMY BUTLER GREENFIELD

MARGARET K. McELDERRY BOOKS
NEW YORK LONDON
TORONTO SYDNEY NEW DELHI

MARGARET K. McELDERRY BOOKS † An imprint of Simon & Schuster Children's Publishing Division † 1230 Avenue of the Americas, New York, New York 10020 † This book is a work of fiction. Any references to historical events, real people, or real places are used fictitiously. Other names, characters, places, and events are products of the author's imagination, and any resemblance to actual events or places or persons, living or dead, is entirely coincidental. † Text copyright © 2013 by Amy Butler Greenfield † Front cover photograph copyright © 2015 by Marie Hochhaus † Back cover photograph copyright © 2015 by Thinkstock † All rights reserved, including the right of reproduction in whole or in part in any form. † MARGARET K. McELDERRY BOOKS is a trademark of Simon & Schuster, Inc. † For information about special discounts for bulk purchases, please contact Simon & Schuster Special Sales at 1-866-506-1949 or business@simonandschuster.com. † The Simon & Schuster Speakers Bureau can bring authors to your live event. For more information or to book an event, contact the Simon & Schuster Speakers Bureau at 1-866-248-3049 or visit our website at www.simonspeakers.com. † Also available in a Margaret K. McElderry Books hardcover edition † The text for this book is set in Granjon LT. † Manufactured in the United States of America † First Margaret K. McElderry Books paperback edition May 2014 † 10 9 8 7 6 5 4 3 † Library of Congress Cataloging-in-Publication Data † Greenfield, Amy Butler. † Chantress / Amy Butler Greenfield.—1st ed. † p. cm. † Summary: "Fifteen-year-old Lucy discovers that she is a chantress who can perform magic by singing, and the only one who can save England from the control of the dangerous Lord Protector"—Provided by publisher. † ISBN 978-1-4424-5703-4 (hardcover) † ISBN 978-1-4424-5705-8 (eBook) † [1. Supernatural—Fiction. 2. Magic—Fiction. 3. Singing—Fiction. 4. Great Britain—History—17th century—Fiction.] I. Title. † PZ7.G8445Ch 2013 † [Fic]—dc23 † 2012012410 † ISBN 978-1-4424-5704-1 (pbk)

FOR T., WHO SINGS
HER OWN SONGS

Chantress

[a. OF. *chanteresse*, fem. of *chantere, -eor*, singer: see CHANTER and -ESS.]

1. female magician, sorceress, enchantress. **2.** A female chanter or singer; a singing woman; a songstress.

—*Oxford English Dictionary*

† † †

A dangerous disease requires a desperate remedy.

—attributed to Guy Fawkes (1570–1606)

CHAPTER ONE
THE SINGING

I was digging in the garden when I heard it: a strange, wild singing on the wind.

I sat back on my heels, a carrot dropping from my mud-splattered hands.

No one sang here. Not on this island.

Perhaps I'd misheard—

No, there it was again: a lilting line, distant but clear. It lasted hardly longer than a heartbeat, but it left me certain of one thing: It was more than a gull's cry I'd heard. It was a song.

But who was singing it?

I glanced over my shoulder at Norrie, hunched over a cabbage bed, a gray frizzle poking out from under her linen cap. As far as I knew, she was the only other inhabitant of this lonely Atlantic island, but it couldn't have been Norrie I had heard. For if there was one rule that my guardian set above all others, it was this one: There must be no singing. Ever.

Sing and the darkness will find you.

We were still dripping from the shipwreck when Norrie first told me this. She had repeated it often since then, but there was no need. The terror in her eyes that first time had silenced me immediately—that and my own grief, so deep I was drowning in it. The sea had taken my mother and had almost taken me. That was enough darkness to last me a lifetime; I had no desire to court more.

Not that I could recall very much about the shipwreck itself. Even the ship that had carried us off from England seven years ago had left no impression on me. Was it stout or shaky, that vessel? Had it foundered on rocks? Had storms broken its masts? I did not know. We had boarded that ship in 1660, when I had been eight years of age. Surely eight was old enough to remember? Yet my only recollections of that night came in broken fragments, slivers that were more sensation than sense. The sopping scratchiness of wet wool against my cheeks. The bitter sea wind snarling my hair into salty whips. The chill of the dark water as I slipped through it.

"Hush, child," Norrie would say whenever I dared mention any of this. "It was a long time ago, and a terrible night, and you were very young. The least said about it, the better."

"But my mother—"

"She's lost to us, lamb, lost to the wind and the waves." Norrie's face would always pucker in sadness as she said this, before her voice grew brisk. "It's just the two of us now, and we must make the best of it."

When Norrie took that tone, there was no refusing her. So

make the best of it we did, and if life on our island was not easy, it was far from desolate.

But we never sang. We never even whistled or hummed. We had no music of any kind. And if anyone had asked me, I would have said I did not miss it at all. . . .

Until now.

It was as if the singing had pierced a hole in me, a hole only it could fill. I sat silent, listening hard. Withered stalks rustled in the warm October sunlight. Gulls shrilled as they swooped toward the bluffs. And then, on the wind, I heard it again, the barest edge of a tune, almost as if the sea itself were singing—

"Lucy!"

I jumped.

From two rows away, Norrie waved her wooden trowel in her gnarled hand. "What's wrong with you, child? I've harvested a whole basket of cabbages in the time it's taken you to root out three carrots."

It didn't matter that I stood half a head taller than Norrie did, or that I thought of myself as nearly grown—she still called me *child*. But I was too used to it to bristle. Instead, I looked down at my meager takings. If Norrie had heard the music, surely she would have mentioned it. Since she hadn't, I wasn't going to. I didn't care to have her scolding me, yet again, for having too much imagination and not enough sense. Was the singing real? I was almost willing to swear it was . . . but not quite. Not to Norrie.

"Well, Lucy, what is it?" Norrie knocked the dirt from her trowel. "Are you ill?"

"No." If anyone looked ill, it was Norrie. Every year the harvest was more of a struggle for her. It scared me to see her cheeks so mottled, her stout shoulders drooping. I knew she wouldn't appreciate my saying so, though.

"You've been working since sunrise," I said instead. "Don't you think you've earned a rest?"

"Rest?" Beneath her rumpled cap, Norrie looked scandalized. "On Allhallows' Eve? Whatever can you be thinking?"

"I only meant—"

"Back to work now, and no more dawdling, please," Norrie said, her face anxious. "We need those carrots, every single one, if we're not to go hungry this winter."

"I'll get them all," I promised, hoping to calm her.

Norrie's brow relaxed a little, but her back was still tense as she bent over her cabbages again.

I wrapped my hands around a frill of carrot and sighed. Allhallows' Eve, the thirty-first of October—every year I dreaded this day. For if Norrie was strict as a general rule, on Allhallows' Eve she was at her absolute worst. From dawn to dusk, she worked us half to death, dragging in the last of the harvest and safeguarding the house against the coming night.

"After sunset," she would say. "That's when the true danger comes. The spirits walk, and mischief is in the air. We have to protect ourselves."

Maybe so. But to me the preparations seemed an endless burden, especially as I had never seen any sign of the mischief Norrie talked about.

Unless the singing . . . ?

But no. If singing was what Norrie had meant by mischief, I reasoned, surely she would've said so. And anyway, the sun was still golden bright. Rather low in the sky, but a good way from night.

Yet I worked a little harder, if only because I owed it to Norrie. For seven years, she had raised me singlehandedly—not without a fair amount of scolding and sighing, to be sure, but always with real affection. Now that she was growing older and her strength was ebbing, I knew it was up to me to return the favor, and look after her. If she wanted the harvest brought in before nightfall, then we would bring it in.

So I piled the carrots high, and when Norrie next turned to see me, she smiled in satisfaction. But while I worked, my thoughts were my own. With part of my mind, I listened out for the singing. The rest of me wished desperately for a life bigger than carrots and harvests and Norrie's superstitions.

I knew, none better, that the island had pleasures to offer— the silky white sand of its beaches; hidden coves speckled with shells; sun-drenched mornings at the water's edge. But they could not compensate for the isolation we endured, or for the relentless drudgery of our daily existence.

Our life in England had not been like this. I remembered a cottage by the sea, bright with my mother's wools and weaving, where guests told stories by the fire. Before that, I had only a scattered patchwork of memories, but they were colorful and varied: a game of hide-and-seek in a castle's great hall, a tiny garret room perched by the River Thames, the green smell of bracken by a forest lodge.

"We moved often in those early years," was Norrie's only comment about that time. "Not that I'm blaming your mother, mind you. She had to look out for herself, what with your father dying before you were even born, leaving her all alone. But the Good Lord didn't mean for a body always to be traveling hither and yon. Best to set yourself down in one place and stick to it, that's what I say."

She was as good as her word. She had rooted herself so deeply on the island that I half feared she would refuse rescue if it were offered.

Me, I would swim out to meet the ship. I longed for new sights and adventures, for a life not bounded by the island's shore. Above all, I longed for freedom—especially as Norrie grew ever more dogmatic about everything from what we had for Sunday breakfast to how many peat bricks we should burn in the fireplace.

With a sigh, I gathered up my carrots. Norrie had countless rules about those, too—not only about how to harvest and sort them but how to store and when to eat them.

A ship, I found myself praying. *Oh, please send a ship.*

But what was the use of praying? I had been waiting and watching and hoping for seven long years, and no ship had ever come.

Seven years, and no rescue in sight. Seven long years on this island. And how many more to follow?

Wincing, I rose and tossed my carrots into the waiting baskets. They thumped as they hit the pile—and that's when I heard the singing again.

The notes cascaded around me, stronger this time and more urgent. For a reckless moment, I wanted nothing so much as to give voice to the music myself, and sing it back to the wind. But then, like a muzzle, came Norrie's warning, the endless refrain I'd heard since childhood:

Sing and the darkness will find you.

I closed my eyes.

"Lucy!"

I blinked, and the music vanished.

Norrie was standing before me. "Lucy, did I hear you *humming?*"

"No. Of course not." I hadn't been humming, had I? I would have known if I had.

"It wasn't me you heard," I said. "It's something else. A sort of singing sound in the wind. I don't know what it is."

Norrie's eyes opened wide.

"Listen! There it is again." This time I took care not to drink the music in too deeply. It wouldn't do for Norrie to guess how it made me feel. "I can't think where it comes from, can you? Could it be a bird—a new one blown in by the winds?" Another possibility struck me, and I glanced toward the bluff in excitement. "Or maybe . . . a ship? I haven't been able to keep a proper lookout today, not with the harvest." This had been a bone of contention between us at breakfast; I had wanted to make my usual observations, but Norrie said we couldn't afford the time.

"Maybe someone is coming to rescue us, someone who doesn't know you shouldn't sing here—"

Norrie's leathery cheeks turned pale. "Child, where is your stone?"

I blinked. "My stone?" I touched my hand to the heavy, clay-red pendant that hung on a silver chain under my dress. It was a gift from my mother, all I had left of her. I never took it off, not even when bathing. "Here, of course. Why?"

Instead of answering, Norrie said, "It's time we went inside."

I looked at her in surprise. "Now?"

"Yes."

"But the cabbages—"

"Leave them be."

I stared at her. That didn't sound like Norrie—Norrie who every year insisted on gathering every scrap from the garden on Allhallows' Eve. "I don't understand."

"What's to understand? We've worked long enough today. You said so yourself. Come inside."

Norrie spoke stoutly enough, but in the late afternoon light, I saw a sheen on her face like the start of the sweating sickness. All thoughts of singing and music flew out of my head. If Norrie was feverish, I must get her to bed.

Tucking her hand in my arm, I steered her toward the cottage.

† † †

Even though it was a good hour or more until sunset, the cottage was half-dark already. Its windows were too few to let in much light. But I would have known Norrie's kitchen anywhere by its smell alone—a rich, earthy mix of peat and tarragon and rue. Usually there was soup simmering too, but on Allhallows' Eve Norrie always insisted that the iron cauldron hang empty while the remains of the old year's fire burned out beneath it.

"You sit down," I told Norrie. "I'll bring you a blanket to keep off the chill."

"No need, child. No need." Now that we were inside, Norrie looked and sounded more like her usual self. But I brought the blanket anyway, and when I came back through the kitchen doorway, I saw her put a hand to her heart.

"You really are ill, then," I said, alarmed.

Again Norrie waved me away. "No, child. No."

"But you're so pale—"

"It's only that it quite takes me aback sometimes, how much you look like your mother. Same gray eyes, same little cat's chin." She looked me over, then added reprovingly, "Of course, your hair is wilder."

I scraped back my tangled curls without protest, not wanting to interrupt. Norrie rarely spoke of my mother, even when pressed—a great disappointment to me, for my own memories of her were few.

But it seemed that Norrie was done with the past. "Goodness!" She pushed away my blanket. "Look at how low the sun is. I must get the seaweed before dark."

It was an Allhallows' Eve tradition that Norrie insisted upon: We always boiled freshly gathered seaweed in a cauldron over the new fire, then drank the broth to protect ourselves from harm. Norrie was exacting about the kind of seaweed it had to be, which made the whole chore more tedious, and another time I might have let her go off by herself to find it. But not now, not when I was so worried about her.

"You rest here. I'll go down to the cove." I reached for a netted sack by the door, handy for carrying the slimy seaweed.

Norrie snatched the bag out of my reach. "No!"

I stared at her. Norrie could be stern, but she rarely shouted and she never snatched.

"You will not go out that door." Norrie blocked the way forward. "Not tonight. Not while there's breath in my body to stop you."

CHAPTER TWO
THE LETTER

I took a step back and stared at Norrie, sure at first that it must be fever that had made her shout. But when I looked in her eyes, it wasn't illness I saw. It was suspicion and fear.

"Norrie, what is it? What's wrong?"

Her shaking fingers tangled themselves in the netted bag, but she didn't answer.

Why was she behaving so strangely? I cast my mind over the afternoon. "It's the singing, isn't it?" I could see from her face I was right. "You think it was me. And now you don't trust me."

"You were *humming*, Lucy. I heard it with my own ears."

"But I told you: That was the singing. It was like birdsong, or the wind in a seashell, only clearer somehow—"

"I heard no singing," Norrie said flatly. "Only you humming."

She said this with such conviction that it stopped me short. Was Norrie right? Had I been humming without knowing it? "You didn't hear the singing?"

"No. And if singing is what *you* heard, that's a very bad sign. Someone or something is trying to beguile you, that's what I think. So it's best you keep indoors today, out of their reach."

"Someone—or something?" I repeated uncertainly.

"An early piece of Allhallows' Eve mischief, most likely."

"But why would I hear the singing, and not you?"

Norrie looked flustered. "You ask too many questions, child. But none of them will change my mind one whit. Tomorrow you can go out again. But not today, not on Allhallows' Eve."

I touched my hand to my stone. Was I being kept inside because of superstition—or something more?

"Don't look at me that way." Norrie's voice sharpened. "Your mother—" She broke off.

"My mother what?" I felt a tingle of fear. "Norrie, you must tell me."

A mistake to use "must" with Norrie. Her broad chin jutted forward. "There's some things best not meddled with, Lucy. You'll learn that in time. All you need to know is this: You won't be going out again today. I may have more to say on the subject someday, child. But not now."

Child. The word suddenly seared like a burn. "I'm not a child," I snapped. "I'm fifteen. Sixteen this winter. That's old enough to hear the truth."

"If you're not a child, then stop fussing like one," Norrie said, unimpressed. "We've no time to waste. It's only an hour before sunset, and I need to gather the seaweed. While I'm gone, I expect you to look after the house." Her face sharpened with worry. "And don't you dare go outside. If you do, you could land both of us in terrible trouble."

These obscure warnings were driving me mad. "What kind of terrible trouble?" When she didn't answer, I said, more insistently, "You know I would never hurt you—"

"Not on your own, no." Norrie shook her head. "But you didn't even know you were humming, child. What else might you do if the singing got hold of you? Have you thought of that?"

I hadn't, not until then. But as she spoke, I remembered how those wild notes had pierced me to the core, and how desperately I'd longed to sing them back.

What else might I do? The truth was, I didn't quite know. Not for certain, not anymore. It was as if everything I knew about myself were no longer rock, but shifting sand. I looked at the battered door behind Norrie, suddenly glad that it stood between me and the wind.

"Very well," I said. "You go. I'll stay."

"Good girl." Norrie wrapped herself in her cloak. "Mind you prepare the hearth exactly as I've told you. And whatever you do, keep your stone close and don't open the door. There's great danger at hand."

"What kind of danger?" I asked again in frustration. "Why won't you tell me?"

But Norrie offered no explanations before she clumped out the door.

† † †

After Norrie left, I stared at the black hearth. With the afternoon almost over and the fire in cinders, the room was cold as death, and nearly as dark. I shivered in spite of myself. Why had I heard the singing when Norrie hadn't? And what was I to do about the fact that some contrary part of me was still longing to hear it again, even if it might lead to disaster?

Well, the answer to the last question was clear enough. For seven years now, Norrie had been instructing me in the rituals of Allhallows' Eve. To keep myself safe, I needed only to follow her instructions to the letter.

Moving sure and fast, I took up the poker and scattered the last embers of the fire. After that, I covered the hearth with lavender and rue and rosemary, herbs of protection that Norrie had picked that morning from our garden. By Norrie's own edict, the new fire could not be lit until the sun set, so there was nothing more to be done there.

I moved on to the sweeping, making quick work of the task. Now and again, however, I stopped to gaze through the kitchen's hatched windowpane, taking care not to disturb Norrie's potted bay tree on the sill. The tiny tree was Norrie's most cherished plant, the only one she never allowed me to touch. A single shiny leaf was enough to shield a person from every kind of wickedness, or so she always said.

Craning my head around the glossy leaves, I saw no sign of Norrie. Of course, it took a while to get down to the cove and back, and Norrie was not exactly fleet-footed. But the wind was rising, and the way it shook the windows made me uneasy. Was Norrie as invulnerable as she believed herself to be?

To quiet my mind and combat the shadows, I lit a bayberry candle.

Rattle went the window, and *rattle* again. I put the broom back in the corner and set the candlestick on the table that hulked in the middle of the room.

Rattle, rattle . . . SMASH!

I whirled around. The wind had battered the window open, and the shattered pane hung crookedly from its hinges. Beneath it lay Norrie's bay tree, a mass of shards and broken leaves.

I stooped down in dismay. Was it chance that it had fallen? Or was it an omen—for Norrie, for me, for us both?

There was no time to contemplate the question, for the window was hanging open and the wind was rushing through. Heart racing, I stuffed it shut with the thick woolen blanket I'd brought out for Norrie. It sealed the wind out, but at a cost: The room became still darker.

I turned back in distress to the scattered debris of the bay tree itself. I scooped up some fragments of clay pot, then stopped as something odd caught my eye. Matted in the tangle of roots was a small, flat box.

I teased it away and took it over to the candle. Slender and no larger than my hand, it shone like silver in spots. Most of it, however, was a rusty black, and the corners were eaten away. I tugged at the lid till it popped off.

Inside the box was a letter. Folded into a packet, badly spotted and water-stained, it bore a single line above its seal:

For my daughter, Lucy, in case I do not return . . .

For a moment, I was so bewildered I could neither move nor breathe. A letter for me? From my mother? After all this time?

Norrie had always told me that nothing remained of my mother—that her possessions had been lost in the shipwreck. And yet here, tangled in Norrie's plant, was this letter.

Norrie must have known about it. Indeed, she must have hidden it herself. Which meant Norrie had lied to me.

A flame of anger shot through me, and my hands tightened on the letter. How could Norrie have kept it from me?

I scanned the line of handwriting again: . . . *in case I do not return* . . .

But that made no sense. It wasn't as if my mother had planned to leave me. My mother had drowned.

Or had Norrie lied about that, too?

Fingers trembling, I broke the seal and flattened out the letter. Entire pages were blotted out by water damage, and the remaining handwriting was so small and faded that it would have been difficult for me to read even in daylight. By candlelight, I could decipher only a few complete sentences at the very start of the letter:

My dearest daughter, I sang you here for your safety.

I stopped and read the phrase again: *Sang you here?* What did she mean?

I will do everything in my power to return for you within a few days, at most a few weeks, but nothing is certain, and I know that if you are reading this, it is because I have failed. The very idea of this pains me almost beyond bearing. My only comfort is that Norrie will look after you, and that when you reach your fifteenth birthday, she will give you this letter. . . .

But she did not, I thought. She did not. She hid it from me instead. And now the letter is almost unreadable. All I could make out on the rest of that page were a few words near the bottom: *singing . . . careful . . . stone . . . Chantress . . . Allhallows . . . magic . . .*

Magic?

On the next page, only a single phrase was legible, but it took my breath away: *. . . when you sing, it will bring you home.*

Home. I thought with longing of England, of the small cottage by the sea where we had lived, and of the castle keep and the River Thames and the other places I remembered mostly in dreams. And then I wondered: *Sing what?*

Frustrated, I leaned closer to the candle, trying to shape stains into words, until the edges of the parchment nearly caught fire. I pulled back sharply, but not before I saw a word after *stone* that looked like *off.*

Take the stone off?

I reached for the pendant swinging against my skin. Was this the stone my mother had meant?

The winds outside the cottage were gathering strength, but I hardly heard them. I folded my mother's letter, tucked it into my sleeve, and peered down at my stone. It looked just as it always did: a dense, brick-red disc about the size of a walnut. Heavy as granite, it was as bumpy and plain as could be. There was nothing magical about it whatsoever. But perhaps it only revealed its powers once it was off its chain.

Never take that stone off, Norrie had told me. *It's meant to protect you.*

But then Norrie had lied about my mother. Who was to say she hadn't lied about this?

There was only one way to find out. Yet my hand slowed as I reached for the pendant. Almost as long as I could remember, I had been following Norrie's rules. The thought of breaking them—deliberately, perhaps irrevocably—made my heart pound.

The wind howled at the cracks in the window, making the candle dance. I thought I caught the whisper of a tune.

This is it. This is your chance to go home. Be bold, and take it.

I grasped the chain and pulled it over my head.

The moment the stone was off, the songs came for me—hundreds of them, humming like bees, flickering like firelight, crossing like shadows. And the strongest one was the wild tune I'd heard in the garden. This time, however, it went on and on. It spoke of the sea and of home and of times long past. It tugged at my heart and my throat and my lips. *Sing me*, it said.

And I did.

I had no idea what the words were, or what phrase came next. But I did not care. A dizzying sense of freedom flooded over me. All I wanted to do was give voice to the notes that came to me, one after another, in an endless stream of sound. We climbed together, strong and sure, rising ever higher. I felt as if I were flying.

Sing and the darkness will find you.

Norrie's warning rang out in my mind. But it seemed to come

from somewhere far away, somewhere very much farther than the music itself.

I hardly even noticed when Norrie herself banged the door open. With a horrified cry, she bounded forward and clutched my wrist, the net of seaweed dripping in her hand.

"Lucy! No!"

But already the wind was rising. It swirled through the room, midnight black, and caught us both in its grasp. As the candle went out, the song rose to a shriek, and everything around us vanished.

CHAPTER THREE

CHANTRESS BLOOD

After the wind seized us, I could see nothing whatsoever. Not the candle, not the room, not even my own bare hands. Worse still, I touched only emptiness. There was no floor beneath me, no table, no walls. From the pressure around my wrist, I guessed Norrie was still with me, yet I could not see or hear her.

I nearly broke off singing then, but the song had a powerful grasp, and it refused to leave me so easily. It filled my throat and opened my lips and insisted on being sung. In that terrible void, it was all I had left, so I clung to it, taking each note as it came, giving each its full measure. And with each note I sang, I allowed myself to trust the song a little more—to believe that I was indeed leaving the island and going home.

Just as my confidence soared, the song fractured, splitting into harmonies I did not understand.

Which line to follow? I hesitated. Only a moment, only a

beat. But thick and strong as rope, the music coiled around me and pulled Norrie away.

I screamed, and the darkness closed in like a shroud on my face. Above me, I saw a gray arch, like the curve of a cresting wave. Was I about to drown?

But no, it was growing light now, and the wave above me was solid, was still, was . . .

Stone.

Above my head, the golden-gray vaulting soared, its interlocking arches meeting in exquisite geometry. And as the last of the darkness lifted, I saw to my astonishment that I was standing in a long and elegant room, facing crimson draperies that hung like drooping sails. Near me, a vast hearth glowed, its flames reflected in glass cases that lined the rest of the room. In those cases were books by the thousands. Books in chains. Books glowing with gilt. Books blackened with age. Books upon books upon books. And not a soul in sight to read them.

My throat convulsed. I had worked magic. I had sung myself off the island. That alone dumbfounded me. But where was I? This was not the small cottage I remembered, or any other place I knew.

More dreadful question still—where was Norrie? For there was no sign of her anywhere.

What have I done?

It was no use telling myself it was Norrie's own fault for keeping secrets. I was the one who'd chosen to sing, and now Norrie was lost. That was the plain truth of it. For all I knew, my magic had killed her.

She lives. It was the merest breath of a song in my ears. I strained to hear the rest, but the notes told me only that Norrie was alive—somewhere.

Oh, Norrie, how could I have lost you?

My hand tightened around my necklace, still twined around my fingers. I could reproach myself all day, but that wouldn't help Norrie one whit. I must act instead. I must find her. But how? With more singing?

I wasn't sure I had the stomach for that, given what my first song had brought about. And in any case, I couldn't hear the music anymore, not properly. It was fading so quickly that the soft notes were half swallowed up by the beating of my own heart.

My bewilderment only grew as I caught sight of the necklace still dangling from my fingers. In place of the dull ochre pendant I'd expected to see, a ruby sparkled. It glowed against my skin like a small red-hot sun.

I stared at it in dismay, then ran my fingers over it. To the touch, it was still my stone, the same size and shape and weight, with bevels and bumps in precisely the same places. But if it was my stone, why and how had it changed? And what was I to do with it?

Keep it around your neck, child. With Norrie's constant admonition ringing in my memory, I looped the necklace back in place. I couldn't tell if it was protecting me, but its familiar weight was comforting.

As I tucked the stone into my bodice, something rustled in my sleeve: my mother's letter, tucked there in haste and forgotten until now. After glancing around to make sure the library truly was empty, I hastened to the fire. Perhaps the letter had changed along with my stone, and now it would give me the guidance I needed.

Even in the bright firelight, however, the letter was no more legible than before. Discouraged, I tucked it back into my sleeve for safekeeping. Only then did I become aware that the last faint music had dwindled into nothing.

Unnerved by the silence, I looked around hesitantly. At the far end of the room, a massive door stood slightly ajar—apparently the only way out. But when I walked toward it, chill air wafted over me, smelling of damp and sawdust and something disturbing that I couldn't put a name to. I took a step back and turned toward the nearest bookcase. Perhaps before leaving I was meant to find something here: a guide to magic, perhaps, or another letter from my mother, or a map. Anything, really, that might help me feel a little less lost.

I pulled out the first book that came to hand, a thick volume that was out of line with the others. Bound in red and black leather, it was titled *Id. Chan.*

Looking for more clues, I leaned toward the hearth light and read the title page:

On the Identification of Chantresses,
Their Physical Marks and Characteristics;
Being also a Guide to Their Habits, Territories, and Powers,
Humbly Submitted to the Lord Protector,
by an Ardent Scholar
and Devoted Friend

Chantress. My mother had used that word in her letter. I pulled the book closer and rifled the pages. Was there anything here that might help me?

I was still scanning the Table of Contents when I heard a clank some distance behind me.

In a flash, I slipped the book back into place.

Where could I hide? The polished tables and cane chairs by the hearth were too bare and open to offer any refuge. And every other square inch of the library was devoted to books . . .

. . . except the draperies.

I bounded to the left-hand bay and parted the yards of flowing velvet. Behind them, a high window sat deep in the stone wall. So bubbled and skewed were its panes, however, that I could see very little through them—only a blurry twilight sky and a high, crenellated wall. Was I in a castle, then, or some grand manor house?

Well, wherever I was, I must take care not to be seen. I crouched under the window and rearranged the draperies. Leaving a tiny slit at eye level, I settled myself—and only just in time, because a panel by the fireplace swung open. A tall boy in dark clothes stepped through it and stole into the room.

At first, I guessed him to be somewhere around my own age, but then I wasn't so certain. Was he a year or two older, perhaps? It had been so long since I had seen anyone but Norrie, and there was an intensity about this boy that made him hard to pin down.

He padded along the line of shelves toward my own hiding place, till he was so close that I could see the fierce light in his eyes.

Crossing to the other side of the room, he scanned the cases, then knelt and removed a moss-green volume. Taking a quick look behind him, he tucked it into his coat. Was he stealing it?

Voices rang out in the hall. The thief—if that's what he was—went still.

"Funny sort of place to meet, a library," a man in the hall complained. "And a library about magic, at that."

"Keep quiet, Giles!" a cross voice replied. "D'you want the whole world to hear you?"

The boy made a run for it, but he was too far from the hidden panel to reach it easily. Instead, he veered toward the draperies closest to him, some distance from mine. He vanished from my sight as the massive library door swung open.

I shrank back against the wall, then wished I hadn't, for I could no longer see anything. But it was too late now to adjust the curtains, for the men were coming into the room.

"Ravendon House is one of the greatest establishments in London, indeed in any city in England," the cross man was saying. "And one of the largest and oldest as well. You must understand, Giles: It's an honor to be invited here."

I heard the word *London* with some relief. At least I was in my home country—if not in any house I remembered.

"I wouldn't take the place on a silver plate, myself," Giles answered. "It's a cursed, drafty old warren. And say what you will, this library is a deuced odd place to meet."

"It's not for you to question Lord Scargrave's judgment. Not if you're the King's man."

"Of course I'm the King's man," Giles harrumphed. "None truer, 'pon my word. I'd not turn spy for him otherwise. Informing on family, on friends—it's not a gentlemanly thing to do, eh?"

"It's for the good of the country," his friend said sharply. "And if our friends and family behave themselves, they won't have anything to worry about. You ought to be pleased that Lord Scargrave has called us here. His invitation is a mark of favor and trust."

"But—"

"Enough. You may have forgotten where you are, but I haven't. And I've no wish to find myself before my lord Spymaster in the Council Chamber. Or worse."

"Forget I said anything," Giles said nervously.

"Let's talk of something else, then. No, wait a moment—I think I hear him coming."

Blinded by the draperies, I could not see anyone enter. But I heard the heavy tread of footsteps on the library floorboards, and the groan of the door swinging shut.

A deep voice said, "Gentlemen, you know why I have called you here."

It was a pleasant voice, even musical, but there was a note in it that made me keenly aware of how very dark and cold it was by the window, and how very thin even the thickest velvet curtains were when nothing else stood between you and discovery.

"You have offered to serve the King," the deep voice went on. "You have offered to serve me."

"Yes, Lord Scargrave," the two men murmured.

"That being so, I give you this simple task: to listen carefully to those around you, and to report any disloyalty to me, so that I may keep His Majesty safe."

More murmuring: "Yes, my lord. Yes."

"And for the sake of His Majesty, I set another task before you as well, a task I ask of everyone in my employ: to keep a watch for anyone who works magic by singing, or any other sign of Chantress blood. You know what to look for?"

"The spiral scar," said Giles's friend promptly. "Raised and white and no bigger than a penny piece, right at the base of the forearm."

My breath caught in my throat as I fingered the scar on my arm. A birthmark, that's what Norrie had called it. But Giles's friend had described it precisely. And what had my song been, but magic?

"Correct. Should you meet any such, you will inform me at once." The deep voice added, "Only me, you understand. Not one word to anybody else."

The answer came in unison, swift and obedient. "We shall report to you—and only to you."

"You had better." The voice was no longer pleasant, but harsh and full of discord. "Otherwise, I shall give you to the Shadowgrims."

CHAPTER FOUR
EDGE AND DROP

I felt a chill that had nothing to do with the cold window above me. I stood still as a deer, not daring to move, except to run my fingertips over the scar on my arm—the scar that would betray my Chantress nature if they found me. Would I, too, be sent to the Shadowgrims, whoever or whatever they were? The very sound of the word made me want to retch.

A matter of a few yards, that was all that lay between me and discovery. A few yards and the flick of the draperies, and I would stand there exposed.

Pulse racing, I trained my ears on the man Giles and his friend. They were falling over themselves to prove their loyalty.

"No need to resort to the Shadowgrims, my lord."

"We will report only to you, Lord Scargrave. You have our word."

"Our solemn word."

"Our *sacred* word."

"I will hold you to it." The harshness in Scargrave's voice had given way to something like pleasure again. "We must each go about our business now. If you serve me well, you shall be rewarded. But remember: I depend on your vigilance and your discretion. And I have little tolerance for error—either of fact or of judgment."

"We understand, my lord."

"Yes, indeed, my lord."

Silence followed—a searching silence that made me wish I could disappear into the stones of the wall behind me.

"Then I bid you good evening," Scargrave said at last. "But do not forget: I will be watching."

Heavy footsteps crossed the floor again, and the library door heaved open and shut. Behind the curtain, I felt my fear lift a little, and I guessed that Scargrave was gone.

In the quiet, Giles asked, "What do you think he means by 'rewarded'?"

"For the right information, he pays even gutter brats in gold," his friend said. "And he has the power to raise gentlemen in both title and estate. Who knows? We may soon be calling each other baron or viscount, if only we supply him with what he needs."

"And if we find him a Chantress?"

His friend laughed. "We may call the King himself our cousin. Truly, Giles, our fortunes would be made."

"Then let's hope we find one soon."

"It's not likely. But we may still be able to better ourselves in small ways, simply by reporting on disloyalty among our own crowd. Speaking of which, it's time we found them again, or they'll wonder where we are."

A chair scraped, and before me the curtains stirred ever so slightly. Had I given myself away? *Please God, no.*

To my relief, no one came running. Perhaps they hadn't been looking—or perhaps it was I who had been shaking, and not the curtains. I steeled myself into absolute stillness, as their voices grew fainter.

"Do you think I could borrow one of these books?" Giles said. "Something that would help me track a Chantress down, I mean to say."

"Honestly, Giles! You're such a dunderhead sometimes. This is Lord Scargrave's private library. No one takes books from it without his permission. That's why he posts guards outside the door: to search us when we go."

"They're going to search us? Our persons, you mean? I say, you might have warned me!"

If Giles was upset, I was even more so. How could I escape this room, let alone the house, if there were guards outside the door—guards who would know I hadn't entered the normal way, who would see my scar if they searched me, who would know me for a Chantress?

As I tried to steady myself, I found the gap in the curtains again, just in time to see the backs of Giles and his friend as they passed out of the room.

No sooner had they left than the thief sprinted out of hiding. I caught my breath; I had half forgotten he was there. Making for the fireplace, he touched the wall beside it with a practiced hand. When the hidden panel sprang out, he ducked down and pulled it shut behind him.

Where did he go? was my first thought.

And then: *Can I follow?*

Shaky-limbed from the enforced stillness, I stumbled out from the draperies. Black and glossy as spilled ink, the wood carvings around the fireplace were a rich jumble of fruits and trailing vines. When I peered closely, I could see the tracings of separate panels, but I had no idea which one hid the passageway, or how to open it.

Apples, pears, grapes. Heart racing, I pushed and pulled at each carved fruit. Nothing moved.

"Why should I remove my coat?" Giles shouted from the hall. "I've not so much as touched one of those poxy books!"

How close he sounded! I looked over my shoulder and saw that the library door was still ajar. At any moment, someone could walk in and see me.

Panic made me hit the next bunch of apples hard. A stem slid to one side, and a panel swung open, revealing a narrow staircase that led down into the dark.

Another bellow went up in the hallway. There was no time to think. I hopped through the panel and pulled it shut behind me.

Alone in darkness, I stood at the top of the stairs. It was too late to go back and get a candle. All I could do now was to try to get out—and not cross paths with the thief who had led me here.

The thief . . . where was he? In this blackness he could be standing five feet away, and I would not know it.

I held my breath and listened. Nothing.

Still, it took me some moments to gather my courage and start down the stairs by feel alone, sliding my worn leather shoes to the edge of each step, then bracing myself for the drop: edge and drop, edge and drop, a score of times and more. The walls, so close together, helped me keep my balance, but when a many-legged creature whisked over my hand, I had to bite back a cry.

What was that?

Whatever it was, it was gone as soon as it had come. But from the murmurs and rustlings around me, I had the sinking feeling there might be worse to come.

Edge and drop.

What if I can't find my way out?

Edge and drop.

What if I'm trapped here forever?

Edge and drop—until I was brought up short against a solid wall.

I ran my hands along it. No, not quite solid. For over on the right, there were hinges. Opposite them, I located a lever.

Before trying it, I listened out. Distant rumbling, and nothing more. I eased the door open, only to find a dimly lit brick wall a few feet in front of me. A new smell came through the door, made up of sweet hay and dung and sweat and something else I couldn't quite remember. I sniffed the air again, and it came to me: horses. A smell I had almost forgotten in my years on the island.

When I edged around the brick wall, I found myself in a shadowy stable full of carriages and carts and hay. At the entranceway, where great doors opened onto the night, a donkey stood waiting, hitched to a two-wheeled cart.

I crept forward and crouched by the doors. Lit only by torches that cast dim pools of light, the stable yard was quiet, except for the guards at the gate some distance away, who were talking among themselves.

Knowing that I could not pass by them unnoticed, I eyed the donkey and cart again. Presumably someone had readied them for a journey—and surely that journey must involve passing through the gates. Moreover, there were several barrels and boxes inside the cart, half buried in straw. Enough straw, indeed, that it could cover a person entirely. Provided she were daring enough to try.

I looked back at the guards, who were still talking. Could I leap into the cart without being seen?

Heart pounding, I hoisted myself over the cart edge and ducked down. No guards came running, and the donkey's only reaction was to flick his ears. I sent grateful thoughts his way and burrowed down into the straw.

And none too soon. Only a few minutes after I had settled myself, the cart rumbled beneath me. I was on the move.

CHAPTER FIVE
THE DONKEY CART

As the cart bumped and rattled its way through the cobbled stable yard, I braced myself against the barrels. When the cart thumped to a halt, the ruby leaped against my skin, and I shivered.

"Papers?" a voice barked.

"Right here," the cart driver replied, his strong, young voice cheerful and easy.

"So you're a ratcatcher, eh?"

"That I am."

"With a pass signed by the Lord Protector himself, I see. Well, that's as good a warrant as one could wish. But what's in the barrels and boxes?"

"Traps and cages and bait. And a few dead rats."

Dead rats? In the barrels right next to me? I forced myself not to recoil.

The easy voice went on, "You can check if you want to."

"Oh, we'll check them, all right. And don't you move till we do."

A long pause. I forgot my qualms about rats and prayed only that I would not be discovered. The cart jiggled as someone jumped on.

My heart thudded so loud I was sure he would hear it. The straw itched at my ankles, but I dared not move. How much did it hide? Could he see my head, my shoes?

Something clunked. "Traps in this one, like he said," a hoarse voice called out. "One with a dead rat in it. You want me to open the rest, sir?"

"No, that will do."

The cart shook again as the guard jumped off.

"Pass on through," the inspector ordered. "But if a Watchman stops you, you'll have to show your papers again."

The cart jerked into motion. Still fearful of discovery, I stayed as still as I could, but my mind was racing. Who were the Watchmen? Would they inspect the cart too?

It seemed an age before the driver spoke again. "Not too far from home now, Aristotle."

Aristotle? Was that the donkey's name? And where was home?

Best if I didn't stay in the cart long enough to find out, I told myself. But when I flexed my numb arms, I discovered that my mother's letter was no longer in my sleeve. A quick search in the straw revealed it wasn't there, either.

I must have dropped it in Ravendon House.

Despair swept over me—and then in its wake, sick fear. Was it the loss of the letter? The aftershock of working magic? Whatever it was, I had never known dread like this.

"Halt there!" A gutteral shout. "Halt for the Watch!"

The cart stopped. Buried in the straw, I went rigid with panic.

"Your pass," a Watchman bellowed. "We must see it."

"H-here," the cart driver said, all easiness gone.

The strain in his voice only whetted my own terror.

"Inspect the cart," the Watchman shouted. "Open everything."

Watchman boots boarded and set the cart planks shaking. Barrels opened and closed. Waves of heat washed over me, and an acrid taste like smoke burned in my throat. I felt roasted alive by fear. They were almost on top of me now, almost—

"Everything's in order," a Watchman called out above me.

"Come down, then," said his commander. "And you, driver, be on your way! Do not dawdle."

The donkey jerked forward, and the cart bounced ahead. My terror dwindled, replaced by a deep languor, as if my limbs had dissolved to jelly. For long minutes, I lay motionless in the straw, too exhausted to do anything but be dimly glad I had not been discovered.

"Whoa." The low command barely disturbed the cold night air. The cart swerved, then halted.

All at once, my languor left me. Had we arrived at our destination—whatever it was? Had I missed my chance to escape?

A soft moan like hinges, and the cart moved again, but only a little. I huddled deep in the straw. I would hide, I decided—hide and hope to flee later, when all went quiet. Hinges again, and the clunk of a door shutting.

"Well done, Aristotle." It was the same strong, easy voice. "That was a close call, and no mistake. But there will be extra hay tonight, you can be sure of that. And perhaps a carrot or two."

The door groaned open again.

"I've been listening for you." A new voice, older and worried. "You are safe?"

"Safe—and successful."

"Oh, well done, Nat!" A hesitation. "And no one suspected . . . ?"

"Not a soul," came the confident answer. "Let me unhitch Aristotle, and then I'll come in and tell you about it."

A moment later, I felt the cart drop beneath me. I flailed about for a handhold, but the straw slipped every which way, and I went with it. I hit the back of the barrels hard and slammed into the floor.

Dazed, I brushed the straw from my eyes. A tall, fierce-eyed boy swam into view, a horrified look on his face. Beside him was an elderly graybeard whose spectacles shone like cat's eyes in the dim lantern light.

"Who is this?" the graybeard asked.

"I've never seen her before," the boy said.

But I've seen you, I thought, gulping in dismay.

He was the thief from the library.

As the old man bolted the doors, I looked around for another way to escape. I could see none. The murky room—a stable, to judge from the manger and stall—was no more than two yards high and a few yards across, and its stone walls had no windows.

The thief-boy drew a knife and hauled me up by my elbow. "How did you get into my cart?"

Before I could answer, the old man flashed the lantern in my face. "Her eyes are normal."

"Not the Raven's Own, then. But some kind of spy, I warrant." The boy tightened his grip on me and brought the knife close. "Who are you? How long have you been following me?"

I knew better than to say I'd seen him steal the book. "I haven't been following you, and I mean you no harm. Let me go."

"Not on your life." His grip was relentless. "You're a spy. Confess it!"

"I'm not. I swear I'm not." I tried not to show how much his knife frightened me.

The old man spoke, his voice quiet but firm. "Release her, Nat."

Nat bristled, but his grip slackened ever so slightly. "Is that wise, sir? If she's a spy, she's a danger to us."

"If she is one, yes. But there are other possibilities, and we must consider them. For the moment, allow her to tell her story in peace."

With a grimace, Nat let go of me. "Don't think you can run," he told me, his knife still at the ready. "I'll be guarding the door. And there is no other way out."

Trying not to show how shaken I felt, I turned to the old man. His glasses caught the light and shimmered, then cleared, revealing a pair of thoughtful and observant eyes. "Let us begin again," he said, his voice careful and slow. "You will tell us your name, please."

Despite his gentle manner, I was wary, especially as Nat continued to watch my every move. I selected a name from thin air. "I'm called Bess, sir."

"And how did you come to be in our donkey cart, Bess?"

The silence stretched out uncomfortably as I tried to concoct a believable reply, one that avoided all mention of the library. "I'm a servant at"—what was the name of the place?—"Ravendon House, sir. But I was badly treated, and I wanted to leave, only I was afraid they would punish me if I tried. So this evening, when my duties were done, I slipped down to the stable yard, where I saw the cart waiting. No one was looking, so I climbed into it. And here I am."

"Her eyes shift when she speaks," Nat observed from his corner by the door.

"So they do," the old man agreed. "But that may be mere nervousness. For now, let us give her the benefit of the doubt." He nodded at me again. "Tell me, Bess, how long have you worked at Ravendon House?"

"Er . . . two years, sir," I said, doing my best to look steadily at him. "Or thereabouts."

"And where did you live before then?"

Telling the truth was out of the question. "In London, sir."

"In which part?"

I racked my brains for an acceptable answer. "By the river."

"On what street?"

"River Street." Surely there must be some such address.

The old man rubbed the bridge of his nose. "I do not know this place. In what neighborhood is it?"

I had no answer.

The old man and Nat looked at each other.

"Under your hand," the old man said suddenly to me, his face stern. "What is it you hide?"

Flummoxed, I found I was covering the spot where the ruby lay hidden under my bodice. I flushed and let my hand drop. "Nothing."

Nat darted forward. "There's a chain around her neck."

I fumbled at my kerchief, but too late. Nat's deft fingers were already closing in.

"Nat, you will leave this to me," the old man said.

As he spoke, I heard a strange snatch of song.

"Ouch!" Nat pulled back in shock. "What was that?"

Did he mean the music?

"It wasn't me." Or had I worked some magic unconsciously? Unsettled by the thought, I whirled away from Nat, only to trip against the cart. As I tried to right myself, the stone slipped out of my bodice, flashing with red fire.

The room went silent. Then Nat whistled and reached for the stone.

"No!" I ducked. "It's not yours."

"And you expect me to believe it's yours?" Nat scoffed. "Who did you steal it from?"

"It was a gift from my mother," I said, stung.

"She must have been a bloody princess, then. Or was she the one who stole it?"

"No." The accusation outraged me. "She was—"

I stopped myself just in time. To say anything more about my mother or myself would be dangerous. And much as I was tempted to name Nat himself for a thief, that too seemed unwise.

As Nat and I eyed each other warily, the old man spoke.

"Neither a princess nor a thief, your mother—but something else entirely, yes? Something which you do not wish to name?"

My heart wobbled in my chest.

The old man's spectacles had caught the light again, glimmering like little moons. "You will please show us your left hand."

I flinched and backed away.

Quick as a wildcat, Nat clasped my left wrist and pulled me into the light. Above his long fingers, the mark showed clearly: a spiral the size of a penny piece, white as bones washed clean by the sea.

Nat gazed at me, eyes wide with shock. "You're a Chantress."

CHAPTER SIX
A SMALL BUT CONVINCING DISPLAY

"It's an old scar, nothing more." I wrenched my arm free and backed toward the door. "Let me go!"

Nat stepped toward me, blocking the way out. "You're a Chantress," he said again. The eager note in his voice made me sick. Was he already counting the reward money in his head?

Time to play my last card. I gave him as fierce a look as he had ever given me. "If you turn me in, I'll tell them about the book you stole."

Nat halted. "What book?"

"I saw you steal it from the library. I saw you go through the secret door, too."

"I didn't—"

"You did. I was there, and I followed you. And if you give me up to that awful Lord Scargrave, I'll tell him everything. So for your own sake, you'd better let me go."

I wanted to scare him. To my dismay, his shoulders relaxed,

and a glimmer of amusement appeared in his eyes. "Hand you over to Scargrave? Believe me, that's the very last thing we'd do."

I let out a deep breath. "So you'll let me go?"

"Oh no," Nat said. "You're not going anywhere. Not if we can help it."

I looked at him in renewed alarm. What did they want from me?

"There, there," the old man said. "We do not mean to frighten you, Nat and I. We are glad you have come to us, Chantress—you cannot imagine how glad."

I could see clearly past his lenses now, and there was no menace in his eyes, only kindness and concern and eagerness.

Or was that a trick of the light?

"Ah, I see you are still afraid," the old man said. "And that is to be understood, for there are many dangers before you, and you are very young. Much younger than I expected. And in trouble, too, it seems, or why would you be hiding in our cart? But we will not betray you. On my life, I, Cornelius Penebrygg, swear it to you. We wish only to help. You will take shelter in our house, yes?"

Though his face was earnest under his floppy cap, I hesitated. What he had said was true, however: I was in trouble—very great trouble. And there was no other help in sight.

"Yes," I said. "I will come with you."

Penebrygg looked relieved, but Nat shot him a worried look. "Sir, are you sure that—"

"Quite sure," Penebrygg said. "But we will do without the lantern on the way, yes, Nat? It is better that we go in darkness."

"Let me settle Aristotle first."

"Of course."

Nat said no more, but as he guided the donkey into the stall, he kept a wary eye on me. And to judge by the prickling in my spine, he continued to watch me even after he blew out the light.

† † †

With Penebrygg guiding my footsteps and Nat following close behind, we made our way across the uneven yard. It was a moonless night, and the gritty air was thick with fog.

Was Norrie somewhere in this city, somewhere nearby? I could only hope so, but every step I took seemed to be taking me farther away from her. I peered around blindly, wondering if I'd made the right decision in going along with Penebrygg, or whether I ought to take my chances and bolt.

Nat's hand came down on my shoulder. Had he guessed what I was thinking?

Penebrygg halted. "Mind the step," he whispered.

Nat propelled me forward, and I passed into a house even blacker than the yard outside, seasoned with damp and smoke and age.

"We'll go upstairs," Penebrygg said.

A flint scraped behind me as Nat lit the lantern again, but its glow was so faint that I had to climb the crooked staircase almost by feel. With a falling heart, I heard Nat locking doors behind us, floor by floor. Not much chance of escape, then, should I need to run.

But perhaps I wouldn't. As we climbed, Penebrygg offered me nothing but kindness, murmuring words of encouragement and steadying me when my footing went awry. Perhaps I'd been right to trust him, after all. From what he'd said earlier, he seemed to know something about Chantresses and their ways. Perhaps— I thought with a leap of my heart—he would even know how I could find Norrie.

When Penebrygg pushed open the door at the top of the stairs, I saw at first only a haze of sullen smoke, almost as thick as the fog outside. Squinting, I finally made out the outlines of a long, slant-roofed room, rife with mysterious shapes and shadows. Against the stone of the hearth, three silver globes gleamed in the haze, attached to a square contraption whose name and purpose I could not even begin to guess at. On the other side of the hearth stood a clock, and I could hear still more in the shadows, whirring and clicking like a flock of invisible birds.

"Here," Penebrygg said, handing me a cloak. "Wrap yourself up, and take the chair closest to the fire. It's a cold night."

As I bundled myself into the chair, Nat settled on a bench across from me, and busied himself with a scrap of wood and a knife—a smaller one than he'd had in the shed. His face was unreadable, and I found myself reaching for my stone as if seeking reassurance. Cool and heavy, it fitted pleasingly against my hand, and I sat up straighter.

Penebrygg motioned toward the small table at my side. "We've bread and cheese and apples here, if you're hungry."

He himself took a slice of bread and cheese, and Nat took an apple, so it seemed safe enough to eat. My stomach rumbled. It had been noon since I'd last eaten, noon on the island with Norrie. . . .

Remembering, my throat closed over, and I found I could barely choke the food down.

Penebrygg eased himself into the only chair left. "Now, then, Bess—"

"No." Having gone so far as to break bread with him, I was reluctant to keep up the pretense. "My name is Lucy. I did not tell you the truth before."

There was a moment's pause, and then Penebrygg said, "A wise precaution, I'm sure."

But Nat frowned. "If she lied to us about that," he said to Penebrygg, "who's to say she hasn't lied about everything? Maybe she's not a Chantress—"

"You yourself saw the mark, Nat," Penebrygg said. "And she has the stone."

"And very convincing they were too. But marks can be faked, and the ruby could be paste. I wouldn't put anything past Scargrave, would you?"

He seemed determined to disbelieve me, but I tried to keep my temper. "I haven't faked anything—"

Nat's knife flashed as he sank it into the wood. "We need more proof."

"Proof?"

"Work some Chantress magic for us," Nat said. "Right here, right now."

To my surprise, Penebrygg chuckled.

"Spoken like a true man of science, Nat. I have trained you well."
He adjusted his spectacles and looked at me. "I myself am inclined
to take you at your word. But Nat is right to be cautious. The stakes
are very high, and we ought to do this one last test: Choose what
song you will, and demonstrate your powers to us. Though you
must sing softly," he cautioned. "We do not want others to hear you."

They wanted me to work magic on demand? Well, perhaps I
could, at that. All I needed was a song to sing.

But what song? At the moment, I could hear nothing but the
fire's crackle and the incessant ticktocking of the clocks.

Take the stone off.

That's how it had worked before, hadn't it? As I took hold of
the stone, it caught the ebbing firelight, flaring red as flame. *Help
me*, I urged it silently. *Bring me magic that will amaze them.* And I
tugged it over my head.

A chill went over me as the room filled with music. Unfor-
tunately, the notes were as soft and indistinguishable as the murmuring I had heard in the Ravendon House library. I could not
make out any particular song, only random notes that faded as
soon as I trained my ear on them.

In the dark recesses of the room, the hidden clocks ticked off
the seconds.

I looked up and saw two faces looking back at me, one full of
skepticism, the other alight with faith.

"We ask for nothing very dramatic, you understand," Penebrygg
said with an encouraging smile. "A small but convincing display
is all that is required."

I looked helplessly back at him. "I can't give you one."

His genial face turned stern, and I saw something of Nat's mistrust in his eyes. "You cannot? Or you will not?"

Miserably aware that I looked not only like a failure but a fraud, I spelled out the problem. "I know nothing about being a Chantress. I am one, truly I am. But I never knew it before today."

Nat raised his eyebrows.

Penebrygg kneaded his bearded chin as if he did not know quite what to think. "Pray tell us more."

I briefly recounted my story. It sounded even more fantastical in the telling than it had in the living of it, and I faltered now and again as I caught sight of Nat's disbelieving face.

Penebrygg, however, listened to me with utter absorption. "So it was seven years ago that you arrived on the island?" he said at one point. "That would make sense."

And when I spoke of how the song had claimed me, and the wind had come for us, he exclaimed, "Extraordinary!"

When I finished my tale, there was silence. Penebrygg rubbed his spectacles on the edge of his sleeve, then pushed them back on his nose with a sigh. "I would give my eyeteeth to observe such magic. But you have not seen your guardian since you arrived? And you have no idea how to find her?"

I shook my head. "Do you?"

"Alas, no. I am only a workaday inventor, with nothing magic about me whatsoever. That said, perhaps we might be able to track her down by ordinary means, if we made discreet inquiries—"

"Stop," Nat interrupted. "Don't you see what she's doing? You asked her to show us her powers, and instead she's spun us a wild story. That doesn't sound like a Chantress to me. That sounds like a spy."

Penebrygg folded his arms across his chest. "What is the first duty of science, Nat?"

With evident reluctance, Nat answered, "To keep an open mind."

Penebrygg nodded. "We must not leap to conclusions—any of us. And I include myself. There is much in Lucy's tale that rings true to me, but it would be wise to gather more evidence." He turned to me. "You know nothing whatsoever about the ruby you carry?"

"Nothing to speak of, except that when I wear it, it's hard to hear the music."

"May I examine it more closely?"

I hesitated. I felt uneasy enough not having the stone around my neck; I couldn't imagine how much worse it would be if I actually handed it to someone else.

"You needn't let go of it," he assured me. "Merely hold it up to the light, so that I may see it better. I shall keep my distance, and I shall not touch it, I promise you."

As I lifted the ruby, Penebrygg pushed himself up from his chair and lit a taper from the fire. Bringing it close, he peered at the stone. "Ah, yes, that's it. And now turn it—no, stop a moment." He squinted. "Remarkable. What a shame that you lost your mother's letter! Let us hope that it lies undiscovered, or at least that Scargrave can make no more sense of it than you could."

"Is there nothing I can do?" I asked.

"About the letter? Not at the moment. But I can suggest another test that will prove whether you are truly a Chantress. Do you wish to continue?"

"Yes." Whatever it took to get their help in finding Norrie, I would do it.

"You are not too tired?"

"No." Despite the late hour and the smoky, shadowy room, I felt wide-awake.

"Very good. Now take the jewel and hold it in your hand. No, not like that. Not in your fist. Let it lie on your palm, like so."

It was difficult to obey Penebrygg, to release my fingers and let the ruby lie there in the open. The necklace had always been my private touchstone, and I wanted to keep it safe and sound, away from prying eyes. I shifted in my chair, forcing myself to keep my palm flat.

"Do not move," Penebrygg commanded. "Be still, and let me try to take it from you."

My fingers closed over the ruby of their own accord. "But it's mine!"

"If it is truly magic and truly yours, no one can take it away from you. Nat tried in the shed, do you not remember? And he did not succeed."

No one could take my stone away from me? Curious now, I opened my hand and let the ruby lie exposed on my palm.

Penebrygg reached for the ruby, but as his hand closed around it, a savage music rang in my ears. Penebrygg's fingers flew back, and his owlish face turned pale.

Nat leaped from his chair. "What have you done to him?"

"Calm yourself, Nat," Penebrygg said, nursing his fingers. "She did nothing. It was the stone."

Nat knelt beside him, his face concerned. "Does it hurt?"

"Not unbearably."

"Let me try."

"No, Nat. I wouldn't recommend it. Not when——"

But even as Penebrygg spoke, Nat's fingers were curving around the stone. The savage notes sounded in my ears again, this time more violently. Nat cried out, and his hand flew upward.

"Ah," Penebrygg said. "What did you feel?"

"Nothing at all, until I was about to touch it." Nat sounded shaken. "And then it was as if my fingers were caught in red-hot pincers."

"Exactly what I experienced," Penebrygg said. "Tell me, did you feel something like that in the shed?"

"When I reached for the necklace?" Nat considered the question. "I felt a pinch, yes. Nothing like as painful, though."

"But you were only reaching for the chain then, and not the stone itself. You did not come so close then." Penebrygg nodded at me. "And what happened on your side? What ran through your mind?"

"Nothing, except . . ."

"Yes?"

"Except that I heard music. Very quick and harsh." I did not add that I had also been possessed by a strange and disturbing feeling, almost as if I were splitting into two Lucys, the one shocked and distressed to see the others in pain, the other darkly satisfied by their failure. It had only lasted an instant, but it was no less unsettling for that.

"It is as I expected, then," Penebrygg said.

"What do you mean?" I asked.

Penebrygg pushed his spectacles along the wide bridge of his nose. "Bear in mind that I know very little about Chantresses. None of us do, not in this day and age. But some of the old stories say that Chantresses were commonly given magical stones by their mothers. And if anyone else attempted to seize that stone, he would feel the pain of fire." He bestowed a sober glance on me. "That is the phrase that is used: 'the pain of fire.'"

"But those stories talk of plain stones," Nat said.

"My stone *was* plain until today," I said.

"But it's a ruby now. And I never heard a story about a gem like that."

"Nor have I," said Penebrygg. "But I once saw a manuscript about a Chantress whose stone was a pearl of immense beauty. So it would seem it is possible. And what other explanation is there for what we have seen tonight?"

"I can think of none," Nat admitted.

Relieved to have proven myself, I asked the question that mattered most to me. "Will you help me find Norrie, then?"

"Of course," Penebrygg said. "We'll do everything we can."

The fear I felt for Norrie did not diminish, but I found I was better able to shoulder it now that I knew I was not alone. I looped the necklace over my head and tucked the ruby out of sight.

While my head was bowed, Nat said quietly, "So we have a Chantress among us, at long last."

Pleased he had accepted the truth of my story, I looked up and smiled. But I saw immediately that it was Penebrygg he was speaking to, not me. And his next words erased my smile entirely.

"A Chantress—but one who knows nothing about magic." He shook his head in frustration. "That's not a help, sir. That's a danger to all of us."

Me? A danger? Hot words rose to my lips, but before I could speak them, Penebrygg rose to my defense.

"Patience, my lad," he said. "To have a Chantress come after so many years of darkness—to have her arrive on our very doorstep, and enter this house safely—to my mind, that is a miracle. And if one miracle has already happened, who knows what others may be possible?"

I had just enough time to wonder exactly what miracles he hoped for, when he leaned forward and patted my hand.

"My dear," he said, "I do believe you are going to save us all."

CHAPTER SEVEN
THE DEVASTATION

"Save you?" I regarded Penebrygg with alarm. "I don't understand. I thought it was me who needed saving—and Norrie."

"We will help you there, never fear," Penebrygg said.

"Of course we will," Nat said impatiently. "But there's more at stake than just you, you know."

I looked from him to Penebrygg. "But that's just it. I *don't* know."

"Small wonder, given the circumstances." Penebrygg pulled his spectacles down the bridge of his nose. "Perhaps it would be best to start at the beginning, then. What do you know about Chantresses?"

I shook my head. "Almost nothing."

"Then I shall tell you what we know. Which is not a great deal, admittedly." Penebrygg sighed and pushed his spectacles back into place. "According to the old stories, the wall between the mortal world and the faerie realms is a strong one, and it cannot be bridged in any enduring way. But long ago, when the wall was easier to cross, there were a few faerie women who married mortal men and bore them children. In doing so, the women lost most of their power. Weak and frail, they rarely lived long. But something of their blood lived on in their daughters and their daughters' daughters. Their voices were magic, and they could sing strange things into being."

"They were Chantresses?" I guessed.

"Yes. Or at any rate, that is the word we use for them now," said Penebrygg. "The old French term for it was *enchanteresse*. And that, in turn, has a root that goes back to Roman times. Nat?"

"Incantare." Nat spoke as if he were used to supplying Latin verbs on demand. *"Cantare*, meaning 'to sing,' and *in*, meaning 'in' or 'against.'"

"'To sing something into being,' in short," said Penebrygg. "Or, if you like, to sing it into a form that bends it against its true nature. Enchantment—that is the work of a Chantress. And has been for time out of mind."

"But what *kind* of enchantment?" I pointed to the fire, little more than a pile of smoky cinders. "Could they—we—make that fire burn brighter?"

"A Chantress could set a lake on fire, if she wished to," said Penebrygg. "Or at least the most powerful ones could. I speak, of course, of the days of Arthur and Camelot, when the faerie blood still ran strong. That was when the Lady of the Lake gave a sword to Arthur, and the Chantress Niniane beguiled Merlin."

"An interfering bunch, the Chantresses," Nat said, eyes on his carving.

"You're too hard on them, Nat," Penebrygg said. "They generally did more good than harm. But in any case, their power waned over the centuries, and eventually Chantresses of any kind became rare."

"Why?" I asked.

"No one knows for sure," Penebrygg said. "It is said that some Chantresses kept themselves apart and never married or mated. Some say, too, that many Chantresses were unusually susceptible to plague and other ills. In any case, by our own time, there were almost no Chantresses left, and their powers were in such abeyance that people had almost forgotten they existed. But they could be found here and there, if you listened to the old stories and had a mind to look for them. Which few people did, until the Great Devastation."

"The Great what?" I asked.

"The Great Devastation," Nat repeated with a touch of impatience. "The explosions at Hampton Court Palace that wiped out King Charles, his heirs, and half the aristocracy almost eight years ago. Surely you remember? By your own account, you were in England at the time."

"I was very young—"

"So was I, but it's impossible to forget."

My reply was choked off by a fragment of memory that suddenly rose in my mind.

Winter sunlight pokes through a basket as I hide beneath it, pretending I'm a chick inside the egg. And then, my mother's hushed voice in the wind, speaking in strained tones.

*"He is dead, Norrie. The King is dead, and his family, and hundreds
more with them, and they say it is magic and treason that murdered
them. And now they are hunting for magic workers—"*

"Have a care, mistress, or Lucy will hear you."

The voices dwindle into whispers.

I swallowed hard. Treason? Murder? Magic?

"I—I do remember a little," I said faintly. "We heard he was
dead. The King, I mean. I remember my mother was very upset."

"As were we all," Penebrygg said. "It was a kingdom in deepest mourning—and deepest shock. No one could quite believe
the scale of the destruction. And people panicked, too, because
the new heir to the throne, Henry Seymour, did not inspire confidence. He was only a distant cousin of the King, and he was a
mere ten years old. To many, the kingdom seemed rudderless.
People talked of civil war. And perhaps it would have come to
that, if Lord Scargrave had not taken young Henry's part."

"Scargrave." I seized on the name. "The man I overheard in
the library?"

Penebrygg nodded. "The very same: Lucian Ravendon, ninth
Earl of Scargrave. A good man, once upon a time. Thoughtful
and resolute, a warrior born and bred, of ancient family and
seemingly incorruptible. Many urged him to claim the throne
for himself, but instead, he threw his support behind Henry, the
rightful heir.

"To safeguard the boy, Scargrave installed him in the Tower of
London, and that ancient fortress became the seat of royal power,
as it was in the days of William the Conqueror. Right away

Henry appointed Scargrave as his Spymaster and Lord Protector, but Scargrave refused to use his new offices for his own gain. His only concern was to protect the King—and to bring the traitors behind the Devastation to justice."

"He was a man possessed," Nat said bluntly.

"And is it any wonder?" Penebrygg asked. "For the Devastation cost Scargrave not only his King and most of his friends but also his wife and only son, who were at Hampton Court that day. To avenge one was to avenge them all."

Nat dug deep into the wood with his knife, but he did not contradict this.

"To find the culprits, Scargrave used every power at his disposal," Penebrygg continued. "But the search proved fruitless— and the failure made the new regime look weak. It was whispered that another attack was coming, that France might invade, that England was doomed. Which only made Scargrave more desperate to track the traitors down. And so he began to take the gossip about magic more seriously."

"What gossip?" I asked. *The gossip my mother had heard?*

"Many said that such explosions could not be the work of ordinary humans, that magic must be involved."

"As if magic were the only power under the sun." Nat sounded annoyed.

"It was muddled thinking," Penebrygg agreed. "And to Scargrave's credit, he ignored it at first. But when the initial investigations led nowhere, he ordered that magic workers be questioned about possible involvement in the Devastation.

Within days, a frenzy of witch-hunting swept over the country. Fortune-tellers, soothsayers, alchemists, even midwives and herbalists—all feared for their lives, and with good reason, for many towns put suspected witches and wizards to death without trial."

"They died like flies," Nat said.

I winced as Penebrygg went on. "And then one day an old woman came to the Lord Protector and told him he must make it stop. 'A person may practice magic,' she said, 'but it does not follow that she is a traitor.' And to prove it, she offered to sing a song for Scargrave that would allow him to catch the real traitors."

A coal crackled in the grate and broke in two.

"She was a Chantress, of course," Penebrygg said. "A frail granddame by the name of Agnes Roser, somewhat addled in her mind, but utterly determined to do what she believed was right. In Scargrave's presence, she offered up a grimoire that she claimed had been hidden by her family for centuries."

"What's a grimoire?" I asked.

I had not liked to expose my ignorance, but Nat answered straightforwardly enough. "A book of spells."

"Yes," said Penebrygg. "And yet the book the Chantress Agnes showed to Scargrave did not appear to be a grimoire. It was instead a Book of Hours, gaudy with bright portraits of kings and queens and courtly life. Very beautiful in its way, of course, but Scargrave chided the old woman for wasting his time.

"But then the old Chantress began to sing, and the illuminated pages shifted and dissolved. In their place, a dull, leather-covered book took shape, mottled with age, with most of its pages bound shut. It was a Chantress grimoire, the old woman said, and only a Chantress could sing its spells to life. But she was willing to sing one for Lord Scargrave.

"And that is when she sang the Shadowgrims into being."

CHAPTER EIGHT
THE SHADOWGRIMS

Shadowgrims. As the word echoed in my mind, another sliver of memory surfaced.

My mother's hushed voice floats up to the loft where I am meant to be sleeping: "I must hide her, Norrie. Hide her where the Shadowgrims can't find her . . ."

An indistinguishable muttering: Norrie replying? And then my mother again.

"What they would do to a child is beyond imagining . . ."

I could remember nothing more. But the fear in my mother's voice stole my breath away.

"In the library, Lord Scargrave spoke of the Shadowgrims." I forced myself to say the word out loud, though it left an unpleasant taste in my mouth. "And I think I remember my mother mentioning them. But I don't know what they are."

"Count yourself lucky, then," Nat said.

It was left to Penebrygg to give me a proper answer. "In the beginning, they were ravens, a type bred by the Ravendon family since ancient times, and which Scargrave brought with him to the Tower of London: clever black birds, large as a man's head, with mocking eyes and dagger-sharp beaks." He paused and added softly. "But now they are something else entirely, and all because of the Chantress's song."

"What did she do?" I asked.

Nat jabbed his knife into the carving. "She made a stupid mistake."

"A grave one, certainly," Penebrygg said. "Her intention, or so she said, was to create truth seekers who would help Lord Scargrave find the true culprits behind the Great Devastation. But instead, her song-spell turned the birds into instruments of torture. By day, they sleep—an enchanted sleep from which none can wake them—but by night, they are hunters like none the world has ever known."

"It's like being in a nightmare," Nat said, his knife still. "The kind where you're caught so fast you can't even scream for help. The terror seizes you first, and then comes the heat, smoky and suffocating, pressing at you from every direction."

My hand went to my mouth. The terror I had felt in the cart, the burning fear . . . had that been the Shadowgrims?

I put the question to Nat and Penebrygg. Nat nodded. "We were near home when two Shadowgrims spotted us. One Shadowgrim swooped down and hovered over us, and the other went to summon the Watchmen. We were out after curfew, you see."

"Weren't you frightened?" I asked.

"Enough that it wasn't easy to talk," Nat said. "Or move. But the ravens kept back while the Watchmen checked us out, and I knew they would only come close if the Watchmen called them down, or if I tried to bolt. Since we had a proper pass—well, almost proper—I thought it would be all right. And it was."

I tried not to stare at his confident face. How could he be so matter-of-fact about an encounter that had terrified me?

Penebrygg guessed what I was thinking. "Nat's more resilient than most," he explained. "I'd not let him go out in the night otherwise. But you shouldn't feel you need to match him. For most of us, the fear is crippling. And it's most paralyzing of all, they say, for Chantresses."

He meant to make me feel better, I knew. Instead, I felt worse.

"I wouldn't have been resilient if the Shadowgrims had come closer," Nat said. "No one can stand up against that. And I would've been more afraid if I'd known you were there. But I didn't."

"Thanks be that the Watchmen accepted your pass," Penebrygg said, "and that nothing more dire happened."

"What *could* have happened?" I asked.

"You really want to know?" Nat met my eyes squarely.

A shiver went through me. "Yes."

Penebrygg shook his head. "Nat, I'm not sure this is the best time . . ."

"She ought to know," Nat said. "She's a Chantress, and she's already felt their fear. Someone should tell her the rest."

Penebrygg bowed his head. "I suppose you are right."

To me, Nat said, "The Shadowgrims kept their distance this time. But if someone tries to run from the Watchmen, or if the Watchmen want to make an arrest, the Shadowgrims come close. And when they do, you feel hotter and hotter, and you hear their wings fanning the flames. Then you're taken prisoner—and if Scargrave wants to know what's in your mind, he orders them to attack."

"And attack they do," Penebrygg said. "But not with beaks and talons. They brush their feathers against your skin, feeding on your thoughts as they once fed on carrion and flesh. Their touch is like fire, scorching and searing you. The terror scalds your very soul. And as you burn, the Shadowgrims pick at your mind, stripping away thoughts they later share with Scargrave."

"They can *speak*?" I said.

"To their master, yes," Penebrygg said. "Not with their raven croak, you understand, but in their own peculiar way, from mind to mind. Memory by memory, thought by thought, they rob you of everything that makes you human, and everything that you hold dear, until at last their dark fire consumes you."

The smoke from the hearth seemed to thicken around me. "You mean, you die?"

"The fortunate ones do," Penebrygg said. "They become nothing more than a pile of ash. But now and again, people live through it—in body, at least. And when that happens, they belong to the Spymaster from then on. Their own minds are gone, and their only thought is to do his bidding. Scargrave has found them very useful as Warders at the Tower, and as Watchmen to guard the city, for they are not paralyzed by the Shadowgrims as the rest of us are, and they obey every command he gives."

"You can see it in their eyes, if you get close," Nat added. "There's a dullness there that tells you they're the Ravens' Own."

I remembered how they had looked in my eyes out in the shed, and how Penebrygg had reported they were normal.

"Why didn't the Chantress undo the spell, or stop it somehow?" I asked.

"To her credit, she tried to undo her handiwork," Penebrygg said. "But when she sang, she stumbled and seemed confused, and the song did not work. Before she could sing another note, Scargrave ordered the ravens to flock around her face. She became their very first victim."

The hairs on my neck rose. Nat, however, was unmoved. "Done in by her own magic," he said. "There's justice for you."

Penebrygg frowned. "Have pity, Nat. No one deserves such a death."

"Maybe not. But she oughtn't to have interfered." Nat chipped off another bit of wood. "She did terrible harm."

"Well, on that we can agree, at least." Penebrygg said to me, "After she died, the Reign of Terror began. Not that many saw it that way back then. Magic workers were deeply mistrusted, and Scargrave was applauded for his quick action against the Chantress. In those early days, he used his new powers with restraint. He caged his ravens in the depths of the Tower—even today, that is where they roost—and he deployed them primarily against those suspected of treason."

"The way people talked, you'd have thought Scargrave was a hero," Nat said in disgust.

"Little wonder, since the Shadowgrims helped him to locate the traitors who had caused the Devastation." To me, Penebrygg explained, "Once they've been in the grip of raven fear, most people will do anything rather than be shut up in their company. And those who resist have their secrets taken from them anyway, once they become raven pickings. So names were supplied, details shared—and within a fortnight, the knaves were found: a clockmaker and his cousins, as it turned out. Nothing to do with magic."

"Why did they do it?" I asked.

"Because they considered King Charles a tyrant, and they wanted to be rid of him," Penebrygg said.

"Was he?" It felt strange to be asking questions like this about my own country, but I had no other way of telling.

"Yes," Nat said. "Not like Scargrave, not with magic at his command. But bad enough in his own way. He bankrupted the country, and he crushed anyone who opposed him. He even did away with Parliament, so the people had no voice."

The whirring in the room echoed in my ears. Clocks everywhere around me . . .

"And it was a clockmaker who killed him?" I said uncomfortably.

"Yes," said Penebrygg. "A member of our own guild, as it happened."

"*Your* guild? Did you know him?"

"Not to speak to," Nat said.

It was not quite the answer I'd hoped for, but Penebrygg's response was more reassuring. "We knew him by reputation, my dear, but no more. If anyone in the guild had guessed what violence he planned, you can be sure we would have done our best to put a stop to it. But he and his cousins kept to themselves. They might never have been discovered if it hadn't been for the Shadowgrims. So people were grateful."

Nat flicked away a shaving of wood. "But it didn't end there. Magic never does."

Penebrygg sighed. "Yes, sad to say, that first hunt served only to whet Scargrave's appetite for more searches and more arrests. None of us could understand it—the Scargrave of old would never have done such a thing—but losing his family like that must have turned his mind. He started sending patrols of Shadowgrims out by night, to ferret out malcontents and agitators and other potential threats to the Crown. If you were to look over London right now, you would see them gliding over rooftops, darting into alleys, crouching under eaves. Though, of course, it's the ones you don't see that you most need to worry about."

I glanced uneasily at the nearest window. "What if the Shadowgrims are perched outside? Could they hear us?"

"Through double solid-oak shutters and two heavy wool curtains?" Nat dismissed my worry. "Not likely. Not if we keep our voices low. Anyhow, if there was a Shadowgrim so close, you would know it. You're a Chantress. Your hair would be standing on end."

If he'd meant this as reassurance, it failed. Indeed, my skin began to prickle as he spoke. And Penebrygg's next words did nothing to soothe me.

"If the Shadowgrims were all we had to worry about, that would be bad enough. But Scargrave has also established a vast web of human spies—"

"Oh!" I gasped.

Penebrygg tensed. "What is it?"

Fear rushed over me. "My skin—it's burning."

CHAPTER NINE
ONLY A CHANTRESS

"Is this a joke?" Nat said, annoyed.

"A jest? Hardly." Penebrygg was already out of his chair. "Look at her, Nat. Something is very wrong."

The heat and the panic were fast overwhelming me; I could barely choke out any words now. "It feels like . . . the cart."

"Shadowgrims, then." Penebrygg spoke hardly above a whisper.

"They're flocking here?" Nat was alarmed now too.

"No. If they were, I would feel it. Even you would be growing uneasy. And no doubt we'd have Watchmen battering at our door as well," Penebrygg said. "No, I suspect this is just a Shadowgrim alighting nearby, nothing more."

Nat glanced back at me. "And that's enough to do this to her?"

"Evidently."

How could they not be burned? The flames were everywhere, I thought dizzily.

"Let's get her downstairs, and see if that helps," Penebrygg said. "Can you stand, my dear? No, I see you can't. Nat, can you carry her?"

Nat had me halfway out of the chair when the burning stopped. One moment I was clutching his shoulders, aware of nothing except the fear and heat in my head; the next, I was meeting his eyes in confusion and jerking away.

As I bounded to my feet, he had to grab at the chair behind him for balance.

"I'm feeling better," I said.

"So I gathered." He rubbed his elbow and moved away.

Penebrygg took my arm, as if to support me. "My dear, are you truly all right?"

"I think so." The terror was gone, almost as if it had never been there. Moments later, however, a wave of exhaustion hit me, and I sat back down.

"I've double-checked, and all the windows are secure," Nat reported to Penebrygg. "And the chimney damper's only open a crack, as usual."

Penebrygg looked over at the fireplace. "Ah, yes, the chimney. I hadn't thought of that."

"It's never been a problem before," Nat said doubtfully.

"But perhaps even a tiny crack is a problem for a Chantress," Penebrygg said. "Especially if a Shadowgrim happened to perch right by the chimney itself."

"Could it have heard us?" I asked in dismay. "Does it know I'm with you?" Even now it might be winging its way back to Scargrave . . .

"No." Penebrygg hastened to reassure me. "It was here so briefly, and we were talking too softly to be heard through such a small crack."

"But perhaps it could sense my presence—"

"No," Penebrygg said again. "You can feel the Shadowgrims, but they can't feel you. Everything we know about them proves that point. It's their one saving grace—that, and the fact that they sleep by day."

I was deeply relieved by his answer.

Nat moved to the fireplace. "So we'll shut the damper, then?"

"Yes, do," Penebrygg said. "And then we'll go downstairs. I think our guest has had enough of the attic for one night."

By the time we settled by the smoking embers of the kitchen fire, I was feeling stronger.

"Where were we?" Penebrygg asked.

"We were talking about Scargrave's spies," Nat said from the bench opposite mine.

"Ah, yes, indeed," Penebrygg said. "His great web, over which he reigns as Spymaster, with the ravens at his side." He straightened his spectacles and looked at me. "I'm afraid that informers are everywhere, my dear. Fear is in the very air we breathe. There is no room for dissent, no freedom to speak one's mind. Even the most innocent acts are now considered sedition and can land a man in front of the ravens."

"Last week a neighbor of ours complained about the price of bread," Nat said. "He was arrested within the hour."

"As if grumbling about prices were gravest treason!"

Penebrygg said, shaking his head. "But no one dares to rise up against Scargrave while he has the Shadowgrims in his command, not even King Henry."

"But why?" I asked. "He's the King, isn't he? Surely Scargrave wouldn't throw *him* to the ravens."

"He would if it suited him," Nat said.

"I think not," Penebrygg said. "The King is not yet eighteen, and he has been led by Scargrave for most of his life. Moreover, he is one of those people who is particularly susceptible to the Shadowgrims, and he lives very near the Tower dungeon in which they are housed. Little wonder he is quiet and melancholy, and he does whatever Scargrave advises."

"Their magic takes some people that way," Nat said. "It's horrible to see."

"Yes," Penebrygg agreed. "The mere existence of the Shadowgrims is enough to unsettle many—especially those who are impressionable, or have little practice in dealing with fear. You can see it in their faces, even in the way they speak and stand. They are easily frightened and easily led, and even by day, when the Shadowgrims can do them no harm, they blindly follow Scargrave because he promises to make them safer."

"But some people stand against him?" I asked. "Like you and Nat?"

"A few," Penebrygg said. "But we, too, fear the Shadowgrims' power. While Scargrave possesses his ravens, we cannot call our souls our own."

I was shaken by the quiet desperation in his voice. "Couldn't you leave England, and live abroad?"

"And leave everyone here to suffer?" Nat said indignantly. "Anyway, Scargrave has guards along the entire coast and in every port; you can't leave without his permission. And even if we did manage to wriggle free somehow, he has ways of finding people, wherever they are."

"The only answer is to fight him here, with every means at our disposal." Penebrygg clasped his hands and looked at me. "That is why we need your help."

"My help? But I don't see how, or why—"

"We have an old saying here," Penebrygg said.

"If harm is done by a Chantress song,
Only a Chantress can right the wrong."

"I don't understand," I said, although I was beginning to.

"It means that the Shadowgrims must be destroyed by the same means they were created: by Chantress magic," Penebrygg said.

Nat jabbed at the wood again. "If we could do it ourselves, we would."

"But we cannot," Penebrygg said. "So we must turn to you."

My heart thumped. "But I wouldn't know where to begin. I know nothing of Chantress spells, aside from the one that brought me here."

"You may know more than you realize," Penebrygg said. "And I am certain there are ways we can help you. Nat, could you bring us the box?"

Nat set aside his carving and went out of the room. Several

long minutes later, he returned with a wide, shallow box. He set it down in the shadows, and I heard the sound of metal against metal, like tiny taps on a pan or the scrape of a key in a lock. When he turned back to us, he held two sheets of parchment.

"It is only a copy," Penebrygg said. "But we believe this to be the song that will destroy the Shadowgrims, provided it is sung by a Chantress. That, at least, is what the papers that we found with it claim. But we cannot make head nor tail of the notation on the parchment itself. Can you?"

I stared at the tiny spots and whorls that were scattered like blots on the page. Meaningless, and yet even as I shook my head, they made memory speak:

The floorboard in my mother's room trips me, and when I reach for it, it wiggles loose. Underneath it, I find scraps of paper with strange blots on them. I know my letters, know that this isn't writing—at least not any writing I recognize. I bring them over to the light, so absorbed that I do not hear my mother's footsteps behind me.

"Lucy, love, give those to me." When I do not immediately surrender them, she takes them gently from my hands.

"What are they, Mama?"

"Nothing for you to worry about. We'll say no more about them."

Penebrygg took hold of the parchment. "You don't know what the signs mean?"

"I think they might be Chantress marks," I said. "But I have no idea what they mean."

Penebrygg and Nat exchanged disappointed glances.

"Well, never mind," Penebrygg said. "In time, perhaps we will work out some way of cracking the code. But first we must know: Are you willing to help us?"

Behind his spectacles, his eyes glimmered with entreaty. And although Nat betrayed no emotion, I sensed that he was listening carefully for my answer.

"But why me?" I was genuinely puzzled. "Why not another Chantress? Someone older, with more skill?"

To my surprise, Penebrygg looked away. "My dear, I thought you understood . . ."

"Understood what?" I asked.

"That there are no other Chantresses left," he said quietly.

The words were like a winter wind, cutting me to the bone.

"Scargrave hunted them down." Penebrygg spoke with great care, as if he guessed how difficult this might be for me to hear. "He wanted no one to threaten his hold on the Shadowgrims and the grimoire that made them. And his task was made easier by the ravens. Before they killed the Chantress Agnes, they robbed her memory of the names and dwelling places of every other Chantress she knew. And Scargrave went after them, capturing them by surprise and binding their mouths shut before giving them to the ravens. So it went, with yet more names gathered and more Chantresses killed, until at last they were all gone."

"But why didn't they fight?" I asked in distress. "If they were Chantresses, if they had power—"

My words hung in the air.

"We don't know," Penebrygg admitted. "Not for certain. But most of those he captured were Chantresses in little more than name. As far as we can tell, they knew only a few weak and worn spells, and they had only a cursory understanding of their heritage. Many were very old, as well, and most lived in remote places. They had little chance against Scargrave and his Shadowgrims. We did hear that at least one young Chantress had been hidden away before the rest of her family was killed, but we thought that was only rumor, until we met you."

"My mother . . ." I whispered. It hurt too much to say anything more.

"What was her name?" Penebrygg asked gently. "There are lists, you see, and those of us who have seen them keep them alive in memory."

I heard myself give the answer, almost as if someone else were speaking. "Viviane Marlowe."

There was a long pause. And then Penebrygg said, "Oh, my dear, I am so sorry."

I stared at my empty hands. I had accepted long ago that my mother was dead and would never come back. It was a sad fact, but a settled one—part of the flint-hard rock on which my life was built. So why did it shake me so much to learn exactly how my mother had died? To know that it was not the sea that had killed her, but Lord Scargrave's Shadowgrims?

No matter. It shook me. I pushed my palms against my hot eyes, and hid my face.

"I think," said Penebrygg, slowly and kindly, "that you need rest and quiet, yes? We must find you a place to sleep and some warm blankets. I shall give you my own bed—"

"No, sir," Nat interrupted, his voice low. "It's not right that you should give up your bed. Your back's not up to it. She can have mine instead."

"That's good of you, Nat."

"But sir?"

"Yes?"

"She still hasn't said whether she'll help us."

"And you would ask her now, when she is mourning her mother?" Penebrygg's hushed voice held a note of reproof. "We have waited a long time for a Chantress, Nat. Surely we can wait a little longer for her answer."

I barely heard them for thinking of my mother, so loving, so gentle, so determined to save me. My mother, surrounded by Shadowgrims . . .

I had spent half my life wanting to come back to this place, this England. I had believed my life would begin here. But I had never imagined anything like this. Desperately I wished myself back on the island, with Norrie at my side, my voice locked away, my magic untapped. This terrible world unknown.

But that was not possible.

Sing and the darkness will find you.

Desolation swept over me. But through my grief and bewilderment, I could sense something else growing in me, something alive, something stronger than fear: a burning and angry resolve.

My hands fell away. I looked Nat and Penebrygg full in the face.

"If you want my help, you have it," I said. "I will do everything in my power to destroy the man who murdered my mother."

CHAPTER TEN
CURIOSITIES

"Lucy?" a voice called.

Fogged by sleep, I thought: *Norrie?* Eyes still closed, I listened for the customary sounds of an island morning—the pots clattering, the cockerel crowing, and Norrie's wide-awake call, "Up now, and no dawdling!"

Instead, I heard dogs yapping, and hammers tapping, and hoarse voices hawking wares: "Had-had-haddock!" "Small coal, penny a peake!" And beneath everything, a rumble like a hundred handcarts rolling by.

Where on earth was I?

London, my sleepy mind said. I was in London with Norrie and Mama, in the narrow garret by the River Thames. Only for the winter, Mama had said, and then we would move out into the country. . . .

"Wake up!" The command was sharp as a slap on my cheek.

I opened my eyes and saw a boy with hazel eyes looming over

me. Memory flooded back: Nat and Penebrygg. Scargrave and the Shadowgrims. The singing and the ruby.

My mother, murdered.

And Norrie lost.

I sat up, and my stone swung forward on its chain. Still there. And still a ruby.

"You sleep like the dead." Nat sounded cross and a bit alarmed. Apparently my commitment last night had made us close enough comrades that he thought it worth worrying about me. It hadn't made him any friendlier, though. "I've been shouting your name, and you never even moved."

"Well, I'm awake now." And feeling at a distinct disadvantage. Neatly dressed in dark breeches and fresh white linen, Nat had the look of someone ready to take on all comers. I, meanwhile, was facing the world with wrinkled skirts, a rumbling stomach, and fingernails that still bore traces of mud from the island garden. I put a hand to my hair and wished I hadn't: It was a scraggle of snarls.

My only comfort was that Nat did not appear to notice.

Striving to sound self-possessed, I asked, "What time is it?"

"Nearly nine. You need to stir yourself." Nat no longer sounded alarmed, only impatient. "Dr. Penebrygg will return anytime now, and he'll want to see you as soon as he's back." He gestured toward a washstand in the far corner. "There's clean water there. And a chamber pot under the bedstead. When you're done, come and find me upstairs."

He sped out the door, leaving me grateful for the privacy—but relieved, too, that he had been frank in addressing the essentials.

I slid out of bed and set about making myself ready. Everything proved straightforward enough, except for my hair. As I struggled to smooth it back, I could almost hear Norrie scolding. *Your hair's a tangle of seaweed, child. Plait it back now, there's a good girl.*

Last night, before I had gone to sleep, Penebrygg had reassured me again that they would do their best to help me find Norrie. "She could be anywhere, I'm afraid. But if you give me a description of her, I will make some inquiries. Very discreetly, of course. Anything else might endanger her—and you."

The nature of those dangers was not something I wished to contemplate. Instead, I remembered my last evening on the island with longing—a fire warming up the hearth, and Norrie and I cozy in our chairs in front of it. Of course, the fire had been built to rule, and I had chafed whenever Norrie gave me pointed reminders on tending it. But we both had been safe, and that seemed a blessing to me now.

However much I wanted to, however, I could not turn back time. And even if I could, it would not undo the Shadowgrims.

What's done is done, and we must make the best of it.

With Norrie's words echoing in my ears, I forced myself to concentrate on the job at hand, plaiting my hair. As my fingers worked, I stood by the tiny window and tried to make sense of the view: a scrap of muddy yard enclosed on three sides, with a sloping shed along the other. Aristotle's stable, I guessed.

There. I'd done the best I could with my hair. As for my clothes . . .

I looked down at my skirts and sighed. No amount of shaking out would make them look anything less than bedraggled.

I did the best I could, gave my plait one last tug, and went to find Nat.

† † †

Upstairs, he had said. So up the narrow flight I went, touching the walls for balance, until I reached the attic room where we had talked last night. Remembering the reason why I'd left the room last night, I couldn't help but feel a certain trepidation as I opened the door, yet it passed the moment I saw the sunlight on the walls. The place felt bright and safe and altogether wonderful—perched so high that it belonged not to London, but to the sky.

I shut the door behind me and looked out the nearest window. In the chinks between the rooftops, I saw a wide river, its banks tight-packed with houses, its quays bustling with skiffs and cargo. Swimming through my memory, I recalled another river view, the one from the London garret we had stayed in so long ago. I could remember nothing else about the city or our stay in it, but for a moment, as I stood at that window, I felt my mother at my side.

"You can see the Thames from there," Nat said, "if you know where to look."

At his words, the fragile memory collapsed in on itself. I swung around and looked at him. He was sitting at a tilted desk at the far end of the room, almost hidden by a horde of curious objects.

The largest was a leather-covered coracle, a good four feet across, improbably stuffed with a set of globes, a cracked bellows, and a long length of poppy-red silk. Next to this stood a pile of bones, several colossal vases overspilling with feathers and grasses, and a cabinet containing scores of smoky-colored bottles with strange inscriptions on them.

Most of the remaining space was a jumble of shelves, books, shells, pulleys, scales, paintings, and pots. And then, of course, there were the clocks: two dozen, at a guess, their ivory and gold faces tucked into every nook and cranny in the room.

As I picked my way toward Nat, I pointed to the smoky vials. "What's in there?"

"Elements of various sorts," Nat said. "And other things. Dr. Penebrygg collects curiosities."

"What does he do with them?"

"We use them for our experiments."

"What kind of experiments?" I asked, with a dubious backward look at the vials.

"Oh, we're interested in almost everything: the nature of gravity, the properties of light, the motion of the planets, the music of the spheres, the circulation of blood."

I stared at him, surprised by the enthusiasm in his voice. For once, he sounded almost friendly. "You really do mean everything."

"Pretty much. New ways of thinking are in the air, and new discoveries are being made every day. It's exciting to be part of it." Enthusiasm dimming, he added, "Well, as much a part of it as our fight against Scargrave allows us to be." He took up a pen and bent over his desk.

I touched a fold of the scarlet fabric inside the coracle. "And this silk? What kind of experiments do you do on that?"

He didn't look up from his work this time. "Do you always ask this many questions?"

"Wouldn't you, in my shoes?"

To my surprise, Nat considered the point fairly. "I suppose I would." He set down his pen, evidently striving for more patience than he had shown me last night. "All right, then. Ask away."

"What do you use this silk for?" I asked.

"Well, we dissolved some in acid when we were studying color. But mostly it's there as a background for the engravings."

"The engravings?"

"We're engravers by trade. Engravers and clockmakers, to be exact. But clockmaking is frowned upon, so we keep that part quiet."

"Is that because of the Devastation?"

"Yes." Nat spun his pen. "After the Shadowgrims ferreted out the conspiracy, clockmakers were ordered to close their shops, for fear they might be nests of rebellion. Anyone believed to have been a close associate of the rogue clockmaker was hauled in for questioning. We escaped that, thankfully, since we'd never had dealings with him. But even if you had no connection with him, you had to apply to Scargrave himself for a permit to reopen your business. Dr. Penebrygg didn't much care for that, so he shut up shop for good and moved here."

"But he kept his clocks," I said, listening to the ticking of their mechanisms.

"He did. And he's taught me how to work with them. But it's mostly engraving that earns our bread these days." He jotted something down with his pen. "And now I really need to get back to work."

Was he working on an engraving? I stepped forward and peeked over the top of the tilted desk. But he was only writing on an ordinary sheet of paper, carefully aligned against the margin of a book. The book's binding, just visible, was a deep moss green.

"The book from the library," I guessed.

Nat's pen stopped. "You don't miss much, do you?"

"What does it say?" I scrutinized the upside-down text. "I can't read it."

"It's in Latin."

"Why did you take it?" I asked.

"It's too complicated to explain right now." Nat looked up from his work and pointed to the far side of the room. "Did I tell you there's food on the table over there? I've had my share, and so has Dr. Penebrygg, so eat as much as you want."

It was a diversion, and I recognized it as such. But I was hungry enough to abandon my questioning, at least for the moment. On the table, alongside chisels, spikes, and sheets of metal, I found a basket of rolls and a wedge of waxy cheese. They made a fine meal, and by the time I had polished them off, I was reconciled to taking a more roundabout approach to getting answers from Nat.

On my way back to his desk, I stopped by a complicated device made up of brass tubes and bits of glass. "What's this?"

Nat barely took the time to look up. "A microscope."

The word meant nothing to me. I leaned in for a closer look.

Now I had his attention. "Careful!" he warned. "It took ages to put it together."

"You made it?" I looked at the tubes with new interest. "What does it do?"

"It lets you look at tiny things. If you get everything lined up properly, a flea looks as big as a lamb."

I boggled at this. "But that's impossible."

"No more impossible than your own magic," Nat flared. "But it takes hard work and patience, not just a few random snatches of song."

He shot me a look so full of resentment that I stepped back from the force of it. My resolve to put him at his ease evaporated.

"You don't like magic, do you?" I said. No point in beating around the bush.

"No."

"Not even good magic?"

Nat shrugged. "Scargrave would tell you the Shadowgrims are good magic. And they are—for him. That's the way magic is, as far as I can tell. It lets a few people run roughshod over the rest of us."

"You wish I'd never come, then."

He balked. "I didn't say that."

"You hate magic, you as good as said so."

"Doesn't matter if I do, does it? We need your magic. I wish we didn't, but we do."

"So you'll pinch your nose and put up with me, so long as I'm useful to you?" I grimaced. "How very noble of you."

"Well, you're getting something out of the bargain too." He crossed his arms. "You need us to keep you safe."

"*Safe?*" I looked back at him indignantly. "That's a fine thing, coming from you. You'd have strung me up for a spy if it hadn't been for Dr. Penebrygg."

"Nonsense." Nat was unrepentant. "I was being careful, that's all. If you had been a spy, and Scargrave found out what we were up to—"

He broke off and took up his pen again.

I stepped toward his desk, skirting the coracle and the pile of bones. "What *are* you up to?"

"I can't say." He wouldn't look at me. "Not yet. When Dr. Penebrygg comes back—"

"And when will that be?" I asked. "I thought he was supposed to be here already."

"He was." Nat glanced at the nearest clock. "He's late. I don't know why."

"Where did he go?"

"I can't say," he said again.

A sudden fear gripped me. Had Dr. Penebrygg been arrested? Or worse still, was he not the friend he had seemed? "You mean, you don't know?"

Nat shook his head stubbornly. "I can't say."

I clenched my fists. First Norrie, now this. No matter where I went, it seemed people were determined to keep secrets from me. "I *hate* being kept in the dark."

"So do I," Nat said unexpectedly. "I hate it more than anything."

Our eyes met, and I felt a spark like the kick of magic or the start of a song.

Or was that only my imagination? Even as the spark shot down my spine, Nat looked away, and his voice, when he spoke, was as cool as ever. "I'd tell you more if I could, but I can't. You'll have to wait until Dr. Penebrygg gets back."

"But—"

"I've said all I have to say." Nat bent back over his work. But something was bothering him. His face was flushed, and I saw his hand go up to loosen his collar.

I started to speak, then stopped, shocked by what I glimpsed as the collar fell away: a scar across his throat, as white as my own Chantress mark.

"Hello, hello!" The door burst open, and Penebrygg rushed in, his cheeks pink with exertion and excitement.

"There you are!" He smiled at me. "We're to bring you with us when the Invisible College meets today. What do you think of that?"

CHAPTER ELEVEN
MOONBRIAR

"What's the Invisible College?" I asked.

"It's not so much a what, my dear, as a who." Penebrygg sat down by the hearth, his floppy velvet cap askew. "We are a band of mathematicians, engineers, philosophers, and alchemists who are dedicated to overthrowing Scargrave. Not that we've had much success yet. But that is our aim."

"And you become invisible?" I asked cautiously, sitting beside him.

"Alas, no. The power of invisibility is beyond us. Although I will say that young Rooke has hopes—"

"Should we be using names?" Nat interrupted, sitting down across from us. His collar was fastened shut again, and I could not see his scar.

"Sir Barnaby thought we should, as long as we did so with care and discretion, never writing anything down—the usual precautions." Penebrygg glanced behind him. "I bolted every door on the way up. And those windows are latched shut, yes?"

"Yes," Nat said, "but—"

"Lucy is part of our circle now. That is the Council's decision. And since she is in our circle, we must be open with her." Penebrygg turned to me again. "It is our rule, you see. We were known to each other before Scargrave's rise, so there was no disguising things afterward. And there is a certain measure of safety in continuing this way. If we were to cloak ourselves in hoods and masks, an imposter might easily slip in among us. But without them, we know exactly where we stand. Our faces are no secret to each other, and neither are our characters."

"I promise I won't betray you," I said.

"But what if she's caught?" Nat asked Penebrygg.

Trust Nat to assume the worst, I thought. Especially where I was concerned.

"If Lucy is caught, we have nothing left to hope for," Penebrygg said. "And that is precisely why we must tell her whatever we can. She is less likely to make mistakes that way. And should she find herself in trouble, she will know who to turn to. Her safety, not ours, must be our utmost priority."

Nat nodded slowly. "Agreed."

I no longer felt like scoffing. It was sobering to realize how desperately they were counting on me—to the point that they were willing to hazard their own lives to keep me safe.

"The Council agrees we must do everything we can to find your guardian, too," Penebrygg said to me. "We cannot afford to have any of Scargrave's spies find her—not for her sake, and not for ours. This very morning we have begun to circulate her description among our allies, and we will be on the lookout for her."

"Thank you," I said, the words a poor reflection of the deep gratitude I felt.

"Now, you were asking why we call ourselves the Invisible College." Penebrygg nodded at me. "It was Sir Barnaby Gadding, the founder of our group, who coined the term, back in King Charles's time. We had no buildings, he said, no faculty, none of the trappings of a regular school. We merely wrote and corresponded and talked. But we shared an invisible link: a deep and abiding interest in investigating the world around us, and in communicating what we learned. For all intents and purposes, Sir Barnaby joked, we were members of an Invisible College." He added, "I think he took pleasure in the abbreviation, too."

I did not quite follow him.

"IC," Penebrygg said, pointing to his eyes. "'I see.'"

"Sir Barnaby loves puns," Nat said drily.

"Pun or not, it is a good motto for men who believe in witnessing events with their own eyes, and not relying on hearsay and superstition," said Penebrygg. "But that is by the by. The point is that ever since Scargrave came to power, the Invisible College has found it rough going."

"Scargrave doesn't like truth," Nat said. "Or doubts or questions. And those are the lifeblood of what we do."

Penebrygg nodded. "That's why he has closed the universities. The breeding ground of rabble-rousers and traitors, he called them. A sad development in a man who once endowed a Cambridge library, I might add. But be that as it may, our Invisible College continues to meet on the quiet."

"And Scargrave has never captured any of you?" I asked.

"Not a one," Penebrygg said. "And for that we have Sir Barnaby to thank. His family is related by blood to both Scargrave and the King, and he is very friendly with them both; he is the last person anyone would suspect of treason. It is his unassailable position that allows us to meet and plot Scargrave's destruction." He pulled his spectacles down and looked at me. "And you come to us, my dear, when our plans are at a critical juncture. Our investigations have revealed that Scargrave is attempting to breed his ravens."

I frowned. "You mean, he's trying to make more Shadowgrims?"

"Exactly," Penebrygg said. "Hundreds, even thousands, if he has his way. The more of them there are, the more fear he can spread. Right now they're sometimes spread rather thin, especially in the far reaches of the kingdom, which is a help to us. But if Scargrave finds a way to fill the skies with them, every street of this country will be under their watch."

It was a dreadful prospect.

"Luckily for us, it's not easy to breed them," Nat said. "The phase of the moon has to be right, and they have to be taken off patrolling duty for weeks at a time to fatten up."

"And then there's the question of diet," Penebrygg said. "They must be fed leaves from the moonbriar tree—*Selenanthus selenei*—or else none of the eggs will hatch. And that is why the Invisible College has destroyed the only three moonbriar trees known to exist."

"So he can't make more Shadowgrims, after all," I said with relief.

"Not at the moment," Nat said. "But there's always the possibility that another moonbriar tree will be located. Or that Scargrave will locate some seeds and be able to grow a tree of his own."

"Can't you do anything to stop him?" I said. "Find the trees, or destroy the seed, or . . . or something?"

"We are doing those things, my dear," Penebrygg assured me. "Insofar as it is in our power. And it's largely due to young Nat here that we have stayed a step ahead of Scargrave. I've lost count of how many missions he's undertaken for the IC."

"Is that why you took the book from the library?" I asked Nat, hoping this time he would answer me.

He looked at Penebrygg. "The Council gave us permission to tell her?"

Penebrygg nodded.

"Yes," Nat said to me. "One of our spies told me it was worth a closer look."

"Spies?" The IC's network was more extensive than I had expected.

"Yes, my dear. We have our spies, just as Scargrave has his," Penebrygg said. "This particular agent was only able to glance at the book, and he was afraid that if he paid any more attention to it, Scargrave would take notice. Stealing it seemed to be the best option."

"Luckily we know the house better than Scargrave himself does," Nat said.

This puzzled me. "But it's his house."

"Only since the Devastation," Penebrygg said. "For centuries before that, it belonged to another family, who endowed it with many hidden stairways and passages. Some of which have been long since forgotten."

"But you know about them?"

"Sir Barnaby does," Penebrygg said. "He knew the house well as a boy. But he's a man of goutish tendencies, and it's impossible for him to do the actual stealing. For that, we needed Nat here."

"I only hope the book was worth the trouble," Nat said. "It's a palimpsest, and they're tricky."

"A pal—what?"

"A palimpsest," Penebrygg said. "That is, parchment from an old book that has been scraped blank and overwritten to make a new book. If you want to read the remnants of the old writing, you need sharp eyes."

"Will you show me?" I asked Nat.

He hesitated. "I suppose we can take a quick look."

I followed him over to the desk.

"Look at the shadows." He ran a careful finger along the parchment page, and I saw them: very faint lines of writing running under and over the heavy black words of the new text.

"I can't read every word," he said, "but there's a mention of *Selenanthus* midway down the page that's worth a closer look. It may identify a moonbriar stand we don't know about."

"More moonbriar trees?" My stomach clenched. "Do you think Scargrave knows about them?"

"Probably not," Nat said. "That's why we stole the book—so that he wouldn't find out. And if the trees do still exist, we'll do our best to uproot them before he even knows they're there."

He sounded confident, but it was clear to me that the situation was a desperate one: a game of cat-and-mouse, with the cat having every advantage.

Yet somehow, as I looked at Nat, and then back at Penebrygg, despair was not what I felt. What bloomed inside me instead was hope, and with it a great desire to be useful.

"What can I do to help?" I asked.

CHAPTER TWELVE
LISTENING

"Ah! I was hoping you would ask that." Penebrygg gave me a great smile and tipped his spectacles back in place. "We've done well to keep one step ahead of Scargrave. But now that you are here, we may perhaps dream bigger dreams, and vanquish him entirely. Depending, of course, on what magic you can do."

"Very little," I said in a small voice. It was all very well to want to help, but what, really, could I offer them?

Penebrygg's kind eyes met mine. "Do not underestimate yourself, my dear. You may not know your own strength yet, but that does not mean it is not there—buried deep, perhaps, but there."

His confidence was like sunshine on a cold day, and I could not help but be warmed by it. And yet knowing he had such faith in me was daunting, too, for I had no idea how to fulfill it.

"Perhaps we could start with the ruby," Penebrygg suggested. "We know from our experiments last night that it has magic in it—Chantress magic."

It seemed a reasonable place to begin. I pulled on the chain till the ruby slipped out of my bodice. It caught the brilliant morning light, dazzling as a sunrise. The three of us stood still for a moment, as we had the night before, watching it sparkle.

"Extraordinary," Penebrygg breathed. Even Nat seemed mesmerized.

Penebrygg tore his eyes from the ruby and looked at me. "If you take the stone off, do you hear music?"

I lifted the ruby over my head with some reluctance. It was becoming easier to remove it, but I still felt fearful when I did—at least until I heard the singing.

"It's still there," I reported. "Very quiet, but there."

"Marvelous," said Penebrygg.

"But I haven't the faintest idea what it's *for*," I said helplessly. "For all I know, it's music that would burn the house down, or . . . or turn us into cats. It's too soft and mixed up for me to hear much of anything."

"I have something that may help." Penebrygg pulled forth a tightly capped glass vial from his sooty black robes.

Nat looked at it in dismay. "Moonbriar seeds? You carried them through London?"

"Only a few of them. And I was quite careful."

I stared at the dark contents of the vial. "I thought the Invisible College wanted to destroy moonbriar seeds."

"As a rule, yes," Penebrygg said. "After much debate, however, we decided to keep a small amount back for experiments. Sir Barnaby thought I should bring a few of them here, so that we can test your powers. From what we have read, we think they may prove very helpful."

"But are they worth the danger?" Nat asked sharply.

"We shall see." Penebrygg held out the vial. "My dear, open this, and tell me if you hear anything."

With great care, I lifted the stopper, half-afraid of what I might hear. "Why, yes. Yes, I do." The music was clear and distinct, with a complex but identifiable melody.

As Nat gave me a wary glance, Penebrygg bent forward, eyes lighting up behind his spectacles. "That's exactly what Sir Barnaby thought might happen. He has an old treatise on magic that says that most Chantresses find it difficult to understand the music of ordinary objects. Songs sung by objects with magical properties—like moonbriar—are stronger and easier to interpret." He rested his hands on his knees. "Can you tell what the song is about?"

Fearful of getting carried away by the music, I was loath to listen too intently. To my relief, however, the moonbriar's music proved less overpowering than the song I'd heard on the island. A hint of its meaning blossomed in my mind as I listened, and I looked up in astonishment.

"I think it's a song for reading minds," I told them.

Nat froze.

"That's what Sir Barnaby and I believed it might be." Penebrygg rubbed his hands in excitement. "A Chantress who can read minds—what a terror that will be for Scargrave!"

"What a terror for everyone," Nat murmured.

"She is on our side, Nat," said Penebrygg. "Do not forget that."

Nat did not appear reassured.

Penebrygg turned to me. "Of course, we do not know yet if the song works. Tell me, my dear, would you be willing to sing it?"

"I'm not sure." The memory of losing Norrie was all too raw. "If I make a mistake—"

"Nothing ventured, nothing gained," Penebrygg said. "Do your best. That is all we can ask. But you must sing softly. Scargrave has forbidden all music, for fear that it might give cover to Chantresses, and we wouldn't want to draw the attention of his spies. For he does have spies—human ones—during the day."

Sing and the darkness will find you.

"There, there, my dear. No reason to look so terrified. The windows here are shut fast, and the streets are noisy, and the lady whose house wall adjoins our own is quite deaf. If you sing softly, you should come to no harm."

I looked at him and then at Nat, who eyed me back warily.

Well, if Nat had misgivings, so did I. But what was I to do? They were depending on me to save them. How could I do that without exploring my powers?

I closed my eyes, the better to concentrate on the music. The delicate melody danced round and round in my head. With a deep breath for courage, I let myself sing it—very quietly.

When I was done, I stayed still for a moment, trying to sense something beyond my own apprehension and eagerness. Nothing.

I opened my eyes.

"Can you read our minds?" Penebrygg said. Beside him, Nat stood braced as if for a fight.

I shook my head. "Nothing's changed."

Penebrygg shared my disappointment, but Nat looked relieved.

"Never mind, my dear," Penebrygg said. "Sir Barnaby warned me the song itself might not be sufficient. He suggested you try touching the person whose thoughts you wished to divine." He held out his gnarled hand. "Here. Tell me if you can read my mind now."

Without much hope, I took Penebrygg's outstretched hand, closed my eyes, and sang the song again. This time, when I finished, something was different. The song seemed to circle round and round in my mind, ebbing and flowing with my own breath. As it resounded inside me, my own thoughts poured out like water, and a new awareness seeped into me.

"I see a man," I said, still hearing the music in my mind. "He has a long chin and an even longer nose, and his dark hair brushes his shoulders. He does not smile." The man walked toward me, as lifelike as if he were in the room with me. "His eyes burn into me, but no . . . no, he is not looking *at* me, but *through* me. He is ambitious, uncompromising. And . . . and . . . ."

Old, the thrumming said. And yet the man looked young. Were his clothes old? His shoes? What could it be? I gripped Penebrygg's fingers more tightly. "Ah, I see." I almost laughed at the absurdity of it. "His name is Oldville."

I heard a gasp. The image shimmered and vanished, and

with it went the music. I opened my eyes. "Did I say something wrong?"

Penebrygg had let go of my hand and was staring at me, his eyes awestruck behind the glimmering glass. "Dear Heaven. It worked."

I felt rather awestruck myself. "I was right?"

"Right? My dear, you were little short of miraculous. That was Isaac Oldville to the life. Don't you agree, Nat?"

Nat nodded, tight-lipped.

Penebrygg strode about the room in excitement. "Oh, what will Oldville say when he hears? What will everyone say when they see you perform?"

I wasn't sure I'd heard right. "Perform?"

"Why, yes. This afternoon, when the Invisible College meets. Oh, but won't they be amazed!"

"But I've only done it once," I said. "I don't know if I can do it again."

"Practice, my dear—that's what you need," said Penebrygg briskly. "We shall devote the rest of the day to it. But we'll need to keep our strength up. Nat, my boy, could you fetch us some more rolls and cheese from the larder?"

He wasn't looking at Nat, but I was. With an expression like thunder, Nat glared back at me, then turned on his heel and walked out.

CHAPTER THIRTEEN

SUN AND MOON

I practiced the rest of the morning. As I had suspected, the incantation itself was only half the battle; it was equally important to sustain the song inside me after I was no longer singing out loud. When I failed to do that, I saw nothing at all. And if I let the song inside fade, the images I saw wobbled and vanished, and I had to go back to listen to the seeds again. Their melody was intricate enough that I worried I would misremember it and make some terrible mistake.

"You're hungry," Penebrygg said after I lost the song three times in a row. "Pass her a roll, Nat."

Nat did, in silence.

But that was the only way he helped. Although Penebrygg was eager to have him participate in our mind-reading experiment, Nat refused, saying he needed to work on the palimpsest.

Penebrygg looked at him in surprise. "Passing up a chance to experiment? That isn't like you, Nat. Come now: It's high time

Lucy honed her skills on something other than my own aged brain."

"You'll have to find someone else," Nat said, retreating behind his desk. "I don't want any part of this." He bent his head over the palimpsest.

"I'm afraid he's out of sorts today," Penebrygg said softly, almost apologetically, to me. "But no wonder—every time I woke last night, he was pacing about the house. I doubt he had more than three hours' sleep. Let us practice some more, and then I shall see if I can persuade him to rest."

As we continued to work, I became increasingly adept at the magic. Soon I could sustain the music in my mind long enough to read Penebrygg's thoughts several times before I needed to sing the song out loud again. Dipping into Penebrygg's head became almost as easy as dipping into a book, and I could identify the image in his mind within moments: a clock; an apple; the River Thames.

"Let's try one more." Penebrygg offered me his hand, and I shut my eyes, the better to concentrate.

Again the image appeared almost instantly, and I began to describe what I saw. "A portly man with a long face and elegant manners. His right foot seems to pain him, and he is leaning heavily on an ivory cane." Gadabout? Was that his name? No, not quite, but I had it now. "Sir Barnaby Gadding, the leader of the Invisible College."

"Yes," Penebrygg said, but I hardly heard him, for I was still deep in the music. For the first time I felt for myself his satisfaction at my progress. Wanting to impress him still more, I pushed myself to go deeper into his mind. "It pains you to see Sir Barnaby hobbled by gout. Fortunately, he has been improving of late." I probed further. "You and Sir Barnaby have been friends for a very long time, and you esteem him greatly. You believe, however, that sometimes his curiosity gets the better of his judgment—"

Penebrygg pulled his hand from mine, and the stream of thoughts ceased.

"Well done, my dear, well done." The words were hearty enough, but when I saw his face, I wondered if I had done something wrong.

"Should I not have said all that?" I asked.

Penebrygg pushed his spectacles back. "You did exactly right, my dear. It is merely that your acuity is, well . . . quite startling. But, of course, it is good news for us. The Invisible College will be most impressed."

So I hadn't displeased him. That was a relief.

Penebrygg caught sight of the nearest clock. "My goodness, is that the time? I'd say another round of refreshments is in order for both of us." He looked around for more rolls. "Hmmmm . . . we appear to have finished everything off. Perhaps Nat—"

But Nat had fallen asleep at his desk, the pen slack in his fingers.

"Best to let him be," Penebrygg decided. "I shall go downstairs myself."

"Let me help you," I said, rising.

"No, no, my dear. There is no need. You must be tired too, after your exertions. Rest until I come back."

Penebrygg was right: I did feel tired, and it was a comfort to sink back into my chair after he left. When Nat mumbled in his sleep, however, I sat up straight, my senses alert.

What was that he'd said? Something about Scargrave?

I rose and went toward the desk where he lay, his troubled face half buried in his arms. Even in his sleep, he looked angry. Angry with me, no doubt. He hadn't liked me from the start, and my mind-reading abilities had only made matters worse.

But why did the mind-reading bother him so much? It was almost as if he had something to hide.

He mumbled again, and I tried to make out the words. *Grim?* Or perhaps . . . *Shadowgrims?*

I looked at Nat again. *Did* he have something to hide?

Nonsense, I told myself. He couldn't be hiding anything. Not when Penebrygg trusted him so completely.

But what if Nat had been corrupted? What if, unbeknownst to everyone, he was now working for Scargrave?

All at once, I became very aware that the mind-reading song still reverberated inside me. If I touched Nat now, I might be able to see far enough into his mind to know the truth. His fingers dangled in front of me, long and muscular and calloused from the pen.

I touched my hand to his.

The connection was instantaneous and shocking, far stronger than anything I had experienced with Penebrygg. Yet the pictures I saw confused me.

At first, they didn't even seem like pictures at all, merely a darkness that glistened here and there, like the bits of jet that sometimes washed up on the island shore. And then I felt myself moving—something that had not happened when I'd practiced with Penebrygg. I was inching upward, my raw-scraped elbows and knees digging into the black walls that surrounded me. A smoky breeze stung my throat, and my neck burned like fire.

Crackle! A blast of bright, searing heat scorched my feet. Suddenly I was shaking with fear, shaking so hard that I felt my knees begin to give way. But I could not fall, I must not fall, for beneath me lay a fiery pit—

"Stop!" Nat roared.

I blinked, and the images vanished as if they had never been. Instead, I saw Nat before me, on his feet and blazing with rage. Penebrygg was at his side.

"How dare you?" Nat shouted.

Still disoriented by what I'd seen, I stared at him blankly.

Penebrygg laid a placatory hand on his shoulder. "I'm sure she didn't mean—"

Nat shrugged him off and looked at me with loathing. "Chantress you may be," he said. "But for my money, you're no better than Scargrave and his ravens."

He slammed the attic door shut behind him.

† † †

"He didn't mean it," Penebrygg said after Nat had gone. "He was merely speaking in the heat of the moment. He'll come to his senses once he cools down."

Badly shaken, I pulled the necklace back over my head and touched my hand to its stone. "He said I was no better than the Shadowgrims!"

"Well, there you are. A silly thing to say, and he knows it. But he'd had a shock." As I started to speak, Penebrygg held up his hand. "I'm not trying to excuse him, my dear. But perhaps it would be best if you explained to me how you came to read his mind."

I wondered how Penebrygg knew I'd been mind-reading.

"You were speaking out loud, my dear," he told me when I asked. "I only heard the end of it, but it was very clear. Tell me: What made you do it?"

My suspicions, which had carried so much weight at the time, seemed less substantial when I explained them to Penebrygg.

"Betray us to Scargrave? Nat?" Penebrygg's shaggy white eyebrows shot up. "The very idea beggars belief."

I heard disapproval in his voice and tried to defend myself. "But he's hiding something. I know he is. Something to do with flames and fire. And the Shadowgrims."

Penebrygg steepled his fingers together and frowned at me. "Nat has his secrets, as every person does. But they are not what you suppose." He shook his head. "I hate to intrude on Nat's privacy, especially after such a violation. But you have so gravely misunderstood him that I think I must explain matters further."

Violate Nat's privacy—was that what I'd done?

I'd only been trying to make myself safe, an inner voice protested. To make everyone safe. Still, Penebrygg had sown enough doubt in me that I was prepared to hear him out.

"Nat has lived through terrors that most of us are spared," Penebrygg began.

A new and dreadful possibility occurred to me. "Was he captured by Scargrave?"

Penebrygg shook his head impatiently. "Do you think Scargrave the only source of evil in this world? He is not. Not by any measure. Others do grievous harm too—like the magician who bought Nat when he was six."

"Magician?"

"Not a real one," said Penebrygg. "A false conjurer who traveled from town to town, fleecing victims as he went along. He needed a boy to help him, and Nat's uncle wanted his nephew off his hands. So Nat was sold for a few shillings to an unscrupulous scoundrel who beat him and taught him to pick pockets and forced him to climb a tunnel of fire to entertain the crowds. An abominable business, however you look at it."

The grime, the smoke, the flames. I felt sick as I remembered the pictures I'd seen in Nat's mind. Even the few moments I'd experienced secondhand had been suffocating. What must it have been like for him to live through them?

"When he tried to run away," Penebrygg said, "his master put a brass collar on him, one with a ring so that a chain could be attached to it. Two years later, when he tried to run away again, it was still locked around his neck."

Two years, I thought. In a brass shackle for two years. And he was only a small boy.

It explained a lot about Nat, from the scar on his neck to his fierceness.

"The second time he was luckier," said Penebrygg. "He got

away at night, when the collar was harder to see, and he broke into the storeroom behind my shop. Thin as a whippet and starving hungry, he was. Yet it wasn't food he was after, but tools—tools to break the collar. I helped him, and he's been my apprentice ever since."

I tried to take this in.

"He can be prickly, I know," Penebrygg said, "but he has a good head on his shoulders and a stout heart. And a true gift for science. There's many a man in the Invisible College who envies me my apprentice, and that was even before we discovered his talents as a spy and thief. Secret tunnels, hidden staircases, dark passages—nothing daunts him."

"No?" I remembered the fear I had felt when I was in Nat's mind, and I wasn't so sure.

It seemed Penebrygg had his doubts too. "At least he's never given any sign that it has. But it's worried me that he's never spoken of his old life, not since that first night. And he won't let me speak of it either. He's put it behind him, he says. Having you see the truth must have been a terrible shock for him."

"Yes." I couldn't help adding, "For me too."

"Of course, my dear. I'm sorry it happened that way. Sorry for both of you. But in truth, it's Nat I'm most concerned about; I wish he'd talk to me about it, but I suspect he won't."

"I expect he'll never want to see me again," I said.

"Oh, he'll come round, sooner or later. And probably sooner. He's a practical soul, our Nat, and he knows that if we are ever to win this battle, we need every ally we can get." Penebrygg gave me an encouraging smile. "And considered in that light, your attempt to read his mind was a great success. When deployed against our enemies, such a gift will wreak havoc."

I thought this over. "Scargrave has the ravens, and you have me. That's what you mean, isn't it?"

"In a manner of speaking, yes." He peered at me over his glasses. "This troubles you?"

I was as bad as Scargrave, Nat had said. As bad as the ravens. Try as I might, I couldn't get the words out of my mind.

"What the song does"—I struggled for the right words—"what I do—it's a little like the Shadowgrims, isn't it?"

It would have comforted me if Penebrygg had rejected the notion completely. Instead, he said, "Perhaps a little. But only as the sun resembles the moon. Celestial bodies both, but entirely different in their mechanics and effects."

I shuddered. I didn't want to be like the Shadowgrims at all.

Penebrygg reached out and put a hand on mine. "My dear, you are doing this for the right reasons. It is thanks to you that we have our first real hope of defeating Scargrave. Nat knows that. And when he has had time to think it over, he will surely find it within himself to hope, as I do, that your power continues to grow."

I wasn't so certain. "But—"

Around us, the clocks clattered to life, chiming the hour.

"Noon already?" Penebrygg rose from his bench. "It's time we made ready to meet with the College." He beckoned to me. "Come along, my dear—I must show you your disguise."

CHAPTER FOURTEEN
THE APOTHECARY'S SHOP

Penebrygg ushered me down to the room where I had woken that morning.

"By rights, you ought to be clothed as a lady of quality. But rich apparel might be remarked upon, so Sir Barnaby and I thought to disguise you as a serving maid instead." He pointed to the bed, where skirts and bodice lay waiting. "I hope that is acceptable to you."

"Of course," I assured him. The plain gray clothing looked warm, and it was considerably less shabby than what I was wearing. "Where does the College meet?"

"At Gadding House." Penebrygg opened the cupboard in the corner of the room and handed me a cap, apron, and cloak. "I'm afraid we're in rather a hurry, my dear. If you could dress right away, and then meet us downstairs?"

The gray skirts were a tad short, but the full-sleeved bodice hid both the ruby and my Chantress mark, and the loose cap

covered my unruly hair. Wrapping myself in the cloak, I went
down the stairs. As I approached the last landing, voices floated
up to me.

"She only did it because she was frightened," Penebrygg was
saying. "When you think about it, Nat, she knows very little
about either of us."

"She knows we've kept her safe. But that wasn't enough for
her. No, instead, she walks into my mind, without so much as a
by-your-leave, as if she owned me body and soul. I could feel her
there—"

"You could?" Penebrygg spoke with quickened interest. "You
surprise me, Nat. I can't feel her, not in the least."

"Well, I could. It was like having my grave walked on."

"Let us hope our enemies are less perceptive."

"As far as I'm concerned, she *is* the enemy."

I stopped short. I had intended to apologize to Nat, but if he
felt like that, what was the point?

Penebrygg spoke calmly. "We need her, Nat. That is an
immutable fact. You must find a way to work with her."

A long silence. "Very well, then. I will do what is necessary.
But if she tries to read my mind again, I—"

The stairs creaked under my feet. They looked up and saw me.

Nat's shadowed face was angry. "You were eavesdropping?"

"I couldn't help it," I said, stung. "Nobody could, coming
down those stairs."

"Then you'll know I'm only working with you because
I have to. And if you read my mind again, I won't answer for

the consequences. If you can remember that, then we can work together."

"I have no wish to be in your mind ever again, believe me," I said.

As peacemaking, it left a lot to be desired. But Penebrygg seemed cheered by it. "We are allies, yes?"

"Indeed," I said coldly.

Nat matched my tone. "Indeed."

From that point on, his manner was polite enough. But as we walked to the door, I noticed that he was careful to keep well away from me. Whenever I stepped forward, he stepped back—and whenever I glanced at him, he glanced away.

Whatever flash of connection we'd shared that morning was utterly gone. That is, if it had ever existed in the first place.

I told myself I didn't care.

† † †

"Quickly," Penebrygg murmured to me as we went out into the street. "Nat will watch our backs while we go on ahead."

As we hurried along, I wondered if Nat really was watching out for us, or if he was so busy keeping his distance from me that he had lost us. But I knew better than to look behind to check. Much better to appear as if I were out for a stroll with my aged grandsire, Penebrygg had told me. Though nothing about Penebrygg's pace was particularly indicative of age. He was so quick on his feet that keeping up with him was a challenge—not least because it was difficult to draw breath when so many putrid smells assaulted me. The city's drains brimmed with dung, sewage, and filth, and a sick-sweet swelter of rancid meat and rotten apples tainted the air.

If London reeked, I soon discovered that most of it made noise as well. My ears rang as dogs howled, pigs squealed, and carts groaned on every side. And the people! They called and screamed and chattered and scolded, for all the world like a vast flock of gulls fighting for scraps.

What struck me most, however, was not the sheer volume of their cries, but the fear I saw in their faces. Even in full daylight, Scargrave and his Shadowgrims held sway.

Soon I, too, was weighed down with a sense of unease. Though I knew my workaday clothes made me inconspicuous, it unnerved me to be walking out in the open. What if someone laid hands on me? What if they found the ruby—or my Chantress mark?

It was then that I saw the woman watching me.

Silver-haired, she stood in an alleyway, her face still as death, except for her eyes, which gleamed as they fixed on me. As I hastened after Penebrygg, she pulled back into the shadows.

Should I mention her to Penebrygg? No, that would be making too much of what was really only a moment's glance. Besides, she was out of sight now.

"Nearly there, my dear," Penebrygg said softly.

A few minutes later—well out of sight of the alley, I was glad to see—he turned down a narrow lane that was darker and quieter than the other streets we had traveled. It felt safer, some-how, though I had no way of telling if it really was.

When we had walked past half a dozen houses, Penebrygg led us down an even narrower alley and nodded at a shop on our left, where a weathered sign depicting a mortar and pestle hung over a blue-black window. "Here we are."

I stared at the shop in puzzlement. Penebrygg had said we were meeting in Gadding House, but this did not look in the least like a great man's mansion. It was not the time or place to ask questions, however, so I followed him silently over the threshold.

The room I entered was almost as crowded as Penebrygg's own attic of curiosities. Boxes and bottles were everywhere, lining the wooden counter and standing on clever little chests with dozens of drawers. The shelves held long rows of blue-and-white china jars, mortars and pestles, and an assortment of beakers and clay pots. Packets of herbs perfumed the air.

As Nat slipped in the door—he'd been right behind us, after all—Penebrygg nodded at the sharp-nosed man minding the counter. "Good afternoon, Master Apothecary."

"A very good afternoon indeed, I hear." The apothecary glanced at me with frank curiosity.

Penebrygg said quickly, "You'll not have met my brother's granddaughter, here from the country?"

"Roger Harbottle, at your service," the man said to me.

"And of course you know my apprentice," Penebrygg added, motioning Nat forward.

The man nodded. "How can I help you?"

"A dram of Tragacanthum, if you please," Penebrygg said, "and some white saxifrage seeds. Oh, and have you any syrup of Sanguis Draconis?" He leaned forward and intoned another phrase, quick and soft as a single breath.

Master Harbottle frowned. "As to the last, I'm not certain. It will take me some time to make a fresh mixture—at least an hour or more. But you may rest in the treatment room while you wait. If you care to follow me?"

He led us through a small doorway into a long room with a table and chairs. At the back stood shelves and crates and wooden racks where herbs hung drying. After Master Harbottle carefully closed the door to the shop, Nat rolled back the red Turkey carpet and pressed on two floorboards. They pivoted smoothly, revealing stairs that led straight down.

"Lanterns and matches on the left, as usual," murmured the apothecary. "Good luck."

Nat was already descending the stairs. Penebrygg motioned to me to go next.

"But where—," I began.

"Not now, my dear," Penebrygg whispered.

Seeing the urgency in his face, I hastened down the stairs. A match flared below: Nat, lighting a lantern. He did not wait for me but kept moving steadily downward. Not wanting to be left behind in the dark, I followed him. Penebrygg brought up the rear, pulling the floorboards back in place behind him.

At the foot of the stairs, Nat unlocked a door, and we passed through into a tunnel. Though it was solidly built, with timber beams that braced the walls and ceiling, it was low enough that I had to bend my head and narrow enough that we were forced to walk single file. The smell of smoky candles and damp earth pressed in on us, and I wished I had my own candle to hold back the darkness.

On we went, Nat's lantern flickering in front, until at last the passage widened in front of another locked door, twin to the one beneath the apothecary shop.

As Nat unlocked it, I whispered, "Where are we?"

"Beneath Gadding House," Penebrygg told me. "In one of the secret tunnels that lead into its cellars."

"There are others?"

"Three others in addition to this one, each well guarded by friends."

"Master Harbottle is a friend?"

"More than that," said Penebrygg. "He is a member of our College. His wife will take his place at the shop so that he can attend the meeting."

Nat had the door unlocked. Behind it, a short passageway led to another door, larger and more ornate. A guard stood before it, armed with sword and pistol.

Penebrygg said something complicated to the guard in a language that I did not know. The guard replied in kind, and let us through into a room with a single door. Penebrygg twisted the handle this way and that.

"I don't seem to have the knack of it," he said to Nat. "Perhaps you could try?"

"Certainly." Skirting around me, Nat leaned into the handle.

"They change the setting each time," Penebrygg said to me. "I often have trouble with it, but Nat's a wonder with locks."

A delicate click: Nat's work was done. We followed him into a vestibule, where his lantern revealed a small marble fireplace with a golden clock on the mantel. The filigree hands stood at ten minutes past one.

"A little late, but no matter," said Penebrygg softly as we approached a door built into the arch of the wall. He turned to me. "Not an easy audience, my dear, but do your best. A great deal hangs on it."

As I braced myself, he raised his hand and rapped on the door.

CHAPTER FIFTEEN

THE INVISIBLE COLLEGE

"A Chantress?"

"That's what I thought I heard Penebrygg say."

"Are you sure?"

"See how young she is."

"Too young."

I stood before the assembled scholars in the small, windowless library, trying not to show how much their comments unnerved me. I had never before been the object of so much attention. Indeed, it had been many years since I even had seen so many people gathered in one place. Not the easiest audience, Penebrygg had said. He had understated the case.

Everyone seemed to regard me with suspicion.

Well, perhaps that wasn't quite fair. One jovial young man with fleshy hands had brightened when I walked into the room, and a man I recognized as Isaac Oldville regarded me with a restless curiosity. But most of the thirty-odd faces in the room bore expressions of dismay and disbelief.

"My esteemed colleagues." A few paces away from me, Sir Barnaby held up an elegant hand. He looked exactly like the picture I'd seen in Penebrygg's head: an immaculately dressed, rotund gentleman, who had a sprightly air despite his ivory cane and bad foot. "I present to you Miss Lucy Marlowe, whom Dr. Penebrygg assures me is a true Chantress."

The room stirred with comment. An anxious voice said, "What if she is a fraud?"

"Or worse yet, a spy?" someone else added.

Until then, I had been too afraid myself to see the fear in the faces before me. But I saw it now.

Sir Barnaby held up his hand. "Silence, please. The Council would not have invited her unless we were convinced it was safe. And Dr. Penebrygg is prepared to submit proof of his claim before you."

The men quieted, though I could still feel their fear and uncertainty.

Sir Barnaby waved his hand at me. "Miss Marlowe? If you will please show us your arm?"

All eyes fixed on me. My hand shook as I rolled back my sleeve and exposed my Chantress mark for them to see.

"Look!"

"The spiral!"

"By Jove . . ."

"It might only be a scar—"

Mistrustful, they rose from their seats and crowded close for a better view. Not one of them touched me, but their scrutiny—avid and minute and utterly dispassionate—made me feel as if I were a butterfly or a beetle, trapped for observation.

Rattled, I turned my head, looking for a familiar face. Penebrygg and Sir Barnaby had been swallowed up by the throng, but I spotted Nat through a gap in the crowd. He stood by a bookcase at the side of the room, his dark eyebrows drawn in a frown. Although he seemed to be keeping to himself, I wondered if he had somehow poisoned the audience against me.

"Perhaps you would be so good as to return to your seats now?" Sir Barnaby called out. "There is more to come."

Chairs and voices rumbled as the men took their seats. "Can she read the manuscript?" someone called out.

"She failed on the first attempt, I understand," Sir Barnaby said.

I saw many eyes narrow.

"If she can't read it, what good is her mark to us?" a man said.

"If it *is* a genuine mark," another added. "What kind of tests has she been subjected to?"

"Be patient, my friends," Sir Barnaby said. "All will become clear. Dr. Penebrygg, will you demonstrate?"

"With Miss Marlowe's consent, yes."

At the sound of Penebrygg's courteous voice, my confidence began to return. Here, at least, was someone who believed in me and wished me well. "I am ready, sir," I said, and he explained to the audience what they were about to see.

At the mention of mind-reading, the men murmured—not exactly with displeasure this time, but with a blend of alarm and anticipation. When I revealed the ruby and pulled it over my head, they quieted again.

To me, however, the room was anything but silent. As I set the ruby down on a small table beside me, notes eddied around me, elusive and maddening. Though I tried not to listen to them, they distracted me, and I found it difficult to recall the moonbriar song. Fortunately, Sir Barnaby had given me a new vial of the seeds on my arrival. I opened it now.

"The demonstration, of necessity, requires two people. Which of you cares to participate?" Penebrygg asked.

Half the men raised their hands. Penebrygg singled out the jovial dandy at the back of the room. "Mr. Deeps, would you be so good as to come forward? The rest of you shall have your chance later."

Deeps shook out his lace cuffs and swaggered forward. "So you wish to read my mind, missy, eh?"

He paused as if expecting a reply, but I was too busy drinking in the moonbriar song to offer any.

"Not got much to say for herself, has she?" Deeps said in a stage whisper to one of the men sitting across from him. "But then she's only a chit of a girl. Not exactly what we were hoping for, what? Even if she is a Chantress."

Let it go, I told myself, as Penebrygg explained to Deeps what was required. But the dismissal ate away at me, making it hard to steady myself for the singing.

Let it go, I told myself again. *Let it go.*

But it was only when I started to sing that I truly released the weight of his disdain. I gave myself over to the music, and when the notes were there singing inside me, I took Deeps's hand and walked into his mind.

It required more effort to read him than Nat or Penebrygg. Was that because I'd only met him a few minutes ago—or because Deeps's mind was so fragmented? His skepticism warred with his pleasure at being an object of attention, and the rest of him was splintered among a dozen different private thoughts.

Remembering Nat's outrage, I decided to be very careful about what I shared. If I exposed this man's secrets, I'd likely earn his enmity forever. Instead, I described in detail the picture he held out to me at the forefront of his mind: an instrument for making music with black-and-white keys—a spinet, his mind called it.

When I finished, I opened my eyes.

"Was she correct?" Penebrygg asked Deeps.

"More or less." Deeps fluffed his lace sleeves fretfully. "But who's to say it wasn't a lucky guess? Everyone here knows I bought that spinet a fortnight ago. Perhaps Penebrygg mentioned it to her—"

"I did not."

"—or someone else did. But in any case, it does not signify. For even if this young miss did pluck the thought from my mind, it strikes me as a rather labored exercise. I doubt if our enemies will be kind enough to sit still and meditate on a single object for minutes at a time, so that she might more easily read their minds."

I regretted that I had held back from voicing his private thoughts. "The spinet was not all that was on your mind, Mr. Deeps." I spoke clear as a bell across the space between us. "Let me tell you what else I saw: You keep a diary. It is written in code, and in it you record the details of—"

"Hey, ho! How did you know that?" Deeps interrupted. The room buzzed with curiosity.

"You are also annoyed with a certain dancing master because—"

"Enough!"

I had expected Deeps to be angry, but strangely enough, he seemed thrilled. "Did you hear that?" he said to his colleagues. "She read my mind. She truly read my mind!"

"You shall have to watch your step now, Deeps," one of the men quipped. "No more light-o'-loves for you."

"Ah, but I have met the lady who puts all others in the shade." Deeps bowed low before me. "Your humble servant, Chantress."

After that, there was a rush to the front of the room. Half the men wanted me to read their minds; the other half wished to converse with me. Delighted to have made such a favorable impression, I did my best to make tactful use of what I learned of their private musings. But my most daring comments were the ones that delighted them most.

"You are thinking of a building that does not exist—or rather, that exists only in your mind," I told a dignified, straw-haired man named Christopher Linnet. "A cathedral with a vast dome that towers over London. Clustered around it are churches, mansions, arcades, and arches, each one of your own devising. Indeed, you almost wish that the city might be razed to the ground, so that you might have a chance to rebuild it."

"That's our man!" a friend called out.

Master Linnet blushed. "I must admit I'd rebuild it rather differently, if I had the chance. . . ."

"A good fire, that's what you need," someone else said.

The rest of the company laughed, save one: Nat. He sat stiffly, back to the wall, every inch of him conveying disapproval.

Well, he might not like what I was doing, but I had won them over, hadn't I? And that never would have happened if I had refused to give voice to their secrets.

I looked down at the brilliant ruby in my lap. The problem with Nat, I decided, was that he was too touchy. Even Penebrygg had called him prickly. And that was putting it kindly.

Doing my best to ignore him, I turned to the next man who wanted his mind read: Isaac Oldville. I closed my eyes and took his hand. "Red—everything I see is red. Red liquids, red light, red carpets. Even, if I am not mistaken, red hangings in your bedchamber. Why, so great is your love for the color red that I do believe . . . yes, you covet my own red ruby."

Hearing them laugh, I was emboldened to probe further. For a long moment, all was darkness, and I thought perhaps I had lost my connection to Oldville. But no, light was dawning . . . and now I had the uncanny sensation that I was actually seeing the ruby through Oldville's eyes. "You cannot take your eyes off it. It lies there on the table between us, not a foot away from you, dazzling in its beauty and its power. The attraction is so strong that you do not care that the others are laughing."

They laughed harder at this.

The picture was not entirely clear—there was a haze there, and sometimes it darkened unexpectedly—but nevertheless, I felt elated. "But you are determined to prove me wrong," I went on. "You *can* look at something besides the ruby. There, you've done it: You are gazing at your friends and colleagues now. You notice that Deeps's lace is askew, and that Linnet is still chuckling. In the back of your mind, however, you are wondering what the ruby is made of. You want to subject it to experiments—"

"So I should."

I opened my eyes. Oldville did not seem in the least flustered. "And so would the rest of you, if you had your wits about you," he said to his colleagues. "Never before have we encountered such a phenomenon, and there is much yet that we do not understand. Tell me, Chantress, can you read minds like that at a distance?"

I stopped to consider the question. "I don't know. I tried once at the start, and it didn't work. But I've had more practice since then."

"You are willing to try now?"

"If you wish."

"Whose mind will you read?"

I knew no one in London except the men in this room. "Let it be your choice."

"Who shall it be?" Oldville, roused now, stood and took suggestions from the audience.

"My wife."

"My son."

A pause, and someone said, "Scargrave."

"Yes, Scargrave!"

There was no need to put the suggestion to a vote; Scargrave it was, by popular acclaim. But Penebrygg looked worried. "It seems a trifle soon . . ."

Success had given me confidence, however, and I wanted nothing more than the chance to prove myself again. What a coup it would be if I could read Scargrave's mind from this room! The battle would be half won on the spot.

"Let me try," I said.

I closed my eyes, quieted my mind, and sang the moonbriar song again, so that it would have fresh life inside me. After so much practice, this gave me little trouble, but after that I was lost. There were thousands upon thousands of souls here in London. How was I to find Scargrave among them?

At last I opened my eyes and admitted defeat. "I cannot do it."

The men seemed crestfallen, especially Penebrygg, though he rallied himself to say kindly, "Never mind, my dear. It was brave of you to make the attempt."

"Perhaps later, when you are better rested, we might try again," Deeps added.

"Or we might try again now," said Oldville, "using stronger magic."

Everyone turned to look at him.

"With other magic, it helps to have something belonging to

the subject to act upon," he said. "Why should this not be true for Chantresses? A strand of hair would be best. But another personal token may also work."

Christopher Linnet raised an eyebrow in mock appeal. "Anyone here happen to have a strand of Scargrave's hair handy?"

"Not a lock of hair," said Oldville impatiently. "A ring. Lord Scargrave gave Sir Barnaby a signet ring last month—a ring that Scargrave himself used to wear."

"Why, so he did," Sir Barnaby said. "It was a present for my sixty-fifth birthday."

I recalled what Penebrygg had told me: that Sir Barnaby's good relations with the King and Lord Scargrave were part of what helped give cover to the Invisible College.

"Do you really think it would work?" Sir Barnaby said.

"We can but try," said Oldville.

"But do I have it here? That's the question." Sir Barnaby rose from his chair and surveyed the shelves, stopping before a case lined with curiosities and miniatures. "Ah, here it is." He showed me the ring: a thick band of gold on which a flat, heavy emerald was mounted. Sir Barnaby pressed the stone, and it flew open, revealing a glowing portrait no more than half an inch wide; it depicted a serious boy whose red-gold hair shone like the sun. "Quite a wonderful likeness of the King, isn't it? But then, Cooper's portraits are always remarkable."

"It's the first time I've seen a picture of him," I admitted.

"He has the Tudor hair," Sir Barnaby said. "And the hands as well, though you can't see them here. But more to the point, the ring was Scargrave's and it has his mark on it." He pointed to the raven incised inside the band.

A jolt of fear ran through me. *It's only a ring,* I said to myself. *No need to be so afraid.*

But it seemed I was not the only one who was affected. A somber silence had crept over the room, and I was reminded of the risks they took merely in meeting here.

"Will you make another attempt?" Oldville asked.

I could not answer.

"Give her a moment," said Penebrygg, who was still standing nearby. To me, he added, "There's no need to rush yourself. This can wait."

Had he sensed my fear? Not sure what to say, I looked up and saw Nat leaning up against one of the bookcases. He looked back at me, and something flickered in his eyes.

Don't do this, his expression seemed to say, louder than any words.

A flash of anger drove my fear away. Who was he, to tell me what to do?

"I am ready." I took the ring from Sir Barnaby's hand.

It was not necessary to sing the song again. Enough of the magic was still with me that something was already happening. I felt myself swimming in darkness, a humming like music in my ears . . . and then, all at once, I found myself in another person's mind.

But not the one I wanted.

CHAPTER SIXTEEN
A MEETING OF MINDS

I knew at once that something had gone wrong, for the thoughts that flowed through me were not those of a man in control of a kingdom. Instead, they were young and sad and confused:

He despises me, I know he does.

No, of course he does not despise me. How could I think that? He loves me as a father loves his son. He would die for my sake. Truly he would.

But he treats me as a child. A weakling.

And then, overpoweringly:

I am King, and yet my word means nothing. . . .

It was beyond doubt, then: I had landed in the mind of young King Henry the Ninth. But how could that be? Did the subject of the portrait somehow matter more than its owner?

The questions flashed through my head, but almost immediately I lost hold of them. I was so deep in the King's head that I saw and heard everything exactly as he did. There was no veil as there had been with Oldville. Was it practice that was making me more powerful? Or was it merely that the King offered so little resistance?

Standing before a gilded mirror, Henry stared anxiously at his own reflection. The room behind him was richly decorated with gilt and silken tapestries, but it was outshone by Henry himself—a Henry noticeably older and even more solemn than the boy I had seen in the ring's miniature portrait. Underneath the magnificent cloth-of-gold trappings and the brilliant red hair, however, his face was pale and unsure.

Someone spoke from a corner of the room.

"Your Majesty, we bring you the account of arrests."

I hardly heard the words, for the voice itself—charming and musical—shook me to my marrow. The last time I had heard it, I had been hiding in Scargrave's library.

Henry wheeled around. "My Lord Protector?"

Through his eyes I saw Scargrave at last: a man in his prime, iron-haired and agile, with the commanding stance of a man born to lead. In the set of his mouth and the breadth of his bones, he showed the calm strength that had made him a kingmaker.

But then my gaze—Henry's gaze—was drawn to Scargrave's eyes. Deep-set and quicksilver gray, they blazed like a wildfire barely contained. Looking into them, I felt a blast of uncontrolled fear.

My fear—or Henry's?

Both, I thought. But for Henry, fear was perhaps the least of it. As he looked on his Protector, I felt his envy and loyalty and hero worship—and also an onslaught of misery, like a heavy, soaking rain.

Scargrave spoke with scrupulous care to his King. "In no way do I wish to rush you, sire. Indeed, if Your Majesty has reconsidered the plan of receiving these reports directly, rather than accepting a summary through me, then I shall be only too happy—no? You are quite sure? Seventeen is, after all, very young."

Henry's revulsion was so quick and fleeting that I barely registered it. "I am quite sure."

Scargrave nodded at a lanky man in velvet. "Very well, then. Lord Winship?"

Winship bowed low before Henry. "If it please Your Majesty."

"You may begin," Henry said.

Shuffling his papers, Winship began reading as the delegation fanned out behind him. "Herein is offered an account of the arrests made in the King's name in the month of October: For treasonous speech against the King and his advisers, four hundred and fifteen arrests. For treasonous writings, one hundred and twenty-eight. For illegal assembly, three hundred and ninety-one. And for suspicion of treasonous conspiracy, one hundred and twelve. These were passed forward to the usual authorities, and the usual methods of interrogation were employed."

Although Winship recited these statistics in a cheery tone, I could feel King Henry's revulsion returning and deepening.

"Threats alone were enough to break fully a third of the prisoners," Lord Winship continued, "while being held to the flame elicited full confessions from most of the others. The rest were, of course, given to the Shadowgrims, with excellent results. After a quarter-hour confinement, thirteen prisoners confessed everything; by then, of course, their confessions were not necessary, since the Shadowgrims had gleaned the relevant information. Subsequently, these prisoners were punished according to their crimes."

My horror was mirrored by Henry's own.

Winship, however, was still buoyant. "Of the remaining prisoners, all but two died in the presence of the Shadowgrims—some almost instantly, others after some time—thereby eliminating their dangerous persons from the kingdom. In every case, vital information was gleaned by the Shadowgrims before the prisoners' demise. The two prisoners who survived have become the Ravens' Own. They have joined the personal guard of the Lord Protector to the great benefit of all parties." Lord Winship looked up from his notes. "I believe that is everything, Your Majesty."

"As you can see, we have matters well in hand, sire," Lord Scargrave said. "It was a typical month, except for the rise in those attempting illegal assembly. We are looking into that, and it will soon be brought under control."

Henry's hands twisted. *And this is all done in my name.*

"Your Majesty?" Scargrave inquired. "Are you well?"

I felt Henry's despair. And then, faint but real, a spark of rebellion.

"I have a question," he said.

Lord Winship's self-satisfaction faltered. "A question about my report, Your Majesty?"

"Yes." At last, Henry sounded like a king. "Were all those arrests necessary?"

Winship stammered a reply. "Oh, er, yes . . . indeed . . . I suppose . . ."

Scargrave's brow creased in irritation, but he spoke gently to Henry, as if humoring him. "Of course they were necessary, Your Majesty. As you have heard, we have the confessions to prove it."

Henry put out a hand. "I want to see the papers."

Scargrave leaned forward. "There is no need—"

I could feel Henry's heart pounding, but he persisted. "As your King," he said to Winship. "We demand to see the papers."

With an apologetic look at Scargrave, Winship handed them over.

"Your Majesty, this is highly irregular," Scargrave said, his anger well controlled but visible. "As I have said before, there is a time and place for everything—"

"This arrest here." Henry's hand shook as he pointed to the lines, but his voice was steady. "It says that the man complained about the price of bread, nothing more. But he was arrested for treason."

"If you will allow me, Your Majesty." Scargrave took the papers from Henry. "Ah, yes. I remember now. That was indeed how it started, with a complaint about prices."

"That is not treason," Henry said.

"It is how treason starts. A complaint about prices is a complaint about the King's policies—a complaint, in essence, about the King himself."

"But he was speaking of bread."

"He was spreading dissatisfaction and discontent. The merest whisper, you might say—and yet it takes only a tiny flame to start a fire. And like flames, such whispers can lead to disaster. They swell and grow and embolden others, until at last the murmur becomes a shout, and people are baying like madmen for the King's blood."

"But this man—"

"This man was arrested and questioned for good reason. And that would be true even if the complaint about bread were the sole charge we had against him. But perhaps it will interest you to know that when his house was searched, he was found to be in possession of incendiary pamphlets by Locke and Grotius on the limits of royal power and the right of subjects to rebel against their King. When threatened with the Shadowgrims, he confessed all, and he has been sentenced to ten years' hard labor on the Isle of Man. You are well rid of him."

"But—"

"You would prefer that we had allowed him to remain free?" Lord Scargrave turned scathing. "Free to read his pamphlets and his books about the natural rights of men, and then to meet with others of like mind, and plot against the lawful rulers of this country? And then to murder you, as the King before you was murdered?"

Henry stared straight ahead. Only I knew how deeply the words bit into him, and how much—at least at this moment—he loathed the Lord Protector.

But it seemed Scargrave sensed something of what was in his mind, for he reined himself in. "Forgive me, Your Majesty." He inclined his head, as if to show deference to Henry. "I spoke too bluntly, and for that I ask your pardon. It was never my intent that you be forced to contemplate such matters. Indeed, I have pledged my strength, my wealth, and my honor in the hope of preserving you from such an end."

I felt Henry's loathing ebb, to be replaced by self-doubt.

"Perhaps my methods sometimes strike you as harsh," Scargrave continued, "but how else can I defend you? And not only you but the very integrity of the kingdom itself? Someday, I hope we can contemplate new ways of governing men, but for now we must take no risks. For you are the last of a long and noble line, Your Majesty, and if we lose you, there is nothing standing between us and chaos."

Henry was now hanging on every word. Caught inside him, I found myself moved by the earnest voice despite myself. I hated Scargrave and everything he stood for, but it was impossible to deny that in his own way he loved his King and his country. It was what he had done in the name of that love that I despised.

"Make no mistake," Scargrave said. "I take no pride in imprisoning my fellow men. I would rather it did not need to be done. But without a king, without an heir, we would succumb either to civil war or foreign invasion. Next to the carnage these would cause, even a thousand arrests are as nothing."

Henry raised his head and met Scargrave's burning eyes.

"I do this to keep you safe," Scargrave said quietly.

"We are fortunate to be under your protection," Henry whispered. The last spark of his rebellion went out.

As he continued to stare into Scargrave's eyes, a great feeling of dread overcame me—a thickening of the air, and a darkening and fluttering on every side, as of many wings. . . .

Suddenly I knew that I must get out.

With a wrench, I damped down the music inside me and pulled myself back from everything in front of me. Back from the King's mind, back from the gilded chamber, back from those burning, restless eyes—

I blinked, and the ring gleamed gold in my hand.

"Miss Marlowe?" Sir Barnaby's face hovered close. "Are you quite all right?"

"Yes." Still dazed by the journey, I pulled the ruby back over my head. "Yes, I am. But why did I reach the King and not Scargrave?"

"The King?" Sir Barnaby said in dismay. "Miss Marlowe, you must tell us everything."

"I didn't speak as I went along?" I had meant to, but perhaps I had gone in too deep for that.

"You said a few words at the beginning only, and we couldn't quite catch them," Sir Barnaby said. "But no one dared disturb you; you were clearly elsewhere."

I told them everything I could recall about my time inside the King's mind.

When I was done, Oldville held out his hand. "May I see the ring?"

Once I had handed it over to him, he played with the clasp. "Nat, take a look at this. There's something odd about the mechanism."

As Nat was drawn into the proceedings, Penebrygg whispered in my ear. "Oh, my dear! What a coup!"

"But it was the wrong person," I whispered back.

"No matter."

Before Penebrygg could say more, Nat held up the ring. "Here's your answer." The portrait swung loose, revealing a secret inner frame with a lock of red-gold hair.

Christopher Linnet whistled. "King Henry's hair."

Sir Barnaby looked at the ring in genteel consternation. "I had no idea it was there."

"Well," said Oldville grimly. "Now we know what went wrong. Few totems are more powerful than hair."

"Ah! But let us look on the bright side," Samuel Deeps urged. "The Chantress may have failed to reach Scargrave, but she most certainly excelled in reading the King's mind. I have never heard anything like it." He bowed before me, silk-clad leg neatly extended. "Chantress, I offer you my keen admiration and my deepest gratitude. You have aided our cause immeasurably."

As a rumble of "Hear, hear" crossed the room, Penebrygg beamed and patted my hand. "Well done, my dear, well done," he murmured.

"You mean, it was important—what I learned from the King?" I asked.

"Yes, it was," Sir Barnaby said. "We have long suspected that the King's heart is with us, and that his true nature abhors the Shadowgrims. But only now do we know it for certain. And that is a great relief. It suggests that if we can but find a way to rid ourselves of Scargrave and his ravens, the kingdom will be in good hands."

Oldville nodded curtly at me. "And that is not all: We now know that you can read minds at a distance. And that means we stand a much better chance of defeating Scargrave." He appealed to his fellow philosophers. "We must procure some artifact of Scargrave's as quickly as possible."

"But how?" Deeps puzzled.

"I am to dine with him later this week," Sir Barnaby said thoughtfully. "But I can hardly take a lock of his hair, can I? At least not without arousing his suspicions."

"Not a lock, no," Oldville agreed. "But perhaps a single strand? One lying loose on his cloak or his hat?"

"I can try," Sir Barnaby said doubtfully.

"Do not take great risks," Christopher Linnet urged. "If you are exposed, we are lost."

From the anxious murmur behind him, I gathered that many members agreed.

Ignoring them, Oldville regarded me with a calculating eye. "Tell me, Miss Marlowe: Would you be prepared to make the experiment at our next meeting—or sooner, if need be?"

There was something about his gaze that made me feel like running away. But I did not want him to know that. "Of course, sir."

A clock chimed.

"Good gad!" Sir Barnaby exclaimed. "Is it that late already? We must begin to disperse this instant, else some of you will be walking home in the dark." He waved a hand in the air. "You know what to do."

It seemed they did, for they were already gathering up their belongings and organizing into groups.

"We stage the departures so that our exodus will not be too noticeable," Penebrygg told me. "But do not fear. We ourselves will be among the first to go."

As I adjusted my kerchief to hide my necklace, I saw Nat coming toward us, his face somber as a funeral. When his eyes met mine, he stopped short, then stepped back.

Others in the room might have changed their minds about me. But evidently he had not.

"Go in safety, and be of good cheer," Sir Barnaby called out as we readied ourselves. "There is much that must still be done, and many dangers that must be faced. But we have seen great wonders tonight—and with Miss Marlowe on our side, no doubt we shall soon see even more."

Penebrygg beamed at me, his smile full of pride. But Nat looked more troubled than ever.

CHAPTER SEVENTEEN
A STEP TOO FAR

On our journey back, we joined the anxious throng trying to get to their homes before sunset. Though no one in particular stopped to stare at us, I felt wary as we approached the alley where I had seen the woman with the gleaming eyes. No one was there this time, but as we passed, I had the dreadful sense that someone was watching me.

The feeling faded quickly, however, and we reached Penebrygg's house in safety. As Nat shot the bolts home, I sighed and tugged off my cloak. Now that the strain of the afternoon was over, I felt shivery and spent—and strangely let down, too.

Penebrygg's response, as usual, was to suggest food. "A meal, that's what we need. Nat, come to the kitchen and help me prepare it." He nodded at me. "You go up and rest, my dear. We'll call you when it's ready."

Grateful for the offer, I leaned forward to hang my cloak up and almost crossed paths with Nat. He pulled back so abruptly that my face flamed.

You would think I was a leper, I thought, but I was too tired to argue about it. Instead, I climbed the stairs away from him. Each step seemed an effort, but I couldn't stop at the bedchamber, not when I knew that the bed I'd be resting on was Nat's. Pushing on, I climbed still higher, to the attic.

The long, high room was still bright, even at this late hour—but through the west window, I saw the sun sinking toward the rooftops, its molten glow setting the city alight.

How long till dusk? A half hour? Perhaps less? On the island I would have known for certain, but not here. Unnerved by the prospect of imminent nightfall, I almost retreated downstairs, back to lights and company and the courage to be found in numbers. But I didn't want to look like a coward in front of Nat.

Instead, I forced myself to remain where I was. If a Shadowgrim were to perch on the roof again, I told myself, I would just ride the fear out. The ravens didn't know I was here; they couldn't touch me. Anyway, they weren't even awake yet. For now I was perfectly secure.

To be on the safe side, however, I allowed myself to shutter the attic windows and to shut the chimney damper. The shutters were simple enough to work, I found, and the draperies that covered them slid easily on their rods. I stopped only to light a candle on the last remnants of the smoldering fire, so that I would not be left in the dark.

Once I had shut out the coming night, I felt safer. Yet as I set my candlestick down, I felt the pangs of homesickness. Was it only yesterday that Norrie and I had been together on the island? Truly, it felt more like a year.

Oh, Norrie, where are *you?*

Though Sir Barnaby had assured me that the Invisible College would do its best to find her, I knew their inquiries might well come to nothing. And there seemed to be no way that I myself could help find her. . . .

Or was there? With rising excitement, I thought of the moon-briar song. If it had allowed me to reach the King, perhaps I could use it to reach Norrie, too. Except that I had nothing that belonged to Norrie here: no lock of hair, no possessions of any sort.

Could I reach her without that, given how close we were?

Unlikely, perhaps, but I had to try.

Slowly, deliberately, I took off the ruby and set it on the table beside me. The room glimmered with beguiling notes: When I listened carefully, I could even hear the moonbriar seeds that Penebrygg had locked away in three nested coffers. By now, I knew their song very well, but to be absolutely sure I sang it correctly, I held the coffer to my ear. Their song was very soft indeed, but it was powerful all the same. I sang it, then tried to see my way to Norrie.

It was no use. Norrie was unreachable.

Trying not to think what "unreachable" might mean, I put the ruby back on again and went in search of more light.

Cradling my flickering candle, I looked around for a proper lantern. Spying one by Nat's desk, I held my candle to it and waited for its wick to catch fire. When it did, the warm light illumined the moss-green cover of the book on Nat's desk.

Scargrave's book.

I stared at it. Yes, it was Scargrave's, beyond a doubt. It had the same device on its spine that I had seen on the ring: a raven strutting, talons out.

Of course, an image alone was not enough to connect me to Scargrave. That much I knew already, from the ring. But I remembered what had been said at the meeting, and I wondered if perhaps there was something inside—some writing, or perhaps even that strand of hair that Oldville was hoping for—that would be of more service.

I looked again at the book—and shivered.

Don't be silly, I told myself. *A book can't hurt you. And neither can a piece of hair. They're tools, nothing more. You needn't use them until you're ready.*

Gingerly, I took up the book.

There. That wasn't so terrible, was it?

As my confidence grew, I felt curiosity stirring inside me, and with it my sense of adventure. Perhaps I ought to wait for Nat and Penebrygg, but what I really wanted to do was to experiment with the book on my own, without Nat glowering at me. I was learning that there was something to be said for facing your fears directly—and discovering that you were strong enough to handle them. So why not face a few more? Why not go in search of Scargrave myself?

Before my courage could desert me, I stripped off the ruby and opened the volume. There on the frontispiece was the proof of ownership, a signature written in a strong, slashing hand: *Lucian Richard Arthur Ravendon.* I placed my fingers squarely on it.

Without warning, darkness swept over me, thick and suffocating as a shroud. I felt myself growing colder and colder and colder. And then the darkness lifted . . .

A book. I was looking at a book.

Not the one I had just been holding, but another, much older one, its ivory cover mottled with spots and stains and veining, like a human hand. A multitude of silvery chains bound it to the stone wall.

The grimoire, I realized. I was looking at the grimoire through Scargrave's eyes. A sense of exultation filled me, bolstered by the mood of anticipation in Scargrave himself.

Anticipation of what? I tried to burrow deeper and find out, but the details eluded me. It was as if I were standing outside a guarded room, lacking the passwords to let myself in. All I had were the images I saw through his eyes—the book, the chains, the stone wall—and a few emotions: the anticipation I had felt earlier, and now a creeping sense of being watched . . .

"Who's there?"

It was Scargrave himself who uttered the words. But they felt almost as if they had come from my own lungs.

I began to feel very afraid. Before this, a core part of me had always stayed separate during mind-reading. However strongly I felt the other person's feelings, I had been aware that they were not quite *my* feelings. But this was different. Still locked out of parts of Scargrave's mind, I nevertheless felt myself falling deeper and deeper into the rest of him.

"Who's there?" he called again, and this time it was a whisper.

The fear of being watched, the fear of being found out: I felt them as if they were my own. And then the sliver of me that was still separate realized what was happening: Scargrave wasn't sensing the presence of an ordinary intruder. Whether he knew it or not, he was sensing *me*.

I silenced my fear and let myself thin out as if I had no existence, no substance. In response, I felt his throat ease, his pulse calm—felt this as if it were my own body.

But in hiding from him, I had lost something essential: The boundaries between us had all but disappeared.

A hand hovered over the silver-threaded book. His hand? My hand? Was there any difference now?

There must be, some submerged part of me tried to say. There must be. But the rest of me was lost in sensation: the flutter of anticipation rising again; the hush of the tomblike room; a chill like ice as the hand neared the book . . .

Hand and book met. A searing flash, like the heat of a thousand suns, and silence split into sound: croaking and cawing and a cacophony of screams.

The ravens, reporting to their master.

No! I did not want to know, did not want to hear . . .

The shock had brought me back to myself, but I had gone too far, and I could not pull myself free. The jabbering Shadowgrims circled, my body burned, and the fiery darkness claimed me.

CHAPTER EIGHTEEN
DARKNESS

It was like death, that darkness—a velvet shroud wrapped hot and thick around me, holding me silent, suspending me beyond time and reason. In the depths of that vast, sweltering silence, I felt the Shadowgrims hovering at the edges of my mind.

Then, out of the darkness, a single intelligible phrase:

"Three days it's been, and she still hasn't responded."

A determined speaker, young and strong. After endless moments, the name came to me: Nat.

Had the ravens caught him, too?

I strained to open my eyes.

"Did you see that?" It was Nat again, a note of excitement in his voice. "She blinked. I'm sure of it."

"So she did." It was Penebrygg.

"That must be a good sign."

"Let's hope so, Nat. But I confess I've never seen a fever quite like this." Penebrygg came closer. "None of us has."

My eyelids were heavy as headstones, but at last I raised them. Yet when I tried to focus, it was like looking through a crooked piece of glass half melted by flames. In it, I saw sunlight picking out the crooked timbers of Nat's bedchamber, and Nat and Penebrygg curving over me.

"Look! She's coming round."

"God be praised," Penebrygg said heavily. "My dear, can you speak?"

I tried to make a sound, any sound, but I could do nothing but shiver and burn.

"I'll fetch another blanket," Nat said.

By the time he was back, I was able, with great effort, to murmur my thanks.

"She spoke." I had never heard him sound so pleased.

"So she did." Penebrygg patted my hand. "Well done, my dear. Well done."

I struggled to speak again. I wanted to tell them about the book, to warn them—

"What's that?" Penebrygg listened to my mumbling, then shook his head. "No, I can't make it out. Can you, Nat?"

"No." One word, but I could feel the strength of his frustration.

"Rest," Penebrygg told me. "Rest and we'll try again later."

Although I did not want to obey, my eyes wouldn't stay open. The hot darkness swept over me again. But this time, in the silence, a breeze came to cool me. And one by one the ravens took flight and left.

† † †

When I woke again, I was alone. But for the first time since the darkness had taken me, I was cool. All that remained of the heat was an ache in my neck and a faint prickling in my hands and feet.

Haltingly I sat up and touched the ruby that hung from my neck. Who had put it back over my head? Penebrygg, I guessed, since I couldn't imagine Nat being willing to. Or had I myself grabbed it, in a last bid for self-preservation? Come to that, who had removed my gray skirts and bodice, leaving me in only my shift? Was that Penebrygg too? I tried to remember, but that only made my neck ache more. So I looked around the room instead.

To judge from the fading light, it was late afternoon. Nearly time, in fact, to shutter the window. Not sure yet whether my tingling limbs could be trusted, I waited for someone to come. But after a while, anxiety got the better of me, and I crawled out of bed, determined to close the window myself. I could not bear to be exposed to the Shadowgrims again.

The window was only a few feet from the bed, but even over that short distance, my feet betrayed me. I tripped, and my shift caught on the bedstead and tore. A fine picture I must make, I thought wryly.

I hoisted myself up and peered out the window. And then I stopped short. Out in the three-cornered yard, a black-clad figure was slipping into Aristotle's shed.

A woman? Or a man in long black robes? The door closed too quickly for me to tell for certain.

I must warn Nat and Penebrygg.

I slammed the shutters closed and slipped into the gray skirts, which I'd spied at the foot of the bed. Tugging on the bodice, I rushed back toward the landing. Below, I heard a clatter of pots. They must be in the kitchen, then.

I headed downstairs, but my feet were clumsy and swollen. I stumbled down one flight of stairs, then skidded and nearly went flying down the rest. As I clutched at the rail, a feverish heat enveloped me, blurring my mind and making me forget my errand. My moments inside Scargrave's head came rushing back, and I heard the flutter of ravens' wings in the air.

And then, a new sound, a sane sound: Penebrygg's voice floating up to me.

"You showed presence of mind in knocking away that book, Nat. That may have been what brought her back to us."

"Who knows? Maybe I only made things worse," Nat said, sounding discouraged. "That's part of the problem with magic. You never know where you are."

"No," Penebrygg agreed with a sigh. "No, you don't."

"I knew trouble would come of her mind-reading," Nat said. "But I thought it was the rest of us who would suffer. I didn't think she would suffer too." A pause. "And worse than anyone else."

"It is only a temporary defeat, Nat." To my surprise, it was Sir Barnaby who spoke. "You said she has woken and that she has even tried to speak. That can only be good news. Let's hope we have her on the mend, and that she'll be singing for us again soon."

His words cleared away the sweltering fog in my mind.

I will never sing again. Not if it means going back into that darkness. Not if it means losing myself like that.

I pulled myself upright, determined to go tell them so. And then, with a shock, I remembered the woman in the shed.

I clattered down the stairs as fast as I was able and burst into the main chamber.

"Lucy!" Penebrygg exclaimed. "You shouldn't be out of bed."

I steadied myself against the wall. "There's someone in Aristotle's shed."

Nat slipped out at once.

"I am right behind you," Penebrygg called after him. "Sir Barnaby, will you guard the back door?" To me, he said, "Hide yourself, my dear. In the cupboard there, you'll find a hidden door that leads to the cellars—a way out, should you need one."

I was still trying to figure out how the cupboard mechanism worked when I heard the back door open. As I ducked down, the door clunked shut, amidst grunting and squawking.

"Do you see it?" It was Nat's voice, low and urgent. "On her arm, there: the Chantress mark!"

Another Chantress? Here?

I crept forward and peeked out. Penebrygg's back was to me, and he had a cudgel in his hand. Facing him, Nat held an intruder fast. I recognized the silvery hair and dead-white face of the woman from the alley—and I recognized, too, the mark on her arm, a bleached-bone spiral exactly like mine.

She twisted, her long necklace of bone beads clacking as she turned. Nat pulled back his hand in surprise. "She bit me!"

Penebrygg spoke in the most thunderous tone I had ever heard from him. "Who are you, madam? And what were you doing in our yard?"

In the candlelight, the woman's eyes gleamed angrily. But she did not speak.

Sir Barnaby stepped into the light. I was shocked to see that he, too, was holding a prisoner, this one veiled by a hooded cloak. "Perhaps this one will tell us more."

"Take off your hood," Penebrygg ordered.

A trembling hand jerked it back.

I gasped.

It was Norrie.

CHAPTER NINETEEN
REUNION

"Do you have any idea how much I've worried about you?" Norrie clutched my shoulders, crushing me to her. "Nearly made myself sick with it, I did."

My only answer was to sigh with relief. Norrie was safe. Norrie was here. My song had not killed her.

"The moment I heard you singing, my heart turned to water," Norrie said. "I didn't know what to do. What your mother would have said to me—"

"Why didn't you give me her letter?" I tried not to sound reproachful, but the words tumbled out. "Why didn't you tell me she was a Chantress?"

"Tell you?" Norrie pulled back. "Oh, child, I couldn't!"

"But if I'd known—"

"I was to keep you safe, that's what your mother said. And I wasn't to let you sing until you came of age."

"At twenty-one?"

Norrie faltered. "Well, no. Chantresses are fifteen when they come into their powers."

"But I *am* fifteen."

"So you are, child. So you are." Norrie's eyes watered, and for the first time since her arrival, I saw the weariness in her face. "And I did think to tell you on your birthday. But how could I send you back into the world that killed your own mother? For killed is what I knew she must be, when she didn't come back. And I was right." Her mouth trembled. "Sweet lady. She didn't deserve what happened to her."

I couldn't bear to think about it. "But what happened to you? Are you all right?"

"I'm well enough, child. I landed in a field by Lord Scargrave's country house in Ealing. A field where they used to burn witches, I'm told." With a look of mingled gratitude and awe, Norrie turned to Nat's captive, now released, though Nat looked ready to grab hold of her again, given half an excuse. "I was lucky your godmother found me there—and then found you."

I blinked. "My . . . godmother?"

"Lady Helaine Audelin," Norrie said, curtseying to the silver-haired woman. "The greatest Chantress of her generation."

Gaunt to the point of emaciation, Lady Helaine stood erect as a queen, her gleaming eyes fixed on me. "So you are Lucy." She tilted her head, as if tracing a resemblance. "You are very like your mother."

Chantress she might be, but there was nothing musical in her voice, which rasped like a rusty chain.

Disconcerted, I said, "I—I don't remember you."

"No?" Lady Helaine did not seem particularly bothered by this. "Well, there will be time enough for us to become acquainted again, now that you are grown." She waved an imperious hand at Nat, Penebrygg, and Sir Barnaby, who were standing behind her. "But first tell me this: These men, who are they? Have they mistreated you?"

Nat balled his fists. "How dare you accuse us—"

"My lady," Penebrygg said at the same time, "we would never mistreat Lucy—"

Lady Helaine's voice grated harshly, silencing them. "Let my goddaughter speak!"

"They're telling the truth," I said, startled by her high-handedness. "They've treated me very well."

"You are certain? If they have done you any harm, they shall answer for it." Lady Helaine had a combative look in her eye.

"They've given me shelter and kept me safe," I said firmly.

"Very well, then." Lady Helaine waved a regal hand at the men again, as if in dismissal. "You may leave us."

"Leave?" I stared at her, not understanding. "Why should they leave?"

Nat's hand went to his knife. "We're not going anywhere."

"My lady, we cannot leave you alone with her," Penebrygg said, "not when we know so little about you—"

"I am Lucy's godmother," Lady Helaine interrupted. "Norrie will vouch for that."

Norrie drew closer to me. "That she is."

"There," said Lady Helaine. "What more do you need to know?"

"Plenty," Nat said hotly. "Everyone knows Scargrave's killed all the Chantresses. If you are who you say you are, how did you escape from him? And how long have you been at liberty? And why haven't you used your magic to destroy the Shadowgrims?"

I gazed at Lady Helaine in alarm, wishing I'd thought to ask such questions myself. Yes, Norrie had vouched for her. But how much did that mean, when Norrie was so newly arrived herself? What if Lady Helaine was deceiving her?

"My magic?" Lady Helaine repeated. Her glance skittered away from Nat to me, and for a moment, she did not look quite sane.

When I stepped back, she snatched at my arm, wild-eyed. "Do not leave me, goddaughter! If you only knew how I have longed to find you . . ."

I sidestepped her, and Nat darted between us, his knife out. Behind Lady Helaine, Norrie gave a little moan of distress.

But Lady Helaine had eyes only for me.

"You wish to know about my magic? My magic is gone." Her hoarse voice cracked, then dwindled to a whisper. "The Shadowgrims devoured it all."

† † †

"Having told you that, I suppose I may as well tell you the rest," Lady Helaine said, with more self-possession than I would have thought possible. Though brittle as glass, she no longer looked crazed.

We had adjourned to the attic with food and drink. Sir Barnaby, Penebrygg, and Nat had insisted on coming with us, and I was glad of their company. Lady Helaine might be my godmother, but she was essentially a stranger to me, and I felt the need for stronger allies at my back than Norrie, who was at present slumped beside me, half-asleep. She had never been one for late nights, dear Norrie, and once we had retreated to this dim, quiet chamber, she could barely keep her eyes open.

I, however, was wide-awake. I was chilly enough to need a blanket—a sign, I hoped, that the Shadowgrim fever had truly broken. Leaning forward over the crumbs of what had once been a full plate of smoked fish and cheese, I sipped at my peppermint tea. I was hungry to hear Lady Helaine's story, and yet dreading it too. If a great Chantress in her prime had been unable to defeat Scargrave, what hope was there for me?

"It began with my cousin Agnes, of course," Lady Helaine said with distaste. "A silly, soft-hearted fool, and that was before she was in her dotage. It was she who sang for Lord Scargrave, without a thought for the trouble she was making for the rest of us." She nodded at me. "But your mother found out and came to warn me."

"How did she know?" I asked.

"She wouldn't say exactly, but if anyone would know the truth about Agnes, it was your mother. Agnes adored her, and your mother used to call her 'Auntie Rose.' Roser was her last name."

Auntie Rose. At the sound of the name, I felt the dab of a doughy hand against my cheek, saw a wrinkled currant bun of a face peering into mine. *Auntie Rose.* How old had I been when we'd gone to visit her? Six? Seven?

"You're just like your mother," she'd said in delight.

Auntie Rose. Cousin Agnes. The woman who, with the best of intentions, had unleashed this horror on the kingdom.

With a sharp look at me, Lady Helaine continued with her story. "Your mother and I went to London to try and undo the damage Agnes had done, and we penetrated the Tower where the grimoire was kept. But before we could lay our hands on it, Lord Scargrave discovered us, and he ordered his filthy birds to attack."

"All of them?" Nat asked suspiciously. "That's not how he usually does it."

"There was no 'usual' then." Lady Helaine's voice became rougher than ever. "The Shadowgrims were newly created, and Scargrave knew very little about them. Instead of going after us with one or two birds, he set them all on us at once."

She turned to me. "Your mother died almost immediately." She stopped, as if struggling for words. "I don't think she suffered. A moment of agony, perhaps, but then there was nothing left but a pile of ash."

I stared at the fire, at the dull glow of the coals and the coat of gray fur on the grate. I felt sick.

"And you?" Sir Barnaby asked Lady Helaine.

"I fought," she said with grim triumph. "The Shadowgrims sapped my magic so quickly that I could not defeat them, but at the last moment, I managed to sing a song of escape—taking care to leave a pile of ash behind me, so that everyone would think that I, too, was dead. But that was the last magic I was ever able to work."

"Still, you held off the ravens," Penebrygg said. "We thought that was impossible, even for a Chantress."

"For most, it is. But I was the most powerful of my generation, and the most learned." She spoke with chilly pride. "No one else had such training, or such skill."

"If you lost your magic," I asked, "how did you find me?"

"By smell." Lady Helaine nodded at Norrie, who was gently snoring. "I found her in exactly the same way."

I was sure I had misheard. "You found us by *smell*?"

"Yes," Lady Helaine said. "I cannot work magic myself, but I have lived too long with enchantment not to be able to sense it in the air, especially the enchantment worked by my own kind. Four evenings ago, I caught the tang of it, fresh currents coming from the east. In the old days, the smell alone might have told me more about you and the magic you were working, but that is lost to me; I could tell only that a Chantress was at work. Yet that was enough. I followed the smell, and it brought me to Norrie. And the next day I caught the scent of it again, coming from this part of London. I traced it to this house, and I have been watching you ever since."

"But why—?" Nat began.

"Enough." Lady Helaine's eyes glinted. "I have answered a great many questions. It is time for me to put some to you." She singled me out with a look. "Goddaughter, Norrie tells me that you took off your stone on Allhallows' Eve. Do you have it with you now?"

In answer, I brought the ruby into the light.

Even Lady Helaine seemed dumbstruck by the sight. She leaned in close and peered into its depths, then asked me to rotate it slowly before her, as if she were a jeweler making a minute inspection. "Oh, that is a very fine one," she whispered at last. "Very fine indeed."

"I've kept it on most of the time," I said. "Except for the mind-reading, but—"

"What?" Lady Helaine's spindly hands stiffened. "What magic have you been working, goddaughter?"

I told her.

"You entered Lord Scargrave's mind with moonbriar magic? Without protection?" In icy fury, Lady Helaine turned on Sir Barnaby, Penebrygg, and Nat. "You forced her to do this?"

Penebrygg looked abashed. "We did not know there was any danger."

"It wasn't a question of forcing," I said. "I wanted to try."

Our words only seemed to increase Lady Helaine's anger. "You have been careless beyond imagining, all of you! No wonder I could smell magic in the air. It is a wonder that all the kingdom did not."

I touched my hand to the ruby.

Lady Helaine glared at me. "Never take that stone off again."

CHAPTER TWENTY
STONES

My hand stilled on the stone. "Never take it off? Why?"

"Because that stone was meant to protect you," Lady Helaine said, her voice ratchety with suppressed fury. "Every Chantress has one. It is created by her mother and godmother, and it protects her from the Wild Magic that abounds in the world."

"Wild Magic?" I asked.

"What's that?" Nat asked warily. Behind him, Penebrygg and Sir Barnaby looked confused.

"Don't you people know anything?" Lady Helaine exclaimed. "Wild Magic is everywhere. Everything—seeds, rocks, wind, rain, even the earth itself—has its own music, its own singing. And in ancient times, we Chantresses listened to that singing, and shaped our own songs from it."

"Then why is it bad?" I asked.

"Because not everything in this world wishes us well," Lady Helaine said grimly. "Indeed, many things wish us harm. And as our Chantress blood has thinned out, it is easier for us to be misled by them, to follow their siren songs even unto our own destruction and death. That is why our ancestresses created the stones. They soak up the songs of Wild Magic and keep them from reaching us—"

"How exactly does that work?" Sir Barnaby interrupted, with interest. "She's not supposed to wear the stone around her ears, is she?"

"Of course not." There was a disdainful edge to Lady Helaine's voice, as if she were explaining the obvious to imbeciles. "It is the heart that hears Wild Magic. And thus it is the heart that must be protected from the songs of those who would harm us. As long as a Chantress keeps her stone close to her heart, she will be safe."

"Er . . . I see." Sir Barnaby nodded uncertainly.

Nat and Penebrygg looked as if they would like to ask more questions, but I was the one who spoke first. "I heard singing even before I took off the stone—out in the garden, on the island. How can that be?"

"That happens sometimes," Lady Helaine admitted. "Especially when the Chantress is young and powerful and very vulnerable, as you are. When the Wild Magic is very strong—on Allhallows' Eve, for instance—it may even discover your own desires and use them against you."

"I don't understand," I said.

"What were you thinking of, the day you heard that music?" Lady Helaine's eyes glimmered. "Were you thinking of how much you wanted to be home? Or were you, perhaps, wishing for adventure? For excitement?"

How did she know? I looked away, not liking to be read so well.

"And the Wild Magic heard you," Lady Helaine said softly. "It heard you and called you home, and then put you in the greatest possible danger. That is what Wild Magic does. That is why you must wear your stone. If any Wild Magic does reach you—and only the strongest magic will—it will be too weak to do any real damage. It is only if you take the stone off and let the magic into your heart that you can be hurt by it."

"Fascinating," Sir Barnaby murmured.

Lady Helaine speared him with an angry glance. "You miss my point, sir, which is this: A Chantress who removes her stone and opens her heart to Wild Magic will soon find herself trapped or betrayed—or worse. As Lucy has learned to her cost."

I felt every eye come to rest on me.

"The first mistake was yours, and yours alone," Lady Helaine said to me. "It came out of ignorance, but it was no less serious for all that. You listened to the wind on Allhallows' Eve—the wind that sings so sweetly and promises so much. And look what came of that. You were swept from your place of safety, and you lost Norrie."

I could not find any words to defend myself. What Lady Helaine said was true: I had bungled things badly.

"But as if that were not bad enough, these men inveigled you into even worse mistakes. Nor can they have been as blind as you to the dangers." She fixed them with an icy stare. "Gentlemen, what were you thinking? To listen to the wind is unwise, but to listen to moonbriar seeds, the food of the Shadowgrims—that is folly indeed!"

Penebrygg and Sir Barnaby looked guiltily at each other. Nat stared at his hands.

Lady Helaine's face was dead white in the dark room, her voice rasping yet strangely melodic. "A Chantress who sings a moonbriar song may enter so deeply into another's mind that she can never find her way back. Her heart will beat with his; she will forget her very existence. And the danger is greatest when the other person has considerable power and intends her harm. In that case, a Chantress may well be destroyed. And even if she does survive, the imprint of the person's mind often stays with her, making her more susceptible to his influence. And this"— she lifted her hands in the air, almost helpless with rage—"this is what you have done to my goddaughter."

I blanched, remembering my last moments in Lord Scargrave's head, with the ravens cawing and croaking.

"And that is not all," Lady Helaine said. "The Shadowgrims can smell Wild Magic being worked, and of all songs, they are most drawn to that of the moonbriar. By encouraging Lucy in her recklessness, you exposed her—and yourselves—to their horrors."

"The Shadowgrims know where we are?" Penebrygg exclaimed.

"If they did, you would already be in the Raven Pit," Lady Helaine said. "From what Lucy says, she sang only by day, when the Shadowgrims were sleeping—except once, when she walked into Scargrave's mind at twilight, as the ravens were wakening.

By the time they were in flight, the smell of the Wild Magic had subsided, and any traces that remained would have been blown away on the wind." She added, "Not far enough, though. Didn't you notice the Shadowgrims circling over the city that evening? Something was stirring them up. Perhaps it was that."

"We had no eyes for anything but Lucy," Nat said roughly. Penebrygg nodded. Both of them looked shaken, however, as did Sir Barnaby. Did the prospect of those circling Shadowgrims horrify them as much as it did me?

"Have we lost already?" I asked. "Have we no hope of defeating Scargrave?"

Standing before the remains of the fire, Lady Helaine looked more tired than ever. "No, we have not lost. Not yet. I can teach you a safe way to sing. A way to sing with the stone on."

A safe way to sing? One that would not land me in Scargrave's mind? I looked at Lady Helaine with new hope.

"Tell us more," Penebrygg said, his bespectacled face brightening.

"It is secret knowledge, to be shared only among Chantresses." Lady Helaine waved a dismissive hand in his direction. "All you need know is that it will take time. Perhaps quite a lot of time." She looked at me. "We must find a safe place for you, somewhere well away from London, as far from Scargrave and the ravens as possible—"

Sir Barnaby, Penebrygg, and Nat looked at each other.

Lady Helaine broke off. "What is it?"

"Bad news, I'm afraid," Penebrygg said. "Sir Barnaby came

here tonight to tell us about the new measures Scargrave put into place against Chantresses today. Something has rattled him—"

"The mind-reading!" Lady Helaine said.

"Possibly," Penebrygg admitted. "In any case, he has ordered that every person who passes in or out of the city must be examined for the Chantress mark."

Fear rose like smoke inside me, suffocating and pervasive.

"No exceptions will be made, no matter how it interrupts trade or business," Sir Barnaby confirmed. "There will be additional watchers at the city gates and on the bridges and along the river. New Chantress-hunters have been appointed, and the Ravens' Own are to help them with their work. It will be like the bad old days, when Chantress-hunting was at its height."

"The Ravens' Own?" Lady Helaine echoed. "Are you sure?" When Sir Barnaby nodded, two red spots appeared on her parchment-white cheeks. "And you expect me to keep her safe against those hellhounds? Without magic, without money, without friends—"

"You have us," Penebrygg said.

"But I have no home, no safe place to shield her," Lady Helaine said. "I am constantly on the move, and even so, I have nearly been caught many times."

Nat, Penebrygg, and Sir Barnaby exchanged glances again.

"What about—?" Nat began.

"Indeed," said Penebrygg.

Sir Barnaby nodded. "Consider it settled." To Lady Helaine, he said, "I know a place that is as safe as any in this city, one where the walls are exceedingly thick and you will not be over-heard. You and Miss Marlowe may stay there, and while you are there, you can teach her what you know."

"And then she will put an end to the Shadowgrims," Nat said.

I heard the faint echo of those jabbering birds and shuddered. Somehow I must find the courage to face them again. Perhaps with Lady Helaine's magic . . .

"No," Lady Helaine said.

Nat's hazel eyes turned cold. "You're saying you have some other plan?"

"I am saying that what you ask is not possible," Lady Helaine said. "I do not have the song-spells for that. The Shadowgrims robbed me of them, and of much else besides. I remember only a handful of songs, and while they will help keep my goddaughter safe, I can assure you they will not allow her to defeat Scargrave."

I sagged back in my chair. Was that the best I could hope for—to live a life in hiding, keeping Scargrave at bay?

As I stared at Lady Helaine in dismay, Penebrygg snapped his fingers. "We've forgotten the manuscript! Nat, will you fetch it for us?"

Nat was already on his feet. In a moment, he was back, cradling two sheets of parchment in his hand.

"Can you read this?" he said to Lady Helaine.

Lady Helaine snatched at the manuscript. "Where did you find this?"

"In a library far to the north, several years ago," Penebrygg said. "A curious case, that. We had heard—"

"Never mind that," Sir Barnaby interrupted. "Can you tell us what it says, Lady Helaine? We are quite sure it is important, judging from how well it was hidden. Is it the song for destroying the Shadowgrims?"

Lady Helaine scanned the pages. "No, it is not."

Disappointment, sharp as an awl, struck hard. It was a bitter blow. And then Lady Helaine looked up, her eyes wide and strangely dazed, and said, "It is something even better."

"Even better?" I repeated. What on earth did she mean?

Lady Helaine hesitated and checked the manuscript again. "I saw this manuscript once, a very long time ago. I memorized every note—and then the Shadowgrims drove it from my mind. You are correct: It is indeed a song-spell of the highest importance."

"But what is it for, my lady?" Penebrygg implored.

Lady Helaine's raspy whisper echoed across the room. "It will destroy the grimoire itself."

CHAPTER TWENTY-ONE
PLANS AND QUESTIONS

"But what about the Shadowgrims?" I asked. "If Scargrave still has them, what does it matter if we destroy the grimoire?"

"Once the grimoire is destroyed, its works will go with it," Lady Helaine said. "Including the Shadowgrims."

"You are sure?" Nat asked.

"Yes. It is how our magic works."

The mood in the room lightened considerably. Penebrygg and Sir Barnaby traded hopeful glances.

"Then we can begin to make plans," Sir Barnaby said. "Lady Helaine, how long will it take to teach your goddaughter the song?"

"At least six months, I should imagine. And quite possibly more." Lady Helaine ran her hand along the long strand of beads that hung around her neck. "Her progress will depend on how gifted she is, and how disciplined. But she is very inexperienced—and what little experience she has is of exactly the wrong sort. So one cannot expect miracles."

This withering assessment took the wind out of my sails.

"Can she sing the song anywhere?" Sir Barnaby asked.

"No. She must hold the grimoire in her hands."

I thought of the book I had seen, bound fast to the wall, when I was in Scargrave's mind. My hand and his hand, blending . . . No! I must not think of that. I must stay myself, with no blurring at the edges. I forced myself back to the present, to the smoky room, and my godmother's rasp, and the reassuring bulk of a slumbering Norrie against me.

Sir Barnaby tapped his fingers against his chin. "So we must find a way to send her into the Tower of London undetected—and into Scargrave's Chamber in the White Tower, where the grimoire is kept. That will be a challenge."

"It will be," Lady Helaine agreed. "But I may be able to help there as well. Among the few song-spells that I remember is one for concealment."

"A spell of invisibility, you mean?" Penebrygg asked.

"Nothing quite so powerful as that. The song makes it unlikely she will catch people's gaze, but those who look carefully in her direction can usually see something—a glimmer, perhaps, or even a ghostly outline—and they may be able to track her down. But still, the song will help her, especially if she can be taught to move carefully and quietly and to seek shelter wherever possible."

"We'll have Nat train her, then," Penebrygg said. "He's done plenty of work for us at the Tower, and he knows his way around its secret places. What do you say, my boy? Will you teach her everything you can?"

"I'll do my best," Nat said, and for a moment, I saw enthusiasm in his eyes. Had he forgiven me, then, for reading his mind?

Perhaps not. Before I could respond, the guarded expression returned to his face.

But why should I have expected anything else? And what did it matter anyway? He wasn't here to make friends, and neither was I. We were here to win a war. And to him—and to everyone here—I was merely a tool in that war.

"But, of course, your chief tutor will be Lady Helaine," Sir Barnaby said to me. "And while you are pursuing your lessons, the rest of us shall be planning a general uprising, to take place when the grimoire has been eradicated."

"Destroying the book won't be enough?" I said, surprised.

"Not if it leaves Scargrave still alive and in charge of the King," Sir Barnaby said.

"It might not," Lady Helaine said. "Scargrave has used the book's powers for so long that he's almost become bound to it. You can hear it in his voice. Destroying it may well destroy him."

"A welcome development, if it happens," Sir Barnaby said. "But we must be prepared to take matters into our own hands."

"It does seem a pity that we must destroy the book, though," Penebrygg said, his face wistful under his floppy cap. "I wish we could at least read it first. Who knows? There might be some good songs in there along with the bad, something worth saving—"

"No." Lady Helaine's voice was rough but insistent. "There is nothing in that book but evil. And the Shadowgrims are the least of it. We will be better off when it is gone."

"I'll agree with that," Nat said emphatically. "But it's a wonder to hear a Chantress take such a stand against magic."

I bristled. "You think we don't know bad magic when we see it?"

"Do you?" Nat said, and I was taken aback to hear more worry than antagonism in his voice.

"Of course we do," Lady Helaine said. "This book is beyond redemption. It must be expunged. And in any case, there is no room in the song for half measures: It is all or nothing."

"Very well, then," Penebrygg said. "We have our answer."

"It is settled, then." Lady Helaine fixed her glowing eyes on me. "I will teach you how to sing safely, goddaughter. And you will destroy the book."

I nodded.

Lady Helaine turned to Sir Barnaby. "Now conduct us to your refuge, so that we can begin our work."

† † †

The place Sir Barnaby had in mind turned out to be a set of rooms in the labyrinthine cellars of Gadding House, some distance from the chamber where the Invisible College had met. But it was too late to go there that day; it was past curfew, and although Sir Barnaby had a pass that allowed him to travel almost anywhere he liked, the rest of us were too big a crowd to slip through the streets unnoticed. We set up makeshift beds for Norrie and Lady

Helaine in the attic, and we agreed that we would leave the next morning instead.

When I woke, it was still dark, and I was sure I would be the first one down to the kitchen. Yet when I wandered down the stairs, I smelled porridge. I opened the kitchen door and saw Norrie at the hearth, stirring the pot.

At the sound of my footsteps, she spun around, hand on her heart. "Lucy!"

"Did I startle you? I'm sorry." I gave her a gentle hug and reached for the porridge ladle. "Let me do that."

On the island, Norrie would have shooed me away. Here she surrendered the ladle without another word and settled on the kitchen bench.

"You shouldn't be cooking for us," I said. "It's too much to ask. Especially when you've only just arrived." I gave the thickening porridge a good paddle.

"I thought my mind might be easier if my hands had something to do," Norrie said quietly.

I shunted the pot away from the fire and came to kneel beside her.

Even after a night's sleep, she looked a good ten years older than she had on the island. Her skin was dull; her eyes were buried in wrinkles. But what upset me the most was how lost she looked. But why shouldn't she? I had taken her away from her home.

"I'm sorry," I said awkwardly. "I'm sorry for dragging you here."

"Hush, child." She shook her head with weary kindness. "The time had come. I see that now. And probably it's for the best. Though I admit I do miss my garden. It's not a very green place, London. I'm glad we'll be leaving for the country soon."

She had been asleep when we'd made our plans last night, I realized. "Norrie, there's something I should tell you . . ."

As I explained how we would be living in the Gadding House cellars, Norrie paled. "We'll be living underground?"

"They think it's the safest possible place."

"Maybe so. But I'm not much of a one for cellars, child. Or for caves, or anywhere under the earth. Gives me the creeps, it does."

"Oh, dear." I couldn't bear to be parted from her again, especially when we'd only just found each other. "They thought it was the best place, you see. A regular house is too dangerous, and they don't think they can get us out of London. Though if it were you alone, perhaps—"

"No, no. I want to be where I can watch over you." Norrie patted my hand. "Never you mind me. I'm tired, that's all. It's been quite a while since I ever was in a cellar, so perhaps I'll feel differently this time. And this is quite a large cellar, didn't you say?"

"Oh, yes."

"And there will be lights?" Her voice quavered.

"Of course."

"Then I'm sure I'll be fine. You're not to worry about it." She gave my hand a last tremulous pat and stood up. "Now, how about some of that porridge?"

For a brief while, it was like being on the island again, just the two of us sitting on a bench together, eating our breakfast. By the time we finished our porridge, Norrie looked stronger and more herself, I was glad to see. Strong enough to put up with a question or two? I wasn't sure, but I thought it was worth testing the waters. There was still so much that I didn't understand.

I set down my spoon. "Norrie, did you ever read the letter my mother gave to you, the one you put in the bay tree pot?"

"Never. It was for you, not me."

I sat back, disappointed. I had hoped Norrie had read it, and that it might have some advice for me. "Did she ever talk to you about her magic?"

"No." Norrie scraped halfheartedly at her trencher. "To tell the truth, child, I didn't want to know."

This was difficult for me to understand. "You weren't curious?"

"It wasn't any of my business," Norrie said. "I was there to look after you, wasn't I? Not to help her cast spells. And anyway, magic makes me nervous, and your mother knew that. Kind soul that she was, she took care not to practice it around me. Except at the end, when she needed to hide us."

"What was that like? The song that brought us to the island, I mean." When I saw the look on her face, I added quickly, "Unless it's too hard to talk about." I'd made things hard enough for her already.

"No." Norrie took a deep breath. "You're old enough to have answers now. And I'm done keeping secrets. It never works out the way you think it's going to, anyway. I saw that clear as day the moment I came in and saw you singing."

Norrie was done with keeping secrets? I could hardly believe it. "So what was it like?" I asked again.

"It was horrible." Norrie stared at the floor. "A whirlwind of singing and howling and wind and water, and things pulling at our hands, trying to part us. It was worse even than when you brought me back. I kept my eyes closed and held tight to you both till it was over."

Frustration gripped me. I had forgotten so much. "Why don't I remember?"

"She didn't want you to."

"Oh?" This had never occurred to me.

"It was too much for a child to carry, she said. And if you remembered, she thought you might put your life in danger by singing. So she sang a song of forgetting to you. She feared it might take too much away—that you might even forget her— but she said it had to be done."

After years of blaming myself for my bad memory, it was a shock to learn it was my mother's magic that had done the damage.

"Can it be fixed? Can I get those memories back?"

"I'm afraid not. They were gone for good, your mother said." Seeing my expression, Norrie added, "I'm sorry, child. She meant it for the best."

A wave of loss crashed into me. My mother had wanted so much to protect me, I understood that. But at what price? My memories of her—and of my own past—were like a smashed stained-glass window, cracked and skewed and missing half the pieces.

"I don't remember Lady Helaine, either," I said, measuring the losses.

"Well, no," Norrie said. "You wouldn't. But that's nothing to do with your mother. You only met Lady Helaine the once, right after you were born, when she and your mother made your stone. As far as I know, you never saw her again."

"I didn't?" The surprise of this distracted me from my sadness. "She didn't mention that."

"She probably didn't want to bring it up right at first," Norrie said. "But the truth is, she and your mother didn't get along very well. Nothing to do with you," she hastened to add. "Their first falling-out came long before you were born."

"What was it about?"

"I don't know. Might have been anything—or nothing. Lady Helaine's a bit high-handed, as you've seen. And your mother was a strong-minded girl who didn't like to be told what to do. It's hardly a wonder they didn't always get on." Norrie eyed me sternly. "But just because your mother argued with Lady Helaine doesn't mean you should. She's a wise woman, your godmother. There're plenty of us who respect her. And your mother did too, at bottom, or else she'd not have gone to her when she heard about the ravens."

Norrie stacked our trenchers and took them over to the sink.

Following her, I asked, "If Lady Helaine never came to visit us, then how did you know who she was?"

"Oh, I knew her years and years ago," Norrie said. "When she and I were young. She's much older now, but she has the same bones, the same eyes, the same . . . presence. She's not the sort of person you'd confuse with anyone else, is she?"

"No." Proud Lady Helaine and down-to-earth Norrie—how on earth had they met each other? "Did you grow up together?"

"Heavens, no. I was a serving girl from the village, working at the big house for your mother's family, and she was a grand young lady who came to visit now and again. She made quite an impression. A great beauty, she was, and the men and boys used to follow her about. Some said it was magic that drew them to her. I don't know about that, but I did once see her turn invisible right before my eyes. Made me go all queasy, it did."

I heard footsteps in the hall.

Evidently Norrie did too. "But that's enough for now," she said. "Answering questions is one thing, gossip another. I shall have to mind the line. Now be a good girl, and fetch me those trenchers up on the shelf there."

As I pulled them down, Penebrygg and Nat came into the room, followed swiftly by Lady Helaine. My time alone with Norrie was over, at least for now.

Once we reached Gadding House, however, I was determined to ask more questions. Answers, gossip—I was eager for whatever Norrie could give me. My memory was riddled with gaps, and I wanted to fill in the holes.

CHAPTER TWENTY-TWO
UNDER THE GROUND

After breakfast, we embarked for Gadding House in two separate groups, the better to pass unnoticed. Nat, Norrie, and I set out first.

"We're in luck," Nat said, right before we stepped into the gray street. "The fog's so thick, it'll keep prying eyes at bay."

Even so, it was a harrowing trip. The creeping mist made me shiver with cold, and the talk I overheard in the sullen, stinking streets chilled me even more:

. . . Ravens' Own . . .

. . . guards at the gates . . .

. . . Chantress-hunters everywhere . . .

I was afraid that we might lose Nat in the fog, but this time he stayed close, only a foot or so away from me. He took Norrie's arm when she began to flag, and she seemed to draw strength from him—enough, at least, to get us to the apothecary shop.

Once we entered the tunnel, however, Norrie balked. "I . . . I can't."

Caught behind her, I could barely see the flicker of Nat's lantern up ahead. Trying not to think of the darkness and what it might harbor, I touched her trembling back. "What's wrong?"

"This." Shielding her eyes, she pointed upward. "All that earth, pressing down on us. Ready to swallow us up . . ."

"It won't, Norrie. It won't. Try not to think about it." I was trying hard not to think about it myself. A difficult job in the still, damp air.

"I can't help it." It was almost a sob. "I'm sorry."

I tried to comfort her, but the tunnel was narrow, and I couldn't do much except pat her shaking shoulders.

A flash of light: Nat was coming back with the lantern. "What's the delay?"

Norrie didn't speak.

"She doesn't like being underground," I said quickly. "It scares her."

I was afraid he might scold her, but instead, he spoke to her gently as a bird. "You're not the first to feel that way, believe me," he said. "But don't worry. We'll put you to rights."

The nightmare I'd seen in Nat's head came back to me. *Walls dark and glistening as jet. Walls so tight they scraped hands and knees . . .*

No, Norrie wasn't the first.

"Take my hand, will you? And now look at the lantern," Nat said to her. "That's it. Concentrate on the light, and think about the sun, warm and bright on a summer's day. The sun on an open meadow, with the sky wide and blue above you. Now take a deep breath . . ."

His voice went on and on, soothing and kind, without any sharp edges to it. I hardly recognized it as Nat's, yet as I listened, I felt my own shoulders relax.

It had the same effect on Norrie. He coaxed her into taking first one step, and then another, until she was walking steadily down the tunnel.

"And now we're almost through. Can you hold the lantern for me while I turn the lock? Keep looking into the light, that's it. Watch that soft, bright flame. And here we go, straight through . . ."

The moment we entered the cellars, matters improved. It was still dark, but the hallways were taller and broader than the tunnel, and fresh currents of air stirred as we walked.

By the light of the lantern, I saw Norrie's expression ease, though she still kept her eyes on the lantern.

"Thank you," I whispered to Nat.

"No thanks needed. She did it herself." He nodded at Norrie encouragingly. "I'd say the worst is behind us now."

I believed him until we reached the rooms Sir Barnaby had in mind. Even as we crossed the threshold, my spirits sank. The first room—the largest, Nat informed me—was small and low-ceilinged and covered with dust, and the dingy walls had no windows. Indeed, once we were inside, it was almost impossible to see where the door was, so carefully was it concealed.

A refuge, Sir Barnaby had called it. It looked more like a prison to me. And from the look on Norrie's face, that's how she saw it too.

Only Nat seemed pleased. He carefully settled Norrie into the sturdiest chair available, resting the lantern on the table beside her. "It's good to see the old place again."

"You've been here before?" I said.

"More times than I can count. It used to be Sir Barnaby's alchemy laboratory."

I regarded the smoke-begrimed walls of the room with dismay. "Are you serious?"

"Yes. But that was a while ago. The IC is more interested in practical experiments nowadays—though there's hardly any time for those, either. It's been over a year since we last met here." He nodded toward the hampers in the corner. "It looks like you're well set for provisions."

"For now."

"I gather you'll be getting regular baskets delivered. The cook here is one of our confederates, and no one bakes a finer pork pie." He glanced back at the half-open door behind us. "Let me check the back room—the pallets should be there, and some blankets to go with them."

I was about to follow him when I saw Norrie shiver.

"Chilly?" I asked.

"A b-bit."

As I wrapped my cloak around her, she covered her face. Not just chilly, then. I knelt beside her. "Norrie, what can I do?"

She kept her hand over her eyes. "I—I need a moment to get used to the place." She shuddered again.

"Everything's shipshape there," Nat said, coming back into the room. He cast one quick look at us and crossed to the fireplace. "Let me see what I can do to warm things up."

He pulled open the doors of a black box that squatted in the middle of the hearth.

"What's that?" I asked, not because I cared very much, but because I thought conversation would comfort Norrie more than cold silence.

"A firebox." Nat stacked coals inside, then kindled a flame. "It gives out more heat than an ordinary fire."

"More heat?" I said, my curiosity piqued despite myself. "That small box?"

"Yes." He stepped back from the fire, now merrily crackling, and shut the door on it.

I looked down at Norrie, wondering what she thought of the device, but her eyes were closed. She seemed to have forgotten us entirely.

"That should do it." Nat twiddled a few levers and looked with satisfaction at the black box. "You won't need to add more coal for another six hours at least."

I started to worry about how I would manage the box once he was gone. "You'll have to teach me what to do. I've never seen one before."

"It's a new design."

"Yours?" I guessed.

He looked a little abashed. "Mostly, yes. Though I had some help from the IC. We needed something safer than an open hearth, and something that made better use of coal. Luckily, there's a good circulation of air here, even though we're underground. We'll have these rooms warm in no time."

I looked at the metal contraption again, thinking that I was in favor of anything that would heat the room quickly. "How long did it take you to build it?"

"Off and on, about a year," Nat said. "Christopher Linnet and some others helped me with the plans, but after that it was a matter of trial and error. Quite a lot of error, sometimes: The second firebox nearly blew us all up."

I gave the walls a startled glance. The grime I'd seen there . . .

"Scorch marks," Nat confirmed. "But you needn't worry. I won't be doing any experiments while you're here, and neither will anyone else in the IC—"

Next to me, Norrie let out a strangled sob.

"Norrie, what is it?" I leaned in close, trying to take her hands in mine, but she was hunched over so tightly that I couldn't reach them. "Is it the room?"

"All that weight on top of us," she gasped. "Like being buried alive . . ."

I tried to reassure her and so did Nat, but this time nothing worked. She only curled tighter and tighter, shaking so hard I was afraid she would do herself an injury.

"Dear Norrie, don't." I tried to stretch my arms around her. "Please don't hurt yourself." But she hardly seemed to know I was there. As her breathing grew shallower and shallower, I looked up at Nat. "What do we do?"

"We'd best get her out of here," he said.

Send Norrie away? "No." The answer flew out of me before I'd had time to think.

Nat looked like he was about to argue with me, but a soft fusillade of knocks interrupted him. He went to the door. "Dr. Penebrygg's signal. He must be having trouble with the locks again."

When Nat pulled back the latch, Lady Helaine swept past us. Penebrygg tumbled in afterward. As Lady Helaine looked the room up and down, Penebrygg came straight to my side. "Is Miss Norrie ill, then?"

I explained what the matter was, rubbing Norrie's back as I spoke. She never stopped shaking. I wasn't even sure she understood what I was saying anymore. "Is there anything we can give her?"

Penebrygg looked down doubtfully. "We might perhaps be able to find some poppy syrup to make her sleep. But that won't solve anything in the long term. If it's being underground that does this to her, she'll have trouble staying here even for a day, let alone months on end."

Shaking out her beads, Lady Helaine came over to view Norrie. "She can't stay here, not like that."

Nat nodded in agreement. "We can't leave her like this. Her heart could give out."

Under my hand, Norrie shuddered again. I had wanted her here beside me—here to mother me, if the truth be told. But not if it meant she had to suffer like this. And certainly not if it meant risking her death.

I turned to Nat. "How fast can we get her out?"

Very fast, was the answer. While Nat improvised a litter out of his cloak and some odds and ends in the room, Penebrygg explained what he had in mind: They would carry Norrie to a secret entrance that led up into the upper cellars of Gadding House. There was a set of hidden rooms there, with half windows that let in air and light. "She can stay there till she's herself again. Then we'll leave through the servants' entrance and take her home with us."

Nat gave me quick instructions on how to work the firebox and turn the locks and everything else he thought I needed to know. By the time he was done, Norrie's breathing was so shallow that she fainted away. We bundled her in blankets and shifted her over to the litter, making as quick a job of it as we could.

Before I knew it, I was giving Norrie's slack hand one last squeeze. Then Nat and Penebrygg braced the litter between them.

I'll come with you, I almost said. But I knew I needed to stay here in the darkness, here in the depths, here with my teacher, Lady Helaine. No matter how much I wanted to be with Norrie instead. I held the door, and they left, Norrie unconscious between them.

By rights, the room ought to have felt more spacious after they were gone, with only two of us left to share it. Yet somehow it felt more confining than ever.

CHAPTER TWENTY-THREE
LESSONS

Trying not to think about how many floors of Gadding House were piled above me, I turned to Lady Helaine. "Will they be all right, do you think?"

"I expect so," Lady Helaine said briskly. "In any case, it does no good to worry about it. We have more important matters to attend to."

More important than Norrie's health? I frowned.

Lady Helaine guessed what I was thinking. "The greatest threat to us all—even Norrie—is Scargrave. And only you can save us. That being so, we cannot afford to become distracted from our true purpose, which is to train you as a Chantress. Every other worry and concern must be set aside."

Heartless though it sounded, there was a certain logic to what she was saying. I silenced my objections and tried to listen.

"Where to begin?" Lady Helaine said. "This is what I have

asked myself. You are foolish, you are impatient, you are shockingly ignorant—and your instincts are deplorable."

I felt as if I'd been slapped in the face.

"Fortunately, all is not lost," Lady Helaine continued. "You come from good stock, and blood and breeding count for a great deal. Your gift, though so far misused, appears uncommonly strong. The stone you bear is a sign of that. Although every Chantress has one, few are as extraordinary as yours. If you will put yourself in my hands, doing everything I tell you to do, then I have every hope we will succeed."

My cheeks stopped stinging, though they remembered the slap. "I will do whatever you ask of me," I promised her. *I will do whatever it takes to defeat Scargrave and make us all safe.*

For a long moment, Lady Helaine regarded me in unblinking silence, as if probing the strength of my resolve. Then she nodded sharply and said in a voice that was even rougher than usual, "We shall begin, then. But where?" She ran an impatient hand over her bone beads. "If you had started your apprenticeship with me at age ten, as is customary, we would have had a full five years to cover the rudiments of Chantress magic. But there is nothing normal about our situation, and time is short. We must concentrate only on essentials. Still, you must understand something of our background, our history. So let us start with a question, an easy one: How is Chantress magic worked?"

It was so easy that I feared there must be a trick. "Through songs?"

Lady Helaine dusted her palms in irritation. "Don't answer like a scared little rabbit."

I did my best to sound confident. "The magic is worked through songs."

"That is correct. Using song-spells, we charm the objects, animals, and plants into doing our bidding."

"Only objects, animals, and plants?" I put the question boldly, since that was the tone my godmother admired. "Not people?"

"Not often, not anymore. Long ago, there were some very remarkable Chantresses who could do it easily. Niniane, for instance, who trapped the wizard Merlin in a rock." Lady Helaine's battered voice subsided in a sigh. "But much that was possible for Chantresses in ancient times is utterly beyond us now."

"Dr. Penebrygg said that in the old days, Chantresses—"

Lady Helaine stopped me with a look. "What others have told you is not to be relied upon. When I think of the damage they did to you, encouraging you to remove your stone . . ." Her lips tightened. "You must forget everything they told you and listen only to me. Is that understood?"

I knew the answer my godmother was expecting. "Yes, Lady Helaine."

"Now, as I told you last night, there are two kinds of magic that a Chantress can work. One involves Wild Magic, and that is forbidden. The other is Proven Magic, and that is what I will teach you." She paused. "But before we begin, let me be sure that I have made the fundamental rule abundantly clear: You must never, ever remove your stone."

"I understand." The stone seemed almost to glow as I spoke. "Is it true that every Chantress has one?"

"Indeed."

"Where is yours?"

For a moment, I thought that Lady Helaine would not answer.

But then she reached past her long string of bone beads, under the thick wool of her gown, and drew out a milky-white stone, clouded and cracked.

"Once it was as clear as your own," Lady Helaine said. "But see what the Shadowgrims did. When my stone had power, it shone like a diamond, and it was as heavy as gold; now it is dull, and no more weighty than a shell on the shore. The magic in it has gone."

"Back on the island, my stone was much duller," I said. "It wasn't a ruby then."

"That is because you had not begun to use your powers," Lady Helaine said. "Our stones change and grow with us, you see, for good or ill. Your stone may change yet again, as our lessons in Proven Magic progress."

"Those are the safe songs—the ones we can sing with the stones on?"

"Yes," Lady Helaine said. "You will learn them by ear, as I did when I was an apprentice."

"They aren't written down?" I asked in surprise. "Like the one Dr. Penebrygg gave us?"

"Written-out songs are very rare. As a rule, we Chantresses have preferred to learn our songs by ear, one generation passing its wisdom to the next. An unfortunate practice, I must say, for it means that as our power has dwindled and our family lines have fragmented, a great many songs have been lost. My own godmother was in possession of only three song-spells, and none of them worked very well."

This did not sound promising. "What did her songs do?"

"They worked magic on locks. Most Chantresses have a specialty, and that was hers."

I was disappointed but tried not to show it.

Lady Helaine looked askance at me. "You had been hoping for something more exciting? No, do not deny it. I can see that you did. But almost everyone locks away something—their most desperate secrets, their dearest treasures. So a talent for locks is nothing to be sniffed at." She paused, then added more kindly, "Nevertheless, I am glad to see in you a hunger for something more. When I was your age, I myself had such a hunger, and that ambition was the making of me."

I tried to imagine Lady Helaine as a girl—the "great beauty" that Norrie had spoken of. It was difficult.

"My own godmother did not understand," Lady Helaine went on. "She told me that locks were my destiny, and that I must accept it. But while I had a greater affinity for locks than for any other objects, I eventually found that I could learn other song-spells too. They did not come easily, but after constant practice, I could work them."

"Who taught them to you?"

"At first, I learned from other Chantresses. But when they realized what I was doing, they turned against me. They were satisfied with what they had, they said, and I should be too." Lady Helaine's lips thinned at the memory. "Of course I wasn't satisfied—why should I have been? The Chantresses of old would never have accepted such limits on their gifts. So I resolved to find another way forward. If present-day Chantresses wouldn't help me, perhaps the ones of the past would."

I felt my neck hairs rise. "You mean . . . you called up the dead?"

"The dead?" Lady Helaine raised her eyebrows. "What a question, Lucy. I am a Chantress, not a necromancer." Shaking her head at my foolishness, she said, "I learned about our past as any serious scholar would: through the perusal of old books and manuscripts."

"So you studied grimoires—like the one that was given to Scargrave?"

"Oh, that one I never saw, believe me," Lady Helaine said bitterly. "Agnes never told me she had that book in her possession, though much trouble would have been saved if she had. As it was, I could only locate scraps of what I wanted: the outlines of a song-spell here, the notation of a melody there. But over time I found enough that I could begin to reconstruct the ancient ways. It required great dedication, however, as well as patience and perseverance. Not to mention endless attention to detail."

I nodded because it seemed Lady Helaine expected me to.

She fixed me with a cool stare. "Can I find such qualities in you, I wonder? Because you will need them, of that you can be sure. I will teach you all that I know and remember, but I cannot work a single particle of magic myself. That will be entirely up to you. And it will be harder than you can imagine."

I met her searching gaze head-on. "Whatever you teach me, I will learn."

"Then let your hands fall to your side, and do as I say."

I obeyed, eager to learn my first song-spell. But what my godmother had in mind was something much more basic than singing.

She looked straight into my eyes. "I must teach you how to breathe."

CHAPTER TWENTY-FOUR
BREATHING

It was no small matter to learn a new way of breathing. The unthinking inhalation, the easy release—I had to forget these, my godmother informed me. From now on, my every breath would require thought and precision.

I strained to follow Lady Helaine's instructions, but as the hours wore on, I started to feel as if I were drowning.

"Not so quickly," she snapped as I exhaled. "Don't pant like a dog." And then, a moment later, "No, not like that, either. You sound like a broken bagpipe."

All afternoon it went like this, until at last Lady Helaine released me. "You begin to grasp the rudiments, I see. Practice every chance you have. Practice even while you sleep, if you can. We will resume our lessons when you have mastered this."

Left alone, I collapsed in a chair, feeling almost as if I'd declared war on myself. To breathe in the normal way seemed the greatest luxury in the world, and now it was denied me. My throat was on fire; my chest felt like a clapped-out bellows. I stared at the black stove and wondered: Could any magic possibly be worth so much pain?

Yes. The answer came from the core of me. A safe magic was worth any price. Anything to avoid being at the ravens' mercy again! And that's what Lady Helaine was offering me: a safe way to sing. Somehow I must find the courage and the resolve to learn it.

Determined to show myself willing, I practiced with all my might, taking care to breathe in the strange new fashion during my waking hours—which were many, especially since I was worried sick about Norrie.

I was still breathing in the new way, with mixed success, when Nat called on us two days later.

The moment he came in the door, I asked, "How is Norrie?" It was awful, not knowing.

"She's well," he said to my relief. "As soon as we came in view of a window, she got better, and now she's cooking up a storm for Penebrygg and me. She misses you very much, of course—to the point that she's almost prepared to brave the tunnel again. But I think it's best if she doesn't."

"I agree." I didn't want to put her through that again. "Tell her I miss her terribly too, but she should stay where she is."

"That I will." Nat secured the door and looked around. "Where's Lady Helaine?"

"Asleep. We were up late last night."

"Oh." He stayed near the door, looking a bit disconcerted. "Maybe this isn't the best time for a lesson, then?"

"I don't mind." But as we settled down by the firebox, I smelled the breath of autumn on him—the last of the leaves, the smoke of London, and a sharp, apple-scented tang utterly alien to this cramped cellar room. It threw my breathing off, and I coughed and gasped.

Nat raised his eyebrows. "Swallow something wrong?"

"Not exactly," I answered. Though he looked interested, I did not say anything more. Learning magic was hard enough as it was, without trying to explain it to someone who hated it. Moreover, Lady Helaine had made it clear that such matters were not to be discussed with all and sundry.

Instead, I concentrated on breathing slowly and steadily as Nat instructed me on the Tower of London and the various detachments of Warders and Ravens' Own that guarded it.

"The grimoire is in Scargrave's Chamber," he said, "which is in the very lowest level of the White Tower, very close to where the Shadowgrims are kept. Not far away is a chamber you'll want to avoid: the Feeding Room."

"The Feeding Room?" I didn't like the sound of that.

"It's where they keep the prisoners they give to the Shadow-grims."

I had to concentrate to keep my breathing even, but Nat didn't notice.

"Its walls are ten feet thick," he said. "Here, I'll draw you a map of the whole Tower."

As he worked, I thought only about breathing. (*Not the Feeding Room, not the Feeding Room . . .*) But when I finally looked down at the sketch he'd drawn, complete with cutaway views and concealed doors and overlooked passageways, I drew a different kind of breath entirely: one of astonishment. He had an artist's hand and an artist's eye, and the sketch was a thing of beauty.

"How did you do that?" I asked.

"Do what?"

"Remember everything, and set it down so precisely." I traced the edge of the sketch with my finger. "It's like a tiny, perfect world."

He turned to me, clearly startled by my praise. I again felt a strong current pass between us, as if we were something more than reluctant allies—as if we somehow knew each other through and through.

But that was nonsense . . .

He looked away. "A dangerous world, more like." He pushed the sketch toward me, though he was careful, as always, not to come too close. "Best if you can commit it to memory. Start now, and I'll quiz you on it when I come back."

I gathered myself together and started to practice proper breathing again. "When do you come back?"

"Saturday," he said. "Look for me."

He'd touched on a sore point. I felt the windowless room press in on me. "How can I look for you when I'm stuck underground like this?"

Was that a glint of sympathy in his eyes? "I'll be here anyway," he promised.

When I looked up from the drawing again—so exact, so delicate—he was gone.

†   †   †

At last, after a wearisome fortnight of breathing practice, Lady Helaine finally allowed me to progress—but only to endless drills in sustaining tones.

For the first time I heard her voice raised in song. Though confident, with an extensive range, it grated like rusty chains. Had the Shadowgrims destroyed that, too? Or had she always sounded that way? I wondered but decided against asking, as I didn't think my godmother would take kindly to the question.

Instead, I kindled notes like fire, fanning them from the faintest flame to a fiery blaze, then banking them down again, or extinguishing them altogether. Note after note after note, the whole day long. It was demanding work but satisfying, because even though I was only singing a single pitch at a time—"no phrases," Lady Helaine warned me, "no tunes"—the song-spells did not seem far off.

I was wrong. From sustaining tones, we went to linking notes, and then to trills and glissandos and exercises that traversed up and down the scale.

Intent on proving myself, I attacked each challenge with outward vigor, trying not to show my impatience. But inwardly I chafed at each new hurdle. I wasn't here so that Lady Helaine could make me into a trained musician; I was here so that I could learn magic. But of magic there was not yet the slightest hint.

Some of the exercises were useful, I was sure. But was it really necessary to tackle them all? Especially now, when the stakes were so high?

"It is precisely because the stakes are so high that we must take care," Lady Helaine said crossly when I asked. "Otherwise, your newfound skills will desert you when the crisis comes. You do not want to find yourself at Lord Scargrave's mercy, do you?"

I did not.

Yet although I did my best to tamp down the spirit of rebellion swirling inside me, the lessons seemed more tedious by the hour, and every day dragged. I had to remind myself constantly how fortunate I was to have a way of learning safe magic.

The fact that I was stuck underground only added to my sense of frustration. Though I never suffered as Norrie had, I understood something of her desolation. After living so close to the open sea, being here was doubly difficult: I thirsted for light and fresh air like a netted fish thirsts for the sea. On good nights, I dreamed I was back on the island again, the western wind tugging at my hair, the ocean bright as the sun itself. On bad nights, I dreamed I was being buried alive. Either way, I would wake to the subdued, damp air of the cellars, like an indelible smudge against my face.

Sometimes I thought I couldn't bear to sing another note. And yet I did. Not once, but over and over and over again, as Lady Helaine prodded and harangued me, relentless as a general.

My only respite came during my other lessons—the ones that Nat gave me.

† † †

After the first visit, my lessons with Nat took place under the watchful eye of Lady Helaine. Intent and purposeful, he quizzed me on the layout of the Tower, taught me how to use a lockpick, and demonstrated how to move quietly around a room—all within the confines of our crowded quarters. But as Christmastide approached, he told Lady Helaine that to fully instruct me in the art of concealment, it was necessary to go farther afield.

"At first, we'll stay here in the cellars," he said. "Later, we'll move around the rest of Gadding House."

To leave these rooms again, to see the sun—it sounded heavenly to me. Of course, there would be danger, too; I understood that. But the reward seemed worth the risk.

Lady Helaine narrowed her eyes at Nat. "You are sure this is necessary?"

"We can't be forever creeping around here, pretending we're on turret stairs," Nat said. "If she enters the Tower without any real practice at lying low, she'll fail. And this is the best way for her to practice."

After some heated discussion, Lady Helaine conceded the point, but only on the condition that she accompany us as chaperone. Together the three of us explored the passageways in the cellars, then made sorties to the dark pantries behind the kitchens. But as I became more and more adept at skirting around staircases and ducking into hiding places, Lady Helaine had trouble keeping up with us. Even so, she would not yield her privileges.

To me, privately, she said over supper one night, "That young man needs watching. I don't like the way he looks at you."

I nearly choked on my pork pie. "Looks at me?"

"It's to be expected, I suppose. You're not exactly a beauty, are you? But you are a Chantress. And he is at a susceptible age."

"No." My face was hot. "You've made a mistake. Nat has *never* looked at me that way."

"I know what I saw."

"No," I said again. "It couldn't be. He only talks to me about the business at hand. And he hates my magic so much he won't come within a yard of me."

This wasn't quite true, I thought, as I set down the pie. What was true was that Nat seemed preoccupied when I was with him, as though his mind were on other matters. But he was not quite as careful about keeping away from me as he once had been. Once or twice, while we were studying the maps, our fingertips had almost touched. But Nat had not appeared to notice, so that didn't count.

"Let us hope I am mistaken," Lady Helaine said. "But that is rare."

"You haven't said anything to him, have you?" My cheeks grew hot again at the thought.

Lady Helaine sniffed. "What do you take me for?"

Well, that was one thing to be thankful for, I thought as I contemplated my plate. I would have died of mortification if she'd confronted Nat with her suspicions. Which, needless to say, were absolutely, positively wrong.

Fortunately, the more time Lady Helaine spent with us, the more apparent this became to her. So I guessed, at any rate, since she eventually reconsidered her position on the necessity of a chaperone.

"God forbid that I should hold you back, goddaughter," she said one afternoon. "Not when the stakes are so high." She fixed Nat with a penetrating stare. "But do not take advantage of my absence, young man. Not on any account."

As my face reddened, Nat said, "She'll come to no harm with me, I promise you."

"I will hold you to that." Lady Helaine wrapped her cloak tightly around her. "If she is not back within two hours, I shall come looking for you both."

As my godmother retreated back down the hallway, I let out a breath I hadn't known I was holding.

At long last, I was to have a taste of freedom.

CHAPTER TWENTY-FIVE
EXPLORATIONS

Once Lady Helaine was safely out of sight, Nat said, "Look here: I think it's time we went up to the attics."

That was six stories up from here. "So high?"

"Yes. Most of the way is secret, so I don't think we'll run across anyone. But remember: Always stay in the shadows. And don't let your nerves get the better of you."

As it happened, we did run across someone—a skinny maid hauling a coal scuttle up the stairs. But the scrape of the scuttle gave us some warning, and the light was so poor that we had no trouble keeping out of her sight.

We mounted the remaining stairs in perfect silence, Nat keeping his distance from me, as usual. Whenever I looked at him, his face was all business.

So much, I thought, for my godmother's suspicions.

Finally, after passing through a series of doorways and storerooms, we arrived at the westernmost end of the attics. The slanted ceiling rose well above my head, but to judge from the dusty jumble of crates and old furnishings, it wasn't much used. On the other side of the room, small mullioned windows let in the late-afternoon light. I stopped for a moment, taking in the sight. After so many weeks of living in darkness, it felt as if I were standing in sunshine, even though the skies outside were gray and glowering.

"Oh, I forgot," Nat said behind me.

I turned, expecting him to give me another tip about how to navigate the house. Instead, he withdrew a rumpled parcel from the recesses of his black coat. "Norrie sent you this."

"Norrie?" I looked at him blankly.

"Yes." A smile tugged at his lips. "She said it was your sixteenth birthday."

I'd been so overwhelmed by my new life as a Chantress-in-training that I hadn't given the day much thought. Lady Helaine hadn't made any mention of celebrating the occasion.

Nat held out the parcel. "Aren't you going to open it?"

I untied the string. A familiar smell of honey, ginger, and cinnamon wafted up to me. "Oh!" Nestled inside the cloth were a dozen sticky-sweet brown stars. "Norrie's gingerbread."

I blinked back tears. When I was small and we were still living in England, gingerbread had been my favorite treat. Norrie had always let me choose the shapes: stars and moons and hearts and crowns. How I'd pined for them to come out of the oven! And how I'd missed gingerbread on the island, where spices were nowhere to be found.

"Here." I offered the stars to Nat. "Have a piece."

"Of your birthday treat?" Nat shook his head with mock indignation. "I should think not. I'm lucky enough to get Norrie's cooking every day, remember. These are all yours."

I closed my eyes to savor the scent. "Is she all right? Norrie, I mean?"

"Right as rain, except for missing you," Nat said. "She talks about you all the time."

"She does?" Disconcerted, I met Nat's eyes. "What does she say about me?"

"Oh, I've heard all about you as a baby," he said cheerfully. "And about the time you fell into the pond when you were four. And about the way you used to pretend to be a mermaid on the island shore—"

"She told you all that?" I looked away, my cheeks flaming. "How embarrassing."

"No, not embarrassing," he said seriously. "Nice. I don't have anyone who remembers me that way." He traced a spiral on the wall. "I'm not even sure what my real name is. My parents died when I was three, and my uncle—if that's what he was—just called me 'boy.' I think my mother called me Nat, but I can't be certain, not after all this time."

I took a deep breath. How silly to be sorry for myself because Norrie had told a few old stories.

"I'm sorry," I said. "I remember almost nothing about my own mother, and I know how that hurts. And what you've been through is much worse."

"Maybe, maybe not." He shrugged. "Anyway, there's no need for us to argue the point. I have a place and a name and a family now, and that's what matters."

"A family?" I echoed.

"Penebrygg. We don't have the same surname—I go by Walbrook, the name of the street where he and I used to live—but he's family all the same." He nodded at the parcel of gingerbread, still open in my hands. "You're going to eat some of that now, aren't you? Norrie'll want to know what you think of it."

"Tell her she's the most amazing cook in the world." I bit into a star. "Mmmmm . . ."

Nat grinned at me, then walked over to the window. I wrapped up my gingerbread and joined him there. Peering out, I saw a vast, elaborate garden that swept down to the Thames, the diamonds and arabesques of its green hedges disappearing into swirls of fog.

"It's later than I thought," Nat said, a note of worry in his voice. "Close to sunset, I should guess, though it's hard to tell with all that mist."

Shadowgrims. He didn't say the word, but I knew they were on his mind. While we'd talked, I'd almost forgotten about them.

How careless of me.

"How will you get back?" I asked.

"Me? Oh, plenty of ways. And if worse comes to worst, I can always bed down here for the night." He turned from the window. "It's you I'm worried about. We need to get you back downstairs. But first I need to show you something."

I followed him back through the series of attic storerooms until we reached a vestibule with many doors but no windows. He lit a candle with the tinderbox he carried in his jacket and pointed to one of the doors. "There's a lock like that in the Tower storerooms. See if you can open it."

He watched while I attacked the lock with the tools he had given me, and I worried my fingers would fumble. But when the lock yielded, he was swift to praise me. "You're a quick study."

"At locks, maybe," I said without thinking.

He caught my meaning. "Not magic?"

"I shouldn't have said anything."

"Those drills and scales getting on your nerves?"

I looked at him in alarm. How did he know about the drills and scales? "Have you been eavesdropping?" My face went hot as I thought of him overhearing my mistakes and failures. "How dare you?"

The pink left his face, leaving it stark white. "That's rich, coming from you. Have you forgotten how you spied on me—on my mind, on my memories?"

"That was quite different."

"Not to me."

His blunt words took the wind out of my sails. If I had reason to be angry, he had a thousand times more. I had ransacked his mind. And the fact that I'd done it with magic didn't make it better. It made it worse.

"I'm sorry," I said slowly. "If it's any help, I meant it when I said I wouldn't do it again."

He searched my face, as if weighing my words for truth. The balance came down in my favor: I saw his tense jaw relax.

"And I haven't been spying on you," he said. "Not anything that would count as spying, anyway. I just can't help picking things up when I visit."

"Picking things up how?" It still unsettled me that he'd overheard so much.

"When I'm right by the door, I hear things sometimes. And Lady Helaine mutters things under her breath when I'm there. She thinks I won't hear, but I do. And then there's your face—"

"My *face*?"

He looked at me across the warm light of the candle. "You're unhappy," he said simply. "Anyone with eyes can see that."

The sudden kindness in his voice undid me. I knew I ought to change the subject and talk about something else—anything but the particulars of my magic lessons. That's what Lady Helaine would expect. But the words burst out of me. "If I have to sing another scale for her, I think I'll throttle myself."

"That bad?"

I eyed the free and easy way he stood, the wind-chapped cheeks, the jacket that smelled of woodsmoke and the outdoors. "You cannot imagine."

"You'd be surprised." He held my glance, and I remembered, with a prickle of shame, the terrible memories he carried. But he went on peaceably enough. "If I were in your shoes, I'd be chafing at the bit too. Penebrygg understands that I like to experiment, and he approves of me thinking for myself." He looked at me, and there was empathy in his eyes. "But Lady Helaine is a very different sort."

I felt again that spark of understanding between us, that deep rapport that went beyond words. But to my confusion, this time it came coupled with a sudden awareness of his strength and grace—of the whole lean length of him beside me.

It was an uncomfortable, fluttery sensation, and I was determined to shake myself out of it. I blew out the candle and darted toward the door that led downstairs. "Let's go."

As I thrust at the handle, Nat leaped toward me. "No, not that door—"

I was already halfway out of it. My foot hit the slick slate tiles of the Gadding House roof, and a hot black fog wrapped around me. I pulled back, but before I could close the door, something screeched and flared like flame in the darkness. I froze as a sudden burning terror seized me, and I heard the fluttering of wings through the mist.

CHAPTER TWENTY-SIX
A BAD TURN

I was on fire, being burned at the stake. The Shadowgrims had found me. They were coming to devour me....

An impossibly long moment later, the door swung shut. The terror released me, and I sagged against the sill.

"It didn't see you," Nat said in the quiet darkness. "Not with the fog so thick and no light to draw it. If it knew you were there, you can bet it would have come closer—and it didn't. It kept flying in the other direction."

I had felt uneasy and awkward with him, I remembered. When I had gone to open that door, I had been only too happy to escape him. And no doubt I would be glad to get away again as soon as I was able to think more clearly. But just at the moment, what I felt was gratitude. He had shut the door. He had kept me safe.

Nat lit the candle again and scanned my face. "Gave you a bad turn, did it?"

"Y-yes," I managed to clack out. "Worse than ever."

"Maybe what happened with the mind-reading makes it worse for you."

"Maybe." It was not a comforting thought. I shivered. "I can't believe they don't bother you."

"That's not quite how it is," Nat said. "It's not as if I don't notice them. Or that I don't feel afraid. It just doesn't overwhelm me. I don't know why."

"But you hate fire—" I stopped. I hadn't meant to remind him of how I'd read his mind. Had I undone all the good of my apology?

His eyes stayed level and calm. "Hate it? No. I wouldn't say that. But I do have more experience of it than most. And perhaps that's a help."

"You mean, it protects you from the Shadowgrims?"

"Oh, I'd go down fast enough if they actually attacked. I expect I'm like everyone else that way. But having them fly close by— I can handle that. It's part of why the Invisible College asked me to spy for them."

"I wish I were made the same way."

"Never mind," Nat said. "The important thing is that you're safe. There's nothing to worry about now."

Not true, I thought. There were a thousand things to worry about—starting with the fact that I had yet to learn a single note of magic that would protect me from Scargrave or his ravens. But at least my heart was no longer racing.

"It's time we got back," Nat said. "Lady Helaine will have my head."

My legs were so wobbly I didn't think I could move. But Nat was right: Lady Helaine would be beside herself. So I stood up, stepped away from him, and made the long journey back downstairs.

†   †   †

By the time we returned, Lady Helaine had worked herself into a frenzy of anger and anxiety, and my stumbling, much-abridged account of what had happened did not soothe her.

"No more of these exploits," she told us. "Not until Lucy's magic is more advanced and she can defend herself."

I thought Nat might argue, but he didn't. "I'll be away anyway, as it happens," he said. "Look for me in a few weeks, and not before."

"The Invisible College is sending you somewhere?" I asked.

"Yes."

I wanted to know more, but I doubted he would tell me, especially not with my godmother standing by. Under her watchful eye, I said stiff words of parting. He replied every bit as stiffly and went away.

Over the next weeks, I missed his company more than I would ever have expected. In his absence, another member of the Invisible College—usually Sir Barnaby or Oldville—came to check on us each week, but these visits were brief and perfunctory, nothing like Nat's.

If Nat confused and challenged me, he was also a breath of

fresh air in my cloistered existence. Sometimes I paged through the drawings and maps he'd made for me, not because I needed to learn them by heart (I already had) but because the very sight of his confident hand reminded me of the world outside this one. I even found myself studying the jottings he'd made on the backs of some of the papers: equations and questions and sketches of new inventions. To me, the very vigor of his writing—the bold lines, the underlined queries—revealed his love of new ideas and experiments.

Most of my hours, however, were spent working with Lady Helaine.

After my moments of terror on the rooftop, I had redoubled my efforts to master each new lesson, no matter how tedious. I did not want to be caught at such a disadvantage again.

All day long, I practiced, and sometimes well into the night— a punishing schedule not only for me, but also for my godmother. Although she still held herself absolutely upright, her face became ever paler and more drawn, and her critiques became ever more biting.

At last, thoroughly worn-out, Lady Helaine took to stealing naps in the afternoons, leaving me to practice in solitude. This, I found, was infinitely preferable to practicing while she was around.

† † †

For a full week, I was diligent even when Lady Helaine was asleep. On the eighth day, however, I reconsidered. Lady Helaine was snoring away in the back bedchamber, with two closed doors between us, and I knew from experience that nothing would wake her for at least another half hour. She would never know if I, too, took a break from our crushing regimen.

I decided I was entitled to a rest.

It was only when I sat down before the firebox, however, that I truly realized how tired I was. Tired and lonely and discouraged. It was early January; Nat had been gone for almost a month. And what progress had I made in all that time? I was better at scales, better at trills, better at breathing and sustaining a tone. But I did not seem to be one jot closer to magic.

A soft knock at the door made me leap to my feet. Wrapping my mantle close, I stepped forward as the door swung open. To my disappointment, however, it wasn't Nat who stood on the other side but Samuel Deeps, his lace in disarray, his buttons done up wrong.

"Chantress, a favor, I beg of you." Deeps's hands shook as he bowed to me; he was all entreaty. "One of our men is lost. A cousin of mine by the name of Josiah Quicke. He left the city a fortnight ago, bearing important news for our allies in the North. He was supposed to return on Thursday, but we have heard nothing from him. We think he may be in hiding, but we have no idea where. Can you find him?"

"Me?" Did the IC want me to go out in the open and search for him? "I'm not supposed to leave Gadding House—"

"I would not dream of asking you to," Deeps said quickly. "I ask only that you use your magic."

"My magic?"

"Your mind-reading powers. Unless you have discovered better magic since then?"

"No, I haven't." It made me blush to admit how little I'd learned. "But—"

"Never fear," Deeps said. "The mind-reading is enough. That should tell us where Josiah is."

"You don't understand," I said. "I can't do that. I can't read minds."

"That's what the Council said—that it's not allowed anymore. But what's the point of having a Chantress if she doesn't do magic? Josiah needs you, madam. We *all* need you. And I've brought everything you require: hair from his own brush, and one of his handkerchiefs." He ran agitated hands along the fastenings of his cloak, and pulled out a vial he'd secreted in its lining. "And moonbriar, of course."

Put that away. That's what I ought to have said. But when I saw that glass vial and the shadowy outline of the seeds within it, a strange silence came over me—a silence borne not only of fear but also of longing, I realized with a shock. After weeks and weeks of nothing but tones and scales, something at the very core of me raged to feel the power of magic—and almost any magic would do. Even Wild Magic. Even moonbriar magic.

"Well, Chantress?" Deeps said, his eyes pleading. "Will you sing the moonbriar song?"

CHAPTER TWENTY-SEVEN

AN OLD SONG
AND A NEW ONE

As I stared at the vial, the door swung open again. I reeled around. "Nat!"

He still had his traveling cloak on, and his boots were muddy; he was glaring at both of us equally. Yet whatever hold the moonbriar seeds had over me, it broke at the sight of him.

"You're back," I said.

"And none too soon, it seems." His voice was dangerously level as he pointed to the vial. "Is that what I think it is?"

"Moonbriar?" Deeps said. "Yes. She's going to sing—"

"No," I said to Deeps. The lure of Wild Magic had faded. "I told you I can't. I'm sorry, but that's how it is."

"I should think so, after what happened last time," Nat said, but his manner toward me gentled.

"Just because she had a bit of trouble when she went into Scargrave's mind," Deeps began.

"A bit of trouble?" Nat repeated incredulously. "She nearly died, Master Deeps."

Deeps suddenly looked rather ill himself. "Nearly died?" he said to me. "Dear lady, I did not know. Sir Barnaby told us only that there had been unforeseen difficulties."

"He thought it best not to discuss her weaknesses in too much detail," Nat said.

"He hasn't wanted to discuss her at all," Deeps said, and there was real grievance in his voice as he turned to me. "We are to leave you alone for six months, he said, so you can learn proper magic. As if you weren't doing proper magic already! It's a waste, a dreadful waste."

"I thought the IC told each other everything," I said to Nat.

"The details of every mission? No," Nat said. "We could not survive that way. And you, particularly, are a well-guarded secret. Only a few of us even know where you are. Deeps is one of them." He gave his colleague a reproachful look. "We thought you could be trusted."

"Of course I can be," Deeps said heatedly. "To the last breath."

Nat pointed to the vial again. "Then why have you brought that stuff here?"

"I wish only to ascertain the whereabouts and condition of my cousin Josiah. Nothing more."

"I heard he'd gone missing," Nat said. "I'm sorry. But you know as well as I do that such things have happened before, without us looking to magic to solve our problems."

"But matters are so much worse now," Deeps argued. "Have

you noticed how many more Watchmen Scargrave has on patrol? And how many people he's sent to the Feeding Room this month alone? He's drawing his net tighter and tighter around London. If he captures Josiah, we'll be the ones netted next, and the Shadowgrims will feast on our every secret. We have to keep my cousin safe."

"Not at Lucy's expense." Nat's voice was quiet, but there was iron in it.

"But surely there's no real risk," Deeps said. "It's Josiah we're talking about, not Scargrave. And we know it's his hair on the brush, and his handkerchief, so there can be no mistake there."

"And what if Josiah is dead?" Nat asked. "Or what if he's been captured? What if he's become one of the Ravens' Own? What happens to Lucy then? I tell you she could die."

There was an uncomfortable silence as we all contemplated this.

"She's the only Chantress we've got," Nat said.

"Poor Josiah," Deeps said with a sigh, but without another protest, he tucked the moonbriar back inside his cloak.

"How did you get hold of those seeds, anyway?" Nat asked. "It's hard to believe Sir Barnaby would allow you to bring them here."

"They aren't his. They're mine." Deeps blushed. "I, er . . . kept a bit back after one of our expeditions."

"What?" Nat looked aghast.

Tugging at his rumpled lace, Deeps defended himself. "I was curious. And it was only a very little bit, you understand. But then my cousin disappeared, and—"

"I can guess at the rest," Nat said.

"I was quite careful with it," Deeps said, still red-faced. "And as you see, no harm was done."

"And no harm will be done," Nat said, "because we're going to give it over to Sir Barnaby right now." He went to the door.

Deeps looked flustered, but he reluctantly followed Nat's lead. At the door, he bowed to me. "Madam."

"I'm sorry." I hated how feeble the words sounded. He'd come to me hoping for help, and I was turning him away with nothing. "I hope your cousin comes home safe."

"I hope so too," Deeps said mournfully. "But we can't risk your life on it, dear lady. I do see that."

Nat put a hand to the latch. "I wish I could come again this week, but I can't," he said to me. "I have to go out again right away. I should be back before the month is out."

Away again, so soon? I tried to cover up my disappointment. "Lady Helaine is sleeping," I said. "If you can get out before she wakes . . ."

There was no need to finish the sentence. Nat was already ushering Deeps out the door. Just before he closed it, however, he looked back at me.

"The seeds didn't hurt you?"

"No. Not at all."

Another searching look, and then the flash of his smile. "Good."

The door shut, and he vanished from sight.

† † †

Minutes after Nat and the others had left, Lady Helaine strode into the room, her manner as regal as ever. Despite her nap, not a single silver hair was out of place. "I heard voices."

"That must have been me." It would do no good if she found out what Deeps had asked of me.

"It sounded much lower than your voice," Lady Helaine said suspiciously.

"I was . . . practicing my low tones. And doing some extra breathing exercises."

Practice. Exercises. No words were more magic than these, not for Lady Helaine.

Her harsh voice lightened. "Indeed? Let me hear what you have been doing."

I didn't please her that time, or the next. "Very close is not good enough!" she scolded. "You must be flawless."

The day after that, she became more irritable still, for Samuel Deeps disturbed our morning practice, saying he had come to check the firebox was operating properly. Although Lady Helaine did not let him linger, on his way out, he managed to whisper in my ear that his cousin Josiah had returned to London unharmed.

The news buoyed me up, for Josiah's fate had been preying on my mind, and I went back to the drills with renewed determination. Aboveground, people were risking their lives to oppose Scargarve; I wanted to try and match their dedication. When Lady Helaine, still visibly annoyed by the interruption, demanded that I run through the full set of exercises, I attacked each one with vigor.

Three very long days later, I executed all the exercises perfectly. What's more, I managed to repeat the feat not just once but every time Lady Helaine called on me to perform it. Elated, I beamed at her.

"You have mastered these, it seems." From Lady Helaine, the dry words qualified as warmest praise. "I think we may perhaps attempt a song-spell next. A very simple one, for kindling flame."

Proven Magic, at long last! Yet something worried me. "What kind of flame?" I asked. "Is it anything like the Shadowgrims' fire?"

"Absolutely not." Lady Helaine looked insulted. "Even if it were within my means, I would not teach you such a thing. The songs I know are for kindling ordinary, useful flame, the kind that lights a candle or a hearth."

I was so relieved that I forgot to modulate my breathing as a Chantress should.

Lady Helaine noticed the slip. "Do not grow lax, goddaughter," she warned. "When a Chantress sings, she must strive for exactitude in every measure, down to the smallest tremor or the slightest breath. Otherwise, the song-spell will not work—or worse yet, it will work differently than she intended."

"I will be diligent, I promise," I said, subdued.

"Very well, then," Lady Helaine said. "We shall begin." She set a candle on a wide shelf of stone. "Let us see if you can light this."

"How?" I began.

"I am about to tell you. Listen." She raised her hand as if to hush me. "Stand before me, and clear your mind."

I took up the position I had been taught, feet slightly apart, arms resting at my side. Lady Helaine took up this stance too, and within seconds, we were breathing in tandem.

"Here is the first line of the spell." Lady Helaine eked out a melody, her rough voice harsh on the ears but precise. "Sing it back to me."

"I don't understand the words."

"There *are* no words, at least not in the way you mean. All you need to remember is this: Each sound is part of the whole, and the whole is worthless unless every part is there."

"But how can I learn the spell if I don't understand what I'm singing?"

"You learn them by rote, like every other Chantress before you," said Lady Helaine. "Song-spells are many-layered and complex, and even a gifted Chantress may take years to understand them fully. Most never do. But the song itself is enough to work magic, even with imperfect understanding. So listen again, carefully, and sing it back to me exactly as I have sung it to you."

For the second time, her rough notes grated on my ears. My voice wobbled as I repeated them.

"Your breathing needs work," Lady Helaine said. "Try again."

The kind of singing she wanted from me was nothing like the Wild Magic I had done before. It made my head buzz, my eyes smart, and my throat burn. But I persisted, singing the phrase again and again and again, as many times as she ordered me to.

At last Lady Helaine's face lit up. "Sing it exactly that way. Again!"

I sang gingerly, straining for the same intonation.

My godmother's pale lips split in a smile. "We'll make a Chantress of you yet."

† † †

Lady Helaine's words gave me confidence that day. In the fortnight that followed, however, that confidence dwindled to nothing. Despite countless hours of practice, I failed to master the kindling song-spell. By late January, Lady Helaine and I were both growing desperate.

"Again," Lady Helaine said grimly, four hours into our fortieth lesson. "Again."

I sang the spell once more. Resonance and intensity and intonation: I knew everything had to be correct for magic to happen. But there was a quaver in my breath, a shortness to my phrasing, that I couldn't seem to fix.

"I don't understand it," Lady Helaine said. "It is the simplest spell in the repertoire. This ought to be child's play." She shook her head at me. "You aren't really trying."

I flushed. "I promise you I am."

"I find that difficult to believe. And if it is true, then we are lost. The song-spells we need to accomplish the task before us—the song of concealment, and the song that will destroy the grimoire— are far more challenging."

I avoided her eyes. "I know."

"Be more resolute," Lady Helaine commanded. "More forceful."

I tried again to plow through the song. But the truth was that this kind of singing did not come naturally to me—and the harder I tried, the more alien it felt, as if I were forcing my body to do something it wasn't meant to do. My throat was rubbed raw, and even the most delicate notes scorched my chest.

Lady Helaine's mouth was rigid. "You must work harder! Again!"

I tried again—and failed.

The silence that followed was more frigid and awful than ever.

"You are holding yourself back," Lady Helaine accused. "You are deliberately holding yourself back."

"I am not." Exhausted and near tears, I tried to keep my voice even. "I am giving this everything I have."

"So you say." Lady Helaine twisted her bone beads so tightly I thought they would snap. "But if that is so, I can only conclude I was wrong about your gift. You don't have the promise and power I thought you did. Perhaps what power you had has been used up already."

I looked at her, horrified. "Is that possible?"

"Anything is possible with Wild Magic." She shut her eyes, as if the very sight of me disgusted her. "Whatever the reason, it is clear my training is wasted on you. Our lessons are over."

"But—"

"No pleading. You are a grave disappointment, a sad end to a great family. And I am done with you." She stalked to the door that led to her bedchamber and slammed it shut behind her.

I stood by the fire, shaking. How could she walk out on me like that?

Because she knows you'll never be worth anything, my mind whispered. *You're the last of your line, an utter failure.*

No. I could not afford to listen to such thoughts. *I will succeed,* I told myself. *I will practice again and again until I succeed.*

But the sentences sounded hollow as I said them. What echoed more loudly were Lady Helaine's words:

You are a grave disappointment.

I am done with you.

I paced the room, trying to drive the sound of her voice away. But the smoky walls seemed to close in on me like a coffin, smothering me until I could hardly draw breath. . . .

I had to get out. I had to. I had to.

I snatched up a lantern, scrabbled at the door latch, and ran off.

CHAPTER TWENTY-EIGHT
PLAYING WITH FIRE

At first, the running itself was all I was aware of, that and the sheer relief of escape. It was a while before I realized where my feet were taking me: to the meeting chamber of the Invisible College.

As good a place as any, I supposed. And since it was well hidden, perhaps better than most.

I slipped into the deserted chamber, set my lantern on a table, and looked around. I had come here several times during my explorations with Nat, but it felt strange to be here alone. The room was built for a crowd, and the chairs were arranged so that it seemed as if I had an audience before me. I remembered the mind-reading I had done here, and where it had led, and I shivered.

Not a comfortable room, in any respect. And to make matters worse, there on the table before me was an unlit candle almost exactly the same size and shape as the one I had been trying to light with Lady Helaine. Norrie would say it was a sign. At least, she would if she were able to bear being here.

But a sign of what? Of my failure? Of my shame?

Was it a sign that I should keep trying?

I gripped the table. What if I were to sing right here, without Lady Helaine standing over me, carping and criticizing? Could I make the song-spell work?

A ghost of a hope, but it put new heart into me. Before my resolve could fade, I focused on the candle and started to sing.

Nothing happened. Three times I tried, but the candle sat cool and lifeless before me.

I covered my face. Was it true, what Lady Helaine said—that my magic was gone? Would I never sing an enchantment again?

I could think of only one way to find out. My hand went to the ruby around my neck. If I took it off and heard no music, then I would know my magic was gone indeed.

But did I truly dare to take it off? The stone was my one protection against the dangers of Wild Magic—dangers that seemed all the more perilous after these long weeks where I had lived safe from its influence. What if I *did* hear Wild Magic? What then?

Mouth dry, I eased the ruby over my head. *I won't listen for more than a second,* I promised myself. *But I have to know if there's any magic left.*

The chain cleared my head. For a desolate moment, there was nothing but silence. My heart fell.

An instant later, the world burst into music—encircling me, charming me, delighting me.

Only a second, that's what I had promised myself. But the joy of hearing Wild Magic consumed me. It was as if I had buried half of myself alive, and only now was whole again.

The songs pulled at me and played with me, begging me to give voice to them.

I will not sing, I told them. And I meant it. But what harm would it do to listen? I let the ruby drop beside the candle as I listened to the melodies flying around the room. Perhaps it was only an illusion, but I felt as if I half understood what they were saying to me. Had I become a better listener because of my training? If so, perhaps those endless drills had been worth it.

As I stood there, wondering, a soft and sparkling melody caught my attention. It spoke of flame and heat and light and warmth, and it came from the candle—or more precisely, from the air *above* the candle.

It was a song for kindling flame.

Or so my mind told me. Unless it was the song itself that spoke to me? Either way, it was impossible not to notice the kinship between this song and the song-spell I had been trying to master.

I listened to the song again. It was cheerful and bright, like a candle in the window on a dark winter's night. There was nothing of terror in it, nothing of the raven's fire. It seemed as safe as a song could be.

I hummed one note, and then another. *One song. How much could it hurt to sing one song?*

It was daytime, so the Shadowgrims were asleep; if I worked a very small bit of Wild Magic now, they would not smell it. And if it worked, then I would know I could still make magic. Surely that was worth something.

I let the song take hold of me. It couldn't be sung in my godmother's style, with my breath rigidly controlled. Instead, it needed me to bend and curve around it, nurturing the music and the spark within.

A last trilled note, and a flash of heat shot through me— nothing like the Shadowgrims' scalding terror but instead a dancing, golden light.

The candle ignited.

I stared at its glowing wick. Fire. I had created fire from song. After the first shock, jubilation coursed through me. I was a Chantress, and my power still burned bright.

"What in Hades was that?"

I whirled around. Nat stood a few feet behind me, bristling like a wildcat.

I took a step back, hiding the necklace in the folds of my skirts. "What are you doing here?"

"I got home last night. I was coming to see you." His eyes swung from me to the flame and then back again. "Why aren't you wearing your stone?"

I didn't want to tell him, but I didn't need to.

"You're doing Wild Magic," he said an appalled second later. He made it sound like murder in cold blood.

I lifted my chin. "And what if I am? It's my business, not yours."

"What you do is everyone's business. Our lives are tied to yours. And here you are, playing with fire." Anger blazed in his face, and he stepped toward me, so close that I could see the gold flecks in his eyes. "Who put you up to this? Your godmother?"

"No! She'd have my head if she knew. Please don't tell her." I spoke quickly, quietly, willing him to understand. "It was an experiment, that's all."

"An experiment?" He sounded incredulous.

"Yes. Like your own."

"But you could have burned us alive, girl. You could have blown up Gadding House—"

"The way you nearly did, with those firebox experiments?" That silenced him. "Admit it: Your work is as dangerous as mine. But that doesn't stop you from doing it. Not when there's something you need to find out. So why shouldn't I do the same?"

"It's not that simple."

"Why? Because it's not science? Because I'm a girl?"

"Because you're doing magic."

I scowled at him. "Why am I even bothering to argue with you? Where magic is concerned, your mind's completely closed. You hate everything about it, me included."

He looked at me, startled. "I never said I hated you."

"You said I was like the Shadowgrims." It still rankled.

He reddened. "That was before I really knew you."

His words caught me by surprise. Was he saying he'd changed his mind?

"Your magic's more complicated than I thought," he said. "It's not free, and it's not easy. You work hard for it, as hard as I work at my own craft. Maybe even harder."

I drew a deep breath. It was the most praise I'd had in weeks—and it was coming from the person I'd least expected to offer it.

"But that doesn't change the fact that your magic is dangerous," he went on, his eyes grave. "What if the smell of it pulls in the Shadowgrims?"

"Whatever smell there is will be long gone by night."

"Maybe so. But your godmother said there were other perils too—that Wild Magic could deceive you and hurt you." He shook his head. "What possessed you, Lucy? Isn't her kind of magic good enough for you?"

"I had to," I said. "I had to know—"

"Know what?"

"Whether I could still do magic." It felt like a confession.

There was a long silence.

"Whatever made you think you couldn't?" he asked.

"Never mind."

He crossed his arms over his chest. "What?" It was clear he would dog me till he got an answer.

"It hasn't been going well," I admitted. "No matter what I try, I can't seem to master Lady Helaine's sort of magic."

He raised an eyebrow. "So you thought you'd turn to Wild Magic instead—despite the risks?"

"It wasn't that risky. Nothing like mind-reading. All I did was light one small candle." Stepping back from him, I blew on the wick. "Look: It's gone out."

I'd meant that to be the end of it, but the song of flame lingered in the air, and the urge to make music and magic was still strong in me.

Nat stepped forward, his voice tense. "You're not going to light it again, are you?"

"It's harmless enough. You'll see." I let the song rise from my lips, sure it would be the same, and wanting to prove to him how very safe it was. But the anger inside me, the tumult of the argument, the weight of Nat's disapproving gaze—all of it fed into the music. I softened my voice and bent into the song, trying to tame it. Yes, that was better. The song was still powerful, yet more controlled . . .

Someone rushed toward me, breaking my concentration.

"What are you doing?" Lady Helaine shrieked. "Stop! Stop at once!"

The song inside me exploded, and flames shot into the air.

CHAPTER TWENTY-NINE
REVELATIONS

As the flame flared and hissed down toward the candle, Lady Helaine roared, "What do you think you are doing?"

Panicked, I slung the ruby necklace over my head. The music in the room vanished, and the flame subsided to a pinpoint of light on the wick. In the sudden silence, all I could hear was Lady Helaine's ferocious growl as she stood before me, fury in her eyes.

"Did you think me a fool, that I would not know the sound of Wild Magic when I heard it?"

My mood of defiance was slipping into shades of doubt, but I held my head high. "I thought you were done with me."

"Not when you behave like this." Lady Helaine turned on Nat. "You." She spat the word out. "What did you do to encourage this?"

"He did nothing," I said before he could speak. "He is as angry with me as you are."

"Then you may go," Lady Helaine told Nat. When he did not move, she raised her voice. "I said go!"

Nat looked at me, and to my surprise, it wasn't anger I saw in his face but concern. "Do you want me to stay?" he asked quietly.

I shook my head. This was my battle, not his. "Please go."

After he left, Lady Helaine said in a low, stony voice, "You drive me to despair, goddaughter. You scoff at everything I teach you, and then you practice Wild Magic behind my back—"

"Only this once! And only because you said I had no power left—"

"I do not wish to hear your excuses," my godmother said, still in that harsh voice. "I know the truth now: Something in you is resisting me. Something in you is determined to follow the wrong path."

"But I—"

"You are just like your mother." Lady Helaine's voice cracked across mine like a whip.

My breath caught in my throat. What did this have to do with my mother?

"She had power enough for both of us, more power even than I. But she would not listen." Lady Helaine's burning eyes looked straight through me, as if she were seeing a ghost. "You must be exact, I told her. You must be careful. You must practice and practice and practice. She was my ward and my apprentice; she was duty-bound to listen to me. But she dismissed me at every turn—exactly as you do. Every gift I offered, she scorned."

Was this true? It didn't sound like the gentle mother I remembered. But Norrie had said that my mother and Lady Helaine had not gotten along, and perhaps this was why. . . .

"Wild Magic was the only magic that interested her," Lady Helaine said. "I warned her to steer clear of it. I told her I would not tolerate such doings under my roof." Her mouth crumpled. "I never thought she would run away."

I did not know what to say. Lady Helaine seemed to be speaking to someone else in the room, not to me.

A moment later, her eyes focused on me, as if she were suddenly remembering I was there. "I saw her only twice after that," she added more calmly. "The first time, she brought you, a babe in arms. She knew that by Chantress law, I was your godmother, the eldest of your close-born kin, and she came to me to make your stone. Even with her love of Wild Magic, she knew you must have one. Young Chantresses are too vulnerable without it; they can be carried off by any devious music that crosses their path.

"I thought we might be reconciled then, but when I learned she was still playing with Wild Magic, I was furious. I tried to make her see that she was risking not only her life but yours. We quarreled, and she went away. For eight years, she hid from me, and she used Wild Magic to cover her tracks. There was no way to find you without using Wild Magic myself, and I knew better than to take that path. So I did not see her again until the night she came to me with news of Scargrave and the grimoire." Lady Helaine's voice wobbled. "She would not tell me what she had done with you, not even when I begged. I find that hard to forgive, even now."

I was still grappling with what she'd said earlier. "She used Wild Magic for eight years?"

It was the first inkling I'd had that Wild Magic did not necessarily lead to swift catastrophe and death.

"She was incorrigible." Lady Helaine's jaw became more pronounced. "Absolutely unrepentant."

"But you said Chantresses who use Wild Magic don't last long."

"She had a flair for it," Lady Helaine said grudgingly. "A few in every generation do, though most have the sense to refrain from making use of it."

"But she didn't. Why?"

Lady Helaine's lips tightened. "Because she was tempted. That is what Wild Magic does. It tempts. It seduces. It gives you power beyond reckoning. No doubt that's what drew her to it. She said she liked the freedom of it and the joy—though what she meant by that, I can't understand."

Perhaps she couldn't, but I could. It made me think of the wholeness I felt when I heard the wild music again, and the hot light inside me when I sang the kindling song. Had my mother felt the same way?

Lady Helaine's mouth soured. "Little good it did her in the end. When the Shadowgrims attacked us, her Wild Magic failed her. That is the way of Wild Magic: For all its power, it is chancy and deceitful. It will betray you when you least expect it. And she had nothing to fall back on, no discipline, no memorized songs, no long years of practice at Proven Magic. Indeed, she'd practiced Wild Magic with such abandon that she couldn't work any Proven Magic even if she had remembered it. Her stone had cracked right through."

"Her stone *cracked*?"

"Wild Magic can damage our stones as badly as the Shadow-grims can, though the pattern of the cracking is different. Given the kind of powerful magic your mother worked, it's surprising her stone lasted as long as it did."

My hand moved to my ruby of its own accord. "Why didn't you warn me?"

"Because I thought there was no need. You had given your word you would obey me."

I held the ruby up to the light, and she and I searched it for damage.

"It's still intact," my godmother said, unbending just a little.

"And the mind-reading earlier, with Scargrave—that didn't damage it either?"

"No. I examined it very closely the night we met, and I would have seen the fault if it had been there. Your stone is a strong one, like your mother's, and it escaped unscathed. But it will not stay that way, not if you keep practicing Wild Magic. Another attempt to kindle flame, another session of mind-reading—anything could be the last straw that starts a crack, or even shatters the stone completely. Then you will be like your mother, up against the Shadowgrims without anything to protect you. And you know what happened to her."

I heard blame in Lady Helaine's voice, and it made me angry. "But you were there. You knew the right songs. Why didn't you save her?"

"You think it is as simple as that? A few songs, and all is well?"

Lady Helaine's face twisted. "Understand this: The songs I sang were among the most complicated I knew. They required craft and cunning and years of practice. Even I, with all my skill, could only barely manage to save myself. Your mother succumbed so quickly there was no way to rescue her." She turned away from me, as if the memory were too much to bear. "And if you think that this does not pain me every day of my life, goddaughter, then you may think again."

Chastened, I stood silent. Thorny-tempered my godmother might be, but her anguish was real.

Lady Helaine squared her sharp shoulders and faced me. "Enough of this. What's past is past." The anger had burned out of her voice, leaving only pain and resolute determination. "I was wrong to walk away from you. You are slow—very slow—to master Proven Magic, but the power is there, that is plain. I believe you have as much raw talent as your mother did, and what's more, you have a self-discipline I never saw in her. If you do exactly as I say, you could become a truly great Chantress."

I frowned. Lady Helaine remembered only a handful of song-spells, didn't she? There didn't seem to be much prospect of greatness in that.

But when I raised the point, Lady Helaine shook her head. "Do not trouble your head over that. If it is meant to be, it will be—provided you give your whole heart and body and mind to what I am teaching you. And provided you never do Wild Magic again."

"I never meant to do more of it, anyway," I said, though I knew this was only half-true. Once the ruby was off, the music had beguiled me, and it had been hard to resist it.

"No one ever means to do more, not at the start. That is the way of Wild Magic."

"I tell you, I won't take the stone off again." I had no wish to end up like my mother—betrayed by Wild Magic, surrounded by Shadowgrims. Perhaps Proven Magic was not as powerful, but it was safe. And ever since I had walked into Scargrave's mind, safety was what I craved most.

My eye fell on the candle in front of me. "Let me try again."

"Try what?"

I blew out the flame. "To light it your way."

"I think you've done enough for one afternoon," Lady Helaine began.

But I had already started to sing, drawing breath in the way that she had taught me.

I can do this.

The song-spell still felt wrong to me, burning and scorching and making my head ache, but this time I didn't let the feeling rattle me. I had learned something from the Wild Magic that carried over here: the sense of how a kindling song was put together, and how it needed to work as a whole. Beat after beat, my voice rang out stark and strong.

And yet still the candle stayed dark.

I trained my whole mind on it and kept singing, concentrating fiercely on each pitch and beat and phrase.

But now the last notes were escaping from my mouth—and

still the wick was cold and black. Heart sinking, I sang the final tone, long and low.

The song was over. It was done. And yet again I had failed. I turned away, hands shaking.

Next to me, Lady Helaine gasped.

I spun around. At the top of the wick, a flame quivered, faint but indisputably there.

I had made the song-spell work.

CHAPTER THIRTY
MASTERY

The next weeks passed in a blur of singing and magic. Every day there was something new for me to learn, and sometimes I could feel myself making progress almost by the hour.

Not that the road was entirely smooth.

"Again!" Lady Helaine continued to bark, day after day, hour after hour. More demanding than ever, she jumped on me for being too loud, too soft, too piercing, too husky, too passionate, too glib, and too reckless. Some days almost nothing I did passed muster.

"Again—and sing it properly this time!" I heard the curt command even in my dreams.

Yet I found that Lady Helaine's criticism did not sting as much as it once had. Slowly, painstakingly, with many stops and stumbles, I was learning the song-spells I needed, and that was what mattered.

And if I took more time over this than either I or Lady Helaine would have liked, I was making faster strides with another magical task: that of reading the Chantress manuscript with the song for destroying the grimoire.

Covered with scratching and hatch marks, the pages appeared indecipherable at first, but as I held the scraps in my hands and listened to Lady Helaine's explanations, I started to grasp the relation between each page of symbols and the sound of the song-spell it denoted.

Lady Helaine tapped her fingers together with excitement. "You have a gift for this."

I scrutinized the pages, my mind absorbed by their mysteries.

"A remarkable gift," Lady Helaine mused, now with an air of quiet calculation. "And a very useful one. It will serve you well."

I looked up from the vellum in my hand. "I thought hardly any Chantress manuscripts were written down—and that Scargrave had burned most of them."

"He burned *my* library." Lady Helaine's voice was smoky with anger and regret. "Still, I expect he has not burned everything. Surely some scraps remain to be found." She pointed to a line on my page. "Enough talking. Sing that to me. And be sure to hold your chin up exactly as I have directed."

As I continued to work with the manuscript, I sometimes caught Lady Helaine looking at me with pride, and occasionally with a certain wary respect as well. And that respect only increased when, after hours of agonizing practice, I finally made the song-spell for concealment work.

"Excellent, excellent," Lady Helaine murmured. "I can hardly see you even full in front of the candles. And you are virtually invisible in the shadows."

To see my own body slip away was shocking, and I nearly lost the momentum of the song then and there. But Lady Helaine's rigorous training stood me in good stead. Though my head throbbed horribly, I kept breathing properly for a full quarter hour, and the magic of the song stayed with me until I lost it in a fit of coughing.

"It is a start," Lady Helaine said when I became visible again. "But we must build your stamina."

Our practice sessions became longer and more intense than ever, and as I became more and more proficient, Lady Helaine unbent a little and began telling me stories. At first, these were mostly gripping yarns about her adventures as a Chantress, but later, quieter tales emerged as well: how the women of our lineage had kept their magical nature largely hidden from their husbands ("Men cannot be trusted, neither husbands, nor fathers, nor sons"); how her own husband, a young nobleman, had considered her taste for books and libraries unseemly ("It was fortunate that I had skill with locks"); how she had never borne children but had longed for them ("Daughters all, if I'd had my way").

She told me stories, too, of the dilemmas my ancestresses had faced and the victories they had won. Instead of dreaming about the island, I now dreamed about Niniane and Melusine and Eleanor of Aquitaine. Knowing their histories—their glories and triumphs, their struggles and defeats—made me determined to prove myself worthy of the long line of Chantresses who had come before me.

Yet even when telling stories, a part of my godmother stayed aloof. If I asked a question she didn't want to answer, she simply ignored it. If I dared repeat the question, she turned sour and taciturn.

But then I kept secrets too.

† † †

One of the secrets I kept concerned Nat.

I had seen him only three times since the day he had found me practicing Wild Magic. Two of those visits had taken place in full view of Lady Helaine, and I had thought that she must be the cause of the awkwardness between us. But on his third visit, in early March, Lady Helaine allowed us to make a brief expedition by ourselves into the upper realms of Gadding House—and the awkwardness remained.

As we made our way to the minstrels' gallery above the Great Hall, I could feel the tension between us. I was much too aware of every move that Nat made, and he, too, seemed to be on edge—though perhaps that was only because I was so hard to see. I had reached the point where I could sustain the effects of the conceal-ment song for a full hour, provided I breathed properly and kept the song alive in my head. If Nat looked carefully, he could usu-ally see a slight shimmering in the air where I was, but that was it.

The first time he bumped into me, I heard him inhale sharply.

"Are you hurt?" I asked.

"No."

"Then what's wrong?"

Nat was silent for a moment. "I hate not knowing where you are."

"But that's the plan, isn't it?" I struggled to keep talking while breathing in the proper way. "The only way I can succeed is if no one can see me."

"Of course." He pulled away from me. "But it's unsettling to have a mind-reader on the loose."

"You're never going to forget that, are you?" I said under my breath.

He swung around. "What?"

He misjudged the distance, coming so near that his lips almost brushed my cheek. Startled, I stopped breathing—and quick as a blink, turned visible.

In that moment of transformation, I saw dismay in his eyes. But I saw something else, too, something that made my breath catch again.

That must be the look Lady Helaine meant.

"Lucy," he said.

But someone was coming, and there was no chance to say more. We pressed ourselves into the shadows—and this time he kept a full arm's length away from me. For the rest of our time together, he was silent, and I felt more unsettled by him than ever.

Perhaps I would have tried harder to say something if I had known what was coming. For when we returned to Lady Helaine, Nat told us that he would be absent for a month or more. The Invisible College was sending him up north to track down another possible moonbriar grove.

Awkward as things were between us, I knew I would miss him terribly.

None of this, of course, did I discuss with Lady Helaine.

† † †

What else did I keep hidden from my godmother? Any number of things, from my occasional explorations around Gadding House while she was asleep to my worries about Nat's safety. Above all, I hid my fears and doubts about my progress as a Chantress. There was no room for doubt with magic, Lady Helaine said. But doubt continued to haunt me anyway.

I was making progress, it was true. Yet despite relentless practice, none of the song-spells came easily to me. When I was tired or worried or sick, they became almost impossible. One week I caught a bad cold, and for two days my voice was too hoarse to do any magic whatsoever. What bothered me most, though, was that even when the songs did work, they felt all wrong.

I had tried to broach the subject with my godmother. "It's like singing shut up in a box," I had protested. "It doesn't feel natural."

"Of course it doesn't," was Lady Helaine's cool response. "You are twisting nature against itself, goddaughter. It ought to go against the grain."

With this as my measure, I tried to interpret feeling wrong as the mark of success. And perhaps it was. But I often thought it wasn't nature I was twisting but myself. When I sang, it felt as if I were forcing my voice through someone else's throat. Even breathing properly was still difficult: On the worst days, it was like drowning over and over again.

All of this turned even simple song-spells into a trial. A complicated spell like concealment—which required rigid breathing the entire time I wanted to remain unseen—was excruciating.

Nevertheless, I was determined to conquer every spell Lady Helaine set before me. And gradually, as the gloom of March receded, and I started to feel the warmth of spring when I sneaked through the upper halls, my skills improved. By early April, I could sustain the effects of the concealment song for a full three hours.

Over the next fortnight, I worked to perfect the other critical song-spell: the song that would destroy the grimoire. As I did so, I tried my best to set aside my worries about Nat. I reminded myself many times that he was canny and brave and skilled in evading discovery. Surely he was safe, wherever he was. Yet as the weeks passed and he failed to return, my fears mounted.

† † †

"I must admit that I'm worried too," Penebrygg told me when it was his week to stop by and check on me. It had done my heart good to see him—and to see the parcel he'd brought from Norrie, with her love—but when he admitted his fears to me, my stomach plummeted. If Penebrygg was concerned, then there was real cause for alarm.

"We had word of them through our chain of allies up until

last week," he said. "There were more soldiers on the move than they'd expected, and more Watchmen, and they couldn't get close to the site. And then, suddenly, no word at all. Nothing for a whole week now."

I reminded myself that Deeps's cousin, Josiah Quicke, had vanished for a full fortnight and still returned to London without injury.

Evidently Penebrygg was calling to mind the same thing. "Not that such silences haven't happened before, of course. No doubt they're tucked safe away somewhere, and we'll hear from them soon. Now tell me: How is your magic coming along?"

"Quite well," I said cautiously, for Lady Helaine was within earshot. She continued to believe that my training in magic was a sacred secret. Whenever a visitor from the Invisible College showed impatience with this, she stated her position again, and promptly showed them the door.

"Will you be ready soon?" he asked.

"Very soon, I should think."

Lady Helaine glided over to us like a chill wind. "Dr. Penebrygg, I am certain you have better things to be doing. And I know for a fact that we do. Lucy will not become better without practice."

"Of course, of course." Penebrygg rose and took my hand. "Take care, my dear. And try not to worry about Nat."

He might as well have asked the stars not to shine.

To keep my burgeoning fears in some kind of check, I forced myself to work harder than ever in the week that followed. My godmother's eyes gleamed as she saw how diligently I practiced.

"Songs of destruction are among the most difficult spells," she said. "And this one especially. But you are coming along well."

When the Invisible College asked me to demonstrate my progress, however, Lady Helaine was furious.

CHAPTER THIRTY-ONE

THE DELEGATION

When the delegation from the Invisible College came to call, I was in the back room, asleep. An unusual circumstance in the early afternoon, but I had worked on the song of destruction into the small hours the night before, and I was desperate for a rest. I awoke, however, when I heard Lady Helaine's ringing tones of outrage: "You wish my goddaughter to perform like a common magician?"

"This very hour, if possible." I recognized Nat's voice immediately. So he had returned at last from his moonbriar expedition! A knot inside me released—then tightened again as I tried to hide, even from myself, how glad I was to have him back.

"Not this hour, or any other," Lady Helaine said harshly.

I was disconcerted by her flat denial. But when I entered the chamber, I was even more surprised to discover that Nat was not our only visitor. Standing with him before the fire were Penebrygg, Sir Barnaby, and Isaac Oldville.

Nat stood silent, face downcast, and did not greet me. Not sure what to make of this, I looked at Lady Helaine. "I do not mind showing them—"

"No." Lady Helaine was obdurate. "Their request is out of order."

"Out of order?" Oldville repeated incredulously, his gaunt frame looming over us. "I think not, madam. We have sheltered you and fed you and kept you safe for months now, at considerable peril to ourselves. It is time you fulfilled your end of the bargain."

"How dare you speak to me that way? My goddaughter is not a servant, working for her hire—"

"My lady, forgive us," Penebrygg said to Lady Helaine. He motioned for Oldville to be silent. "We are under great strain, and our words are not always well chosen. We have had bad news, you see."

Nat looked up then, his face haggard.

"You didn't find the moonbriar grove?" I guessed.

"It was there, all right," Nat said. "But Scargrave found it first."

I put my hand to my mouth. This was disaster indeed.

Nat winced. It was only then that I saw what I ought to have noticed right away: his left hand, half hidden by his jacket, crisscrossed with a bloody bandage.

"You're hurt!" I said.

He pulled the hand back, as if to keep it from sight. "It looks worse than it is."

"What happened?"

"The Ravens' Own were guarding the moonbriar grove. We didn't see them until it was too late."

"We lost two of our best men." Sir Barnaby's well-bred face betrayed no emotion, but his hand was tight around his ivory cane.

"They were caught?" I asked.

"Trapped," Sir Barnaby said. "So they shot themselves."

"Shot themselves?" I repeated blankly, still staring at the crimson bandage on Nat's hand.

"Anything rather than be sent to the Shadowgrims," Penebrygg said. "Then everything truly would be lost."

"You said you would protect us." Lady Helaine's accusation took in the entire delegation. "You said—"

"We did our best," Sir Barnaby interrupted, tapping his cane fretfully. "But no one is perfect. In any case, we cannot afford to waste time in recrimination. Scargrave has stolen a march on us: Our spies say he is breeding the Shadowgrims again—and this time there are eggs."

Eggs? Fear hammered at my throat. In a voice I did not recognize as my own, I asked, "How many are there?"

"At least a hundred of the cursed things," Oldville said.

"And how long do we have before they hatch?"

"We cannot say for sure," Sir Barnaby said, "for we do not know exactly when the eggs were laid. Ordinarily, however, raven eggs take about three weeks to hatch."

"So it may only be a matter of days," I said faintly.

"More than that, almost certainly." Penebrygg adjusted his

spectacles, trying to put the best face on things. "It will be five or six weeks until the hatchlings leave the nest for the first time, and months more before they are adults. And we believe that it is only then that they come into their full powers."

"Do not obscure the truth," Oldville said sourly. "We know nothing for sure about Shadowgrim hatchlings. It may be that they come out of the eggs with their powers already developed. Or they may have even more monstrous appetites than grown Shadowgrims do. It remains to be seen. Every day we delay may tilt the balance in their favor."

Dour he might be, but at least he had made the situation clear. "You mean that I must seize my chance now."

The look Penebrygg gave me over the rim of his lenses was full of worry. "Only if you are ready."

"Which is why we have come here," Sir Barnaby said. "To see for ourselves where you are. If you will show us—"

"Of course," I said.

"No." Lady Helaine gripped my arm. I could feel how much she hated being answerable to these men, and how much it distressed her to share Chantress rites with strangers. And in truth, I felt some sympathy with her, for it was not easy for me to share such private things either.

Lady Helaine spoke over my head to Sir Barnaby. "She overestimates herself, poor child—"

My sympathy vanished. "Let me show you what I can do," I told Sir Barnaby. I shook off Lady Helaine's hand, and I started to sing.

"No." Lady Helaine grabbed at me. "You mustn't—"

But the song of concealment was already doing its work. My outline was thinning, my body dissolving into air.

"Heaven above," Penebrygg murmured.

Even Oldville's skeptical face looked impressed. "There's a faint glimmer . . . no, now I've lost it."

Sir Barnaby sat down and clutched his cane in excitement. "Nat tried to prepare us. But truly, it is beyond belief."

"That is enough, quite enough," my godmother said.

"Oh, I'm not done yet," I said, working hard to keep my breathing right. All but invisible, I sang most of the songs she had taught me. I charmed open the locks that Nat had given to me for practice. I turned keys without touching them. I kindled the flames of candles and set a torch alight and made the fire burn brighter. Everyone but Lady Helaine stood open-mouthed in wonder and awe.

Oldville recovered himself first. "Chantress?" He addressed the query to the air.

"Over here," I said, trying not to chuckle as Oldville's eyes wandered, unable to locate me. "By the fire."

"Ah." He still couldn't quite place me, I saw, and it was making him a bit cross. "I notice you haven't sung the song to destroy the grimoire."

"How could she, without the grimoire to sing it to?" Penebrygg said reasonably.

Oldville turned to my godmother. "The song will not work on other books, then?"

"Of course not," Lady Helaine snapped. Her anger, I guessed, was as much for me as for Oldville. "The grimoire is utterly unlike other books. Anyone knows that."

"But this is hypothesis only? You have not attempted any experiments?" Oldville pressed.

"No, we have not," I put in from my place by the fire, for this was a sore point. I found it frustrating to practice a song when I could not judge its effects. "But I should like to try."

Oldville palmed a small book from his pocket and waved it in my general direction.

"No," Lady Helaine barked. "A most ill-advised idea."

"I don't see why," Oldville said. "This volume is the work of dunderheads; I've disproved all its theories myself. It's ideal for our purposes."

"No," Lady Helaine said again. "You must not—"

If I waited for her permission, I would wait forever. No one could see me; I could do as I wished. I plucked the book from Oldville's hand, dodged Lady Helaine's outstretched arm, and let the song of destruction flow through me.

It was an incredibly complex song, closer to Wild Magic than any other I knew, with vivid, joyful syllables that I did not in the least understand. It had taken me ages to memorize, and I was determined to perform it perfectly.

To my astonishment, however, the spell took effect far sooner than most. Before the end of the first phrase, the book disintegrated in my hands.

I broke off, bewildered.

Nat let out a whoop. "She did it!"

A cat's grin spread across Lady Helaine's face.

Penebrygg and Sir Barnaby looked ready to do a jig. Even Oldville appeared satisfied.

I smiled mechanically, but my mind was stepping through the notes of the song I had just sung. Why had it worked in such a strange way?

The question preoccupied me so much that I forgot to breathe in the proper Chantress manner. When I saw the shadow of my hand appearing in midair, I caught myself and tried to call the magic back. But too late: My grip on the concealment spell had slipped past recovery. Sighing, I let the remaining strength of the song leave me, and I became visible once more.

My godmother continued to smile as the others crowded around to offer their congratulations.

"A most astounding performance." Behind the glimmering glass, Penebrygg's eyes were proud.

"Most impressive," Oldville said. "Most impressive indeed."

"Here, here," Sir Barnaby agreed, pounding his cane. "If we were to send you into the Tower tomorrow, I wager you would come up trumps."

"Tomorrow?" Lady Helaine's smile disappeared. "No. There can be no question of that."

"The sooner the better, my lady," Sir Barnaby said. "Time is of the essence."

"Another week," Lady Helaine demanded. "A week to perfect her training."

"We can afford to wait that long, I expect," Penebrygg said cautiously.

"It will give us time to do our part too," Sir Barnaby agreed. "It is no easy task to set a rebellion in motion, even after so much preparation."

Oldville looked disgruntled, but he nodded. "Very well. But only a week, no more."

Lady Helaine inclined her head. "Very well. And now you must go, and allow us to be about our business."

As she began herding them out the door, Nat turned to me again.

"Your hand," I began.

"It will heal," Nat said, his voice brusque. "Don't fret about it. You've enough to occupy you already."

What he said was true. There were songs I must rehearse and maps I must review and a thousand details I must see to before I went to the Tower.

But still I worried as Nat took his leave, shielding his hand from sight. I thought of the battle he had lost and the weary set of his shoulders. I thought of how he had never quite met my eyes. And I thought, too, of the men who had fought beside him, who had shot themselves rather than face the Shadowgrims.

CHAPTER THIRTY-TWO
A QUESTION OF POWER

After the delegation left, I turned and saw Lady Helaine looking into the fire. Her mouth was quirked in that little cat's smile again. She was like someone hugging a secret to herself, one too delectable to share.

"What aren't you telling me?" I asked.

She looked at me, and her smiled deepened, until she looked exactly as she had when I had destroyed Oldville's book with my song.

"That song." It was a shot in the dark, but I was certain I was right. "Why did it destroy the book so quickly? The pages practically flew apart in my hands."

Lady Helaine shrugged. "An ordinary book can hardly be expected to last as long as a Chantress grimoire."

"There's more to it than that, I think."

"Why should you?"

"Because the song didn't feel right."

Lady Helaine rolled her eyes. "No song ever feels right to you."

"This was different," I tried to explain. "It didn't feel the way a song of destruction should."

"How would you know? You haven't the skill or training to tell."

It was true that I didn't have the deep understanding of songs that a great Chantress would. But with every practice session, I was honing my ear as well as my skills, and there were constellations of notes that now held meaning for me.

"There was so much life in the music," I said. "Don't you think that's strange in a song of destruction? And there was something else odd about it." I went silent for a moment, trying to put my finger on what it was that had bothered me. "Something that sounded almost . . . possessive."

I half expected my godmother to roll her eyes again. Instead, her face went very still, with an expression that was half-apprehensive and half-proud.

"How very perceptive of you," she finally said.

"Perceptive?"

"Sit," she told me. "I have something to tell you."

Something I did not want to hear, I was suddenly certain. But I sat.

"What do you know about the grimoire?" Lady Helaine asked.

"Scargrave's grimoire?"

"Do not call it that," Lady Helaine interrupted. "It was never Scargrave's."

"But—"

"He stole it, but that does not make it his. It is *ours*. It is the greatest-known compendium of Chantress Magic in existence—a treasure trove of Proven Magic. It was composed by one of our own kind, a Chantress who understood the songs of living creatures, and who used that knowledge to craft song-spells of great power. The song-spell for the Shadowgrims was but one of them. There are hundreds more, all set down in the grimoire—all tested and proven and safe for the singer. But the book has been lost to us for centuries."

"But it was only a little over seven years ago that Scargrave—"

Lady Helaine shook her head impatiently. "It was not Scargrave who took it from us, not at first."

"Who, then?"

"Some stories say it was the Chantress herself who sequestered it, for reasons of her own. Others say it was a council of Chantresses who spirited it away. Whichever it was, the stories agree that the grimoire was bound shut with a rare and powerful song-spell, one meant to last for at least twenty-one generations." Lady Helaine shook her head in sorrow. "Of course, no Chantress in that Golden Age could conceive of the decline that was to come. By the time that twenty-first generation rolled around, the binding song-spells and much other lore had long since been forgotten. Even the grimoire itself was only a shadowy legend. By my calculations, I was born to the twenty-third generation, and no one took any interest in the old story except me."

I thought of the woman who had opened the grimoire for Scargrave. "And your cousin Agnes?"

Lady Helaine paused. "Yes, you could say she took an interest too. But she never said a word about it to me, so I had to piece the history together for myself. I was twenty-five before I knew about the grimoire, but from that time on, I dedicated myself to searching for it.

"I never succeeded in finding it, of course. But somehow Agnes did. And fool that she was, she opened the book to aid Scargrave—and gave our power away." Lady Helaine crossed the room and put her hand on my shoulder. "You will right that wrong, goddaughter. The song I have taught you will not destroy the grimoire. Instead, it will do something far better: It will allow you to claim it."

I stared at her in disbelief. "Claim it?"

"Yes," my godmother said, her rough voice deepening. "It is your heritage, your birthright."

I clutched at the chair arm as if I were drowning. And truly it felt as if the seas had closed over my head. "You lied." I stood up. "You lied to me—to us—from start to finish."

"Of course. Those men would have stopped me otherwise."

"But you even lied to me!"

"You might have blurted the truth out to that boy. You are too impulsive, goddaughter. And you trust too easily."

"Evidently," I said. "Since I trusted you."

"Better me than anyone else," Lady Helaine said. "Those

people you call friends—they would have you risk death, and for what? To serve them and their interests? We can do better than that."

I searched her face. If she had lied to me before, perhaps she was still lying now. Or perhaps not lying exactly, but hoping and believing in something that wasn't true. "How can you be sure that song is what you think it is? What if you've made a mistake? Oldville's book came apart in my hands, remember?"

"And wasn't I glad of it!" Lady Helaine said. "I was furious with you for offering to sing for them. I didn't know what the song would do, or whether hearing it might awaken doubts and suspicions in them. But I should have known that it would be beyond their understanding—and that it had such power that an ordinary book would be blasted to pieces by it. Have no doubts: When you sing that song, you will claim the grimoire. In that moment, its magic, past and present, will revert to you. Scargrave's hold on the Shadowgrims will end; they will become yours instead."

The Shadowgrims, mine? Their jabbering cries once again inside my head? I put out my hands, as if pushing the grimoire itself away. "No!"

"You do not want power?" Lady Helaine's gravelly voice grew agitated. "Lucy, are you mad? Power protects us. Power keeps us alive. Without it we are at the mercy of our enemies. Surely that is not what you desire? The Chantress line is almost dead. We are hunted; we are prey; if you do not succeed, our kind will die out forever. Is that what you want?"

As I stood there, speechless, she touched her bony hand to my cheek. "And you are my goddaughter, too, do not forget. I want you to have what your mother did not: a rich life, a powerful life, a life where no one dares harm you, or your daughters, or the many daughters who come after them. If you claim the grimoire, you will have all this. It will be the start of a new Golden Age for Chantresses. No one will dare stand against you."

Because I would have the Shadowgrims.

"No," I said again.

"What do you mean, *no*?"

"I mean, I don't want these powers. I won't claim the grimoire." I pulled away from her. Had she thought she could box me in so easily? Well, I would show her I was no one's pawn. Not hers, not anyone's. "There must be some other way to defeat Scargrave."

"No," Lady Helaine said harshly. "There is only one song. If you wish to defeat Scargrave, you must sing it—and claim the grimoire and its powers."

"But no magic is unbreakable, you said." I recalled the lessons she had taught me. "An end is woven into everything."

"But sometimes it is beyond our powers to find it," my godmother said. "And this is such a case. You must face facts, goddaughter: There is only one way forward, and that is to claim the grimoire."

"No," I said stubbornly.

Lady Helaine's eyes darkened. "You are so like your mother."

"My mother?"

"Yes. She balked at this too."

I stared at her relentless face. "You wanted my *mother* to claim the grimoire?"

"No," said Lady Helaine, lifting her chin. "It was I who knew the song; I who had the skill; I who wanted to take the book from Scargrave. But your mother stopped me—and then Scargrave came with his ravens, and we were lost."

Lady Helaine came toward me, her bone beads clicking as she walked. "I will not let that happen again. I will not be overruled. Do you understand me? You will sing that song, and you will claim the grimoire, and you will make the name Chantress great again."

"No," I whispered. *I will be no one's pawn.* I backed away from her, my spine bumping against the wood panel of the door.

Still she came toward me. "You will claim the grimoire and be glad."

"No." I pressed the latch behind me.

Her hands reached for me, and I bolted.

CHAPTER THIRTY-THREE
PURSUIT

I ran without heed, my only thought to put distance between my godmother and me. Behind me, I heard footsteps. Was she following me? I glanced back and saw the distant swirl of her gown. To shake her off, I went upward, ducking through dusty archways and climbing cobwebbed stairs. Higher and higher I rose in the house, until at last I reached the small storerooms in the attic.

Stopping to catch my breath, I heard a commotion of men and horses in the courtyard below. As I went to see what was happening, my shoulder was seized from behind.

"What in the devil's name are you doing here?" Nat hissed. He did not wait for an answer but instead steered me toward the door. "Get back to the cellars as fast as you can."

I pulled away and confronted him. "Why should I?"

"Because Scargrave is here."

I froze. "Here? In this house?"

"A surprise visit," Nat said grimly.

"Does he suspect something?"

"No one knows. He's made visits without warning before, merely out of friendship. But this time he's brought many more men than usual. They're in the courtyard now, and Sir Barnaby is attempting to discover what it is they want. No—don't look out the window at them! They might see you. Get yourself back downstairs, and stay out of danger."

"What about you?"

"Oldville has already left, and Penebrygg and I will leave as soon as we safely can. It is you that we fear for."

"I'll go, then," I said, and then I stopped short.

"What is it?" Nat asked.

"Lady Helaine!" Angry as I was with her, I didn't want her to fall into Scargrave's hands.

"What about her?"

"I ran off, and she followed me. And she may still be wandering somewhere—"

"You ran off? Why? No, never mind. There's no time. Tell me: Where did you last see her?"

"By the old river staircase." I faltered as the implications hit me. "The one with the secret passage that connects to the banqueting house and the gardens. And I think she may have gone through the door . . ."

Nat swore under his breath.

"I'll go and bring her back," I said.

"That's the last thing we need," Nat said. "Go back downstairs, and leave your godmother to me. It would be a disaster if Scargrave found either one of you."

"But if I sang the song of concealment—"

"With servants running everywhere and Scargrave at the door? No," said Nat. "That will only make matters more complicated. I will go search for your godmother. And if you're quick, you can get downstairs without magic. That's the quickest way to safety for all of us. But you'll have to stop talking and *go*."

It pained me to admit it, but he had sense on his side.

"All right, then," I said. "I'm leaving. But my godmother—"

"I'll bring her to you."

†   †   †

By the time I had descended the first staircase, it was clear that I'd already run out of time. The path that led to the secret staircases I needed was bustling with servants. As I watched from behind a tapestried alcove, housemaids and footmen rushed by, scurrying to and fro, making ready for the Lord Protector's sudden visit. The tapestries fluttered in their wake, making me feel more exposed than ever.

I wish I were invisible.

Well, why not? I had invisibility in my power—or something very close to it. Nat had advised me against using it, of course. But then he was always wary of magic, and he had not appreciated quite how dangerous the house would be. If singing myself out of sight was a great risk, remaining in the open was an even greater one.

I closed my eyes, calling to mind what I knew about this house from my explorations with Nat. The secret passage that opened into Lady Gadding's sitting room—that would be the best place to work the song-spell. It was close by, and it had thick walls that would help block any faint strains of singing.

Waiting for my moment, I darted into the next room, where the secret passage began. Once inside, I felt my way until I judged myself to be roughly in the middle of it. As quietly as I could—it was hardly more than a hum—I started to sing.

The spell twined in soft loops around me, separating me from the rest of the world. I could feel myself dissolving into air.

When the song ended, I slipped out again, smiling with relief. Though my lungs were already burning from the breathing required to maintain the song's power, the song of concealment had never worked better. As I passed by the mirrors hanging on each side of the fireplace, I could see only the faintest shimmering in the air where my heart was. And though I listened out, I heard no sounds of alarm.

I was almost safe home.

Yet my disguise was not foolproof. If people bumped into me, they would know I was there. And ahead lay the busiest place in the house, the stairs that led to the kitchens, which buzzed like a hive. I would have to search out another, quieter way down—but to do that, I would first have to cross the minstrels' gallery that overlooked the Great Hall. It was not ideal, for Sir Barnaby received guests in the hall, but I could see no other way forward.

As I neared the gallery, deep voices resounded from below.

Had Sir Barnaby's guests come into the Great Hall already? Should I wait till they moved on to other rooms?

No. The gallery itself was empty now; I must seize my chance.

But as I edged onto it, a single voice separated from the rest and stopped me in my tracks. Shocking as a draught of powerful medicine, it was shatteringly familiar.

With a whirling head, I glanced into the hall below and saw Scargrave standing on the black-and-white tiles. In his black cloak and riding boots, he looked like a king on a chessboard—a king who was winning the game.

"You have no notion why I have come to you?" he said.

"None at all, my dear Scargrave." Sir Barnaby spoke with admirable coolness, his hand steady on his cane.

Scargrave's spurs grated on the floor. "Not one word of my news has reached you?"

I clutched at the railing, certain of one thing only: I must get safe away.

Before I could move, however, one of the men beneath my balcony—one of Scargrave's escort—mumbled something about ravens' eggs.

"Hush, Giles!" his companion said.

Was it the same Giles I had overheard in Scargrave's library? The would-be Chantress-hunter? I leaned over the railing, hoping to hear more—and my foot slipped on something small and hard and round. Marbles? Nuts? Whatever they were, they made a terrible rattle as they rolled and dropped to the floor below.

"What's that?" Scargrave shot around, scanning the room. To

my horror, his gaze ran along the gallery—and stopped at me. "Up there! Look! Something is shimmering."

I ducked down below the railing and made for the opposite gallery door. Below me, the Great Hall was in utter confusion.

"A ghost," one of Scargrave's men moaned.

"A devil," said another.

"A Chantress!" Scargrave bellowed. "After her!"

As I ran through the doorway, an arrow thunked into the wood beside me.

I pelted down the hall, making for the hanging staircase, only to be confronted by a detachment of Scargrave's men rushing up toward me.

"The first man to capture her wins ten thousand guineas!" their captain shouted behind them. "Be bold! And take her alive, if you can, so that we can give her to the ravens."

"I see something," a man cried. "There, at the top of the stairs!"

Another arrow whistled in the air.

I ran so fast that my ruby slapped hard against my chest. Because I knew the house better than they did, I stayed one step ahead, but my overtaxed lungs were no longer breathing properly, and the concealment spell was ebbing. My left hand had become plainly visible, and my shadow could be seen on the floor. I had no chance of reaching the cellars now. Instead, I raced for the nearest shelter on offer: the secret passageway by the sitting room.

I had only reached the screen in front of it when my pursuers entered the room.

"Listen," one of them called out. "Is that singing?"

"She's behind us," another advised. "Go back."

"No, she's here. I'm sure she's here."

Although I was hidden by the screen, they were so close to me that I dared not push on the panel of the passageway. Indeed, I dared not move in any way.

And then, as I waited there, rabbit-still, I heard a far-off cry.

"What's that?" said one of the men.

A door opened, and another man reported, "The hunt's been called off. They've found her!"

Oh no, they haven't, I thought.

But the man was very sure of himself. "They need us below. Quick!"

They left the room at a fast pace.

Afraid that it was a trap, and that they might be lying in wait for me, I stayed silent behind the screen. But as I waited, I felt the house become still around me. Finally, I swung my stiff, ghostly limbs into action and peered out. No one was there.

"Hurrah!" The cry came through a cracked-open window.

Masking myself in the draperies to keep out of view, I peeped at the scene below. The courtyard was full of soldiers, with more arriving by the second. At Scargrave's orders, they were herding three prisoners onto a cart.

Gagged and bound as these captives were, I did not recognize them instantly. But when I did, my stomach twisted. My godmother, Penebrygg, and Nat—Scargrave had them all.

CHAPTER THIRTY-FOUR
THE TOWER

Under my shocked gaze, the pandemonium of soldiers resolved into a marching formation. A ring of men surrounded the cart.

"To the Tower!" they bellowed. "To the Shadowgrims!"

As the soldiers stepped smartly, the cart jerked forward, knocking Lady Helaine, Penebrygg, and Nat to its floor.

I reached for my ruby and bit back a cry. How could I save them?

Follow them to the Tower, a resolute voice inside me said. *And then use your magic to rescue them.*

But what if that meant claiming the grimoire?

Don't think about that now.

Just go.

The cart rolled out the gate, guarded by soldiers.

Yes, I would go.

First, however, I must sing. The invisibility song-spell had ebbed so much that I could see not only my hands and feet but the outline of my skirts and bodice. Altering my appearance would cost me time, but there was no other choice.

Retreating to the secret passage, I sang myself out of sight again. This time I drew on every bit of intensity and self-control I could muster, determined to weave the strongest possible magic. But as the last note left me, and I went toward the door again, it clicked open. Someone had come for me. One of Scargrave's soldiers? One of his spies?

I turned to run for the opposite door. Behind me, a cane tapped.

"Miss Marlowe!" The softest of whispers, but I knew the voice. No soldier, this, but a friend.

I spun around. "Sir Barnaby?"

"The very same," he said in the darkness. "I was in Lady Gadding's room and heard you singing—faintly, my dear, only faintly—and I guessed where you must be."

"How did Scargrave find them?" I murmured.

"I gather they were in the banqueting house. The servants say your godmother ran out the door into the garden, which I find hardly credible—"

I did not. I could only imagine how much my flight had angered and upset her. If Nat and Penebrygg had approached her the wrong way, she might have done almost anything.

"—but I wasn't there to see it myself, or I'd have been taken prisoner too," Sir Barnaby continued. "Scargrave has posted his soldiers about the house, but so far I have managed to elude them. And now that I have found you, I shall keep you safe, never fear. Come with me—"

"I'm going to the Tower," I said.

"The Tower?" I could hear his dismay. "My dear Miss Marlowe, you cannot possibly. Not now, not when Scargrave is on the alert as never before. You could not hope to reach the grimoire safely."

"But I have to save our friends."

"No, Miss Marlowe. You do not." He was emphatic. "Believe me when I say this: The only thing you must do is save yourself."

I was silent. Was he really telling me to abandon these people who meant so much to me?

"They would agree with me," he said. "All three of them. They have always known Scargrave would kill them if he could. What would destroy them—destroy all of us—would be if you, too, were killed. It would be the end of all our hopes, of everything we've worked for."

"I can't simply walk away—"

"That is *precisely* what you must do. Only I am afraid it won't be so easy as that. I have sent messengers to our IC members. Most will escape the city immediately, taking your guardian with them, I should add—"

Thank goodness for that. It would be easier to act, knowing that Norrie was being looked after.

"—but a few of us will remain here to defend you. There are a few London boltholes, known only to myself, where we have a decent chance of hiding you. What would be better still would be if we could get you out of the city entirely. Now that you have this trick of turning invisible, I think it may be possible. For now, however, I am going to conduct you through one of our tunnels to . . ."

I missed the rest of what he was saying. I was moving out of earshot, as swiftly and silently as I could.

"Miss Marlowe?" A furious whisper. "Are you there?"

I had reached the door. The peephole showed no one outside.

"Miss Marlowe!" Sir Barnaby was coming after me, but his stick and the darkness slowed him down.

Before he could reach me, I slipped out of the secret passage, my mind concentrated on the task ahead: invading the Tower.

†   †   †

By the time I reached the courtyard, Scargrave and his prisoners were gone.

Despite my best efforts, I could not quite catch up with them. The soldiers marched down the main streets, but I had to pick my way carefully, taking the quieter alleys where I was less likely to bump into anyone.

As I reached the Tower drawbridge, I saw the cart roll under the gatehouse arch, soldiers stationed on every side. I sprinted across the drawbridge but not fast enough. The Tower gates clanged shut before me.

Afraid my slight shimmer would give me away, I pressed against the gatehouse wall. What was I to do now?

Luck was with me. Already another company of men, this time mounted on horseback, was approaching the Tower. I slipped in behind them as they passed through the gate, hoping that an almost-invisible Chantress wouldn't spook the horses. A few moments later, the gate slammed shut behind me, almost catching my skirts.

But I was in.

I followed the company through yet another guarded gate, but they outstripped me, and so I took shelter against a wall and surveyed the Tower Green. The Tower's special guardians, the Warders, were everywhere, as were Scargrave's soldiers, many of them the Ravens' Own.

Hastily I called to mind the Tower maps that Nat had made for me. Ahead of me was the centerpiece of the entire place, the massive White Tower for which the palace itself was named. And up its staircase, three prisoners were being carried: Nat, Penebrygg, and my godmother.

As the door shut behind them, I stared up at the Tower. Stark and uncompromising, it had been built over five hundred years ago, and reinforced by a score of kings and queens since. It had never succumbed to attack, Nat had told me. And no wonder, for its implacable stone walls soared nearly one hundred feet high—a fact that had been overwhelming enough when I first heard it from Nat, but that seemed immeasurably more so as I stood at their foot, wondering how to get in.

For it was into the White Tower I must go. Deep in its dungeons lay the Feeding Room, where my friends would be sent to await the Shadowgrims. And not far away lay Scargrave's Chamber, where the grimoire itself was bound to the very foundation on which the Tower was built.

Not that I wanted to claim the grimoire. Anything but that.

But I would have to enter the White Tower if I were to learn what other possibilities of rescue existed.

A bell chimed, marking the time. Sunset was barely three hours away. Above me, the Tower flags—black ravens against red—snapped in the wind, as if the Shadowgrims themselves were beating their wings in triumph.

I could not let that happen.

I pushed away from the wall and headed toward the White Tower as fast as I dared.

† † †

To my surprise, getting into the Tower proved easy enough. I merely had to follow on the heels of a company of men with the King himself at their center. The guards were so busy bowing and saluting his jeweled magnificence that they did not notice the slight shimmer well behind him.

Once I was inside the Tower, however, my troubles began in earnest. Warders were everywhere, rushing about three and four abreast, their halberds and swords at the ready, and I had to flatten myself to breaking point to slip by them.

Three false starts and five near-collisions later, I finally reached the staircase I was headed for, the only one in the Tower that led down to the dungeons. A Warder stood by it but not—I saw thankfully—in front of it.

As I gauged how best to sidestep him, a weedy page scampered down the stairs and out past me.

"Make way, make wa-a-y!"

Behind him, a company of men poured out of the staircase. Ten men, a dozen? I did not wait to count them but retreated into a gap in the corner, underneath a rack of helmets.

"Make way for the King and the Lord Protector!"

Scargrave was here in the White Tower?

My heart clattered as he entered the room, his voice heavy with irritation and anxiety. "Your Majesty, you should not be here. Please leave at once."

And Henry, apprehensive but determined: "A King must be allowed to attend his own Councils, my lord."

"Not so." Scargrave did not hesitate to contradict him. "Not if his very life is in danger. And in danger you most certainly are, my Sovereign. Until it has been reported to me that the prisoners are locked away in the Feeding Room, you will best serve your kingdom by remaining safe in your own rooms, with your guards . . ."

His attention was on Henry; everyone else's attention was on him. I crept past them and took to the stairs.

I have to save them.

Moving swiftly and softly, I raced down the winding steps, breathing hard. When the steps opened out onto a dim passageway, I stopped short. I had gotten away. But where was I now?

Heavy iron gates rose before me, blocking the way forward to the Feeding Room and Scargrave's Chamber. I could sing them open but only at the cost of revealing that I was there. Better to wait for someone else to pass through them, especially since I could hear footsteps coming.

I stepped back against the wall, then froze. I could see the haziest suggestion of fingertips on my left hand.

Perhaps I should retreat. But no, more people were coming down the winding staircase; I could not go back now.

I shoved my hand into my right sleeve and concentrated on sustaining the magic I had left. A few not-quite-translucent fingertips were not a disaster, not if I could keep the rest of the magic together until I could reach my friends and get them out. *Please come quickly,* I begged the footsteps.

And they did. A dozen Warders running down the hall, keys at the ready. When they unlocked the gate, I ducked through before anyone else did. I took off down the hall . . .

. . . and careened straight into a room that heaved with Warders. Reeling back, I watched them brandish their pikes and halberds in the half light of torches. At the center of the writhing, shouting melee, a high, scratchy scream was cut short.

My throat went cold. The scream had sounded uncannily like Lady Helaine.

Backing into the shadows, I searched for her figure, but I could not see it in the tumult. What I saw instead was a colossal black door yawning wide on the far side of the room, with a raven carved into the stone above it. Beyond it lay another set of doors, squat and square, that opened like a grave into darkness. I recognized it from Nat's sketches: It was the entrance to the Feeding Room.

For a too-long moment, I stood and stared at it, rooted to the spot, forgetting to breathe. And then, summoning all my power, I came back to myself. But I could feel that my magic was fading.

Shouts and yells broke out. A Warder's pike shot out at me.

"A head! D'you see it? A head and hands, by God!"

"It's another Chantress!"

"Capture her!"

They were after me.

Seeing no other chance of escape, I dove into the melee of Warders, going down on my hands and knees. I emerged by the door and found Nat in front of me, still bound and gagged and limp on the stone floor. Six men seized him and shoved him through the opening.

Then they saw me.

"What the—?"

"Your life if she escapes!" came the cry from behind.

Brutal hands snagged and squeezed me, and I felt my magic break. I was completely visible now. There was no time to sing another song; the gag went on before I could even draw breath. Rope sliced into my arms, binding them together, and the Warders slit my sleeve to see the Chantress mark.

A cheer went up as they held a torch to it. "That'll mean gold for us, my lads!"

After trussing my legs, they tossed me into the dark hole like so much kindling. I hit the floor, and everything went black.

CHAPTER THIRTY-FIVE
TRAPPED

I woke to darkness and the sound of something rustling in the rancid straw. My godmother, Penebrygg, Nat? Or maybe something else . . .

Rats?

My stomach tightened. I would not let them find me on the floor, utterly at their mercy. Wrenching my tied-up arms and legs as best I could, I rolled until I was half sitting, half leaning against a wall. But the ropes around me were still tight as wire.

Well, if the ropes wouldn't yield, what about the gag? I rubbed it against the rough rock wall, trying to work it loose. But I only scraped my cheek raw.

The rustling grew louder. Something was coming toward me, so close I could hear its breathing soft in the air next to me. I jerked my bound legs, hoping to frighten it away.

"It's me," Nat whispered.

His voice was astonishment enough, but then his hand brushed against my cloak, searching for the gag. I had a moment to think, *He's free,* and then I flinched as the gag rope bit deeper into my cheek.

"Easy now," he said, and the gag slipped away. His fingers went to the knots around my wrists, though he avoided touching my skin. Was that because he knew it was chafed and sore—or because he was still determined not to come too close, even in these desperate circumstances?

"How did you get free?" I whispered.

"Tricks of the trade," he said softly. "Bracing my muscles, knowing the knots they use. And a bit of luck. They weren't quite as careful with me as they should have been. Maybe the bandage threw them off."

"Your hand," I said, remembering. "They can't have done it any good."

"It still works. That's all that matters. And if it made them underestimate me, then I should count myself lucky it happened." He gave my wrists a last tug. "There. That should do it."

As the rope slid off, he went to the bands around my legs.

I stretched my numb arms and shook out my lifeless fingers. "How are the others?"

"I've already undone Penebrygg's knots," Nat said. "But he's still out cold. There's a lump big as an egg on his head, and I don't like the way he's breathing."

The rope fell away from my legs, and I flexed my prickling feet. "And my godmother?"

Nat said nothing.

"You haven't freed her yet?" I asked.

When he still didn't answer, I frowned. There was no love lost between them, I knew, but—

"She's gone," Nat said.

"Gone?" It took a moment for his meaning to hit me. "You mean . . . dead?"

"I'm sorry," he said softly.

"No." My voice cracked.

"Don't let them hear you," he warned in a voice barely louder than breathing.

Heartsick, I murmured, "What happened?"

"She panicked when we came up to the Feeding Room and buckled against the Warders. In the struggle, her gag got loose, and she shrieked."

I remembered the sound of that scream. I buried my head in my arms.

"They thought she was singing," said Nat. "They panicked and bashed her over the head. You could hear the bone crack. I think she was gone even before they threw her in here."

"She's here?"

"Lucy, don't—"

But I was scrabbling around in the dark already. I found the edge of her gown, and then her sleeve. "Lady Helaine?"

No response. But it was only when I touched her cold, lifeless hand that I accepted Nat was right: She was gone. All the fire in her—all her rage and ambition and passion—had winked out.

It seemed an age before Nat spoke. "Lucy? We need a plan."

"A plan?"

"To get you to the grimoire."

Overwhelmed by loss, I almost spilled out the truth then and there: that I could only claim the grimoire, not destroy it. But something kept the words back. Perhaps it was the cold weight of Lady Helaine's hand, or perhaps just the fear of Nat's reaction. For Nat would be angry; of that I was certain. He would think I'd deceived him. And he would be even angrier if he knew that I had reached the point where I was willing to make the grimoire mine.

It was not desire that prompted me but desperation. Every other plan had failed. Scargrave was about to kill us all—and who knew how many others besides. Lady Helaine had been right: There was only one way forward, and I had to take it.

Releasing her hand, I turned to Nat. "I'll conceal myself again. I can sing softly, and these walls are thick—"

"No," he said. "They'll hear you. There are airholes—"

"If they hear me, so much the better; we won't have to open the doors ourselves. When they come to see what's wrong, I'll slip out and go to the grimoire."

"Past two prison doors and two more iron gates, with the whole place packed with Warders?" Nat's voice was rich with skepticism. "You'd never make it. They're on the lookout for an invisible Chantress now. They'd take you down the moment they saw a single glimmer."

"I have to try," I insisted.

"It's not worth the risk. Not when there's another way."

"There's another way?"

"Yes," Nat said. "But you're not going to like it."

CHAPTER THIRTY-SIX

MADNESS

He was right. I didn't like it. Not one bit.

"Go through the Raven Pit? Are you mad?"

"It's the only other way out," Nat said. "Remember the maps?"

In the darkness, I recalled the line of three rooms he'd sketched out for me: the Feeding Room, the Pit, and Scargrave's Chamber, where the grimoire was anchored in the wall.

"There's a door in here that opens into the Pit," Nat said, "and on the other side of the Pit, there's another door that leads to Scargrave's Chamber. And the beauty of going this way is that there are no guards."

"Because they have the Shadowgrims instead," I reminded him. "And that's much, much worse."

"They won't wake until sunset, and that must be a good hour away. Maybe two."

I considered this. "What about the eggs?"

"They haven't hatched yet," Nat said. "I quizzed Sir Barnaby, and he said he'd stake his life on it."

"But he's only going by rumors."

"He has better sources than that," Nat said. "He's our spymaster."

"But what if you're wrong about the time, and it's later than you think? What if we get caught in the Pit at sunset?"

"If it's that late, then our goose is cooked—whether we're in the Pit or not. But we have time. I'm sure of it. I heard the clocks chiming as they brought us in."

I shook my head. "It's a mad plan."

"It's our best plan."

"That too," I conceded with a sigh. "All right, then. Where is this door?"

† † †

It turned out Nat knew exactly where the door was. Not only because his memory for maps was superb but because he'd come across it while he was untying Penebrygg.

"Two paces forward and one to the left," he directed me.

He went first. A moment later, I heard a quiet scratching. "It's not the easiest lock, but I think I can pick it."

"With what?"

"Pins and things. I keep them in a jacket seam, and they missed them in the search. Probably because they were in such a hurry to tie me up. Check on Penebrygg, will you?"

I had just found my way to him when I heard the lock click.

"There it goes," Nat whispered. "How is he?"

"Still not moving," I reported. "Maybe you should stay with him." Though I did not relish the idea of going on alone, I felt honor-bound to make the suggestion.

"And let you face the dangers alone?" Nat sounded almost angry at the notion. "Now, that really *would* be mad."

"But—"

"No." The anger left his voice, leaving only warmth. "We go together. And that's that. Penebrygg would say the same if he could."

We go together. His words made me feel less alone in that black midnight of a cell. For the first time in hours, I smiled.

And when you claim the grimoire? What will he say then?

I pushed the thought away, but my smile went with it.

†   †   †

After we made Penebrygg as comfortable as we could, Nat tugged at the door. I almost lost my nerve as it swung wide. Would the ravens crowd in?

The only thing that rushed toward us, however, was an ashy stench that made me gag.

"Moonbriar fruit," Nat told me. "Lots of it, to judge by the smell. They must still be feeding it to the ravens. Maybe they're having more trouble getting viable eggs than we thought."

Cheered by this possibility, we felt our way forward into a narrow, stone-lined passage. Ten feet or so later, with the stench growing ever stronger, this ended at another door.

"Locked." Nat fiddled at the keyhole. "I can't get it to open."

"What's wrong?" I knelt by the door. At the keyhole, I was astonished to find the faint but smoldering smell of magic, almost veiled by the foul odors coming from the pit. I tried to call to mind what my godmother had taught me about such smells.

"There's magic at work here," I said. "A charm to protect the ravens, I think."

"Scargrave's doing," Nat said.

"But you said he can't do magic."

"Not himself, no. But before he executes magic workers, he tries to pull their secrets out of them. And sometimes he persuades them to work a charm or two before they die."

I didn't want to think about the nature of those deaths. Instead, I focused on the lock. "Lady Helaine taught me a song that should break it. Will anyone hear me?"

"We'll have to risk it," Nat said.

We were a long way from the Warders by now, but to be on the safe side, Nat closed the door behind us. In the choking air, I struggled to sing the right unlocking spell.

When the lock clanked, I wrenched at the handle. It turned with a squawk, but the door didn't budge. "Maybe it's stuck."

As I tried the handle again, Nat heaved himself at the door.

It gave way suddenly and completely, sending us sprawling over the threshold. Then it swung shut again with an ominous click.

Flat on the stone floor, I was nearly overcome by the smell of the place: not merely ashes now but festering fumes like clotted smoke. Then I heard a sound in the darkness that made my heart go still: the whirr of ravens' wings.

"Lucy? Are you all right?"

Something was wrong; I could feel it in the air, which was growing warmer by the moment.

"Light," I said shakily. "I need to see." But when I tried to kindle a flame, my voice trembled too much to hold the tune.

"Why isn't it working?" Nat asked. "What's wrong?"

"I think the Shadowgrims might be waking—"

"They can't be. Believe me, we'd know it if they were."

Mewling clicks in the darkness nipped my mind like flames . . . and suddenly I knew the truth.

"The new ravens," I breathed. "They've hatched—and they're trying to feed on me. I can feel them. Their voices—can't you hear them?"

Nat listened for a moment. "No."

"Then maybe I really am going mad—"

"No," he said swiftly. "Don't say that."

The tiny voices strengthened. I could hear the words now. *We are small. We must grow. We must feed by night and day . . .*

"Lucy?"

I shuddered in the rising heat. "Oldville was right," I gasped. "The rules are different for hatchlings. And . . . and I think there are more of them than we ever imagined."

Searing and greedy as fire, their ravenous voices assaulted me: *We are hungry—oh, so hungry. And the magic in you feeds us . . .*

"Lucy, whatever they're saying, remember: They can't reach

you." Nat's voice was sure and calm. "Neither the grown ones nor the hatchlings. Sir Barnaby says there's a grille that walls them in, and that must be right. Otherwise, the birds would have flown out when we opened the door."

I understood that he was trying to drive the hot, painful whispers away. But they were too ferocious to be hemmed in by reason.

"So you're safe, you see," Nat continued steadily. "They can't get to you. And we're going to walk right past them to the next room, to the grimoire. And then you'll be able to put an end to them forever."

An end to the Shadowgrims: For a brief moment, I felt brave again, coolly confident. But then I remembered that my song was for claiming, not destroying. With the next breath, the heat and fear were back, worse than ever. I could not move. I could not breathe.

"Lucy! Lucy, listen to me!"

I could not hear the rest. Only the feverish whispers reached my ears, powerful as an incantation. They robbed me of movement and filled me with dread.

Our parents fed on your mother. We will feed on you.

Something tugged my hand, pulled against my neck. I wanted to scream, but I was too deep in the ravens' hold to make a sound.

Yes, we will feed on you . . .

"Lucy. It's me."

I could hardly hear the voice, it was so distant. But then Nat took my hand. A shock went through me as our fingers touched. My heart beat like a hammer, and I struggled again for breath.

"I've found the door, but the lock's like the other one," he said. "It won't give way. You're going to have to sing it open."

I did not understand one word in ten. The fear was tearing me away again.

You are ours.

With steady fingers, he pressed a seedy, stringy pulp into my palm. Gripping my other hand, he used it to snag my necklace and lift it above my head.

No! I buckled to my knees as the world became a boiling sea of sound. The voracious song of the hatchlings swirled around me, even louder and greedier than before.

But then I heard something else: the moonbriar song rising from the pulp in my hand and from the floor around me. Cool and sweet and clear, the song wove itself like a shield around me, as Nat clasped my hand in his. When I gave voice to the music, the ravens lost their hold on me. Instead, I fell into Nat's mind, tumbling into it without effort, just as I had done on that long-ago day in Penebrygg's attic.

But this time was different. This time Nat was inviting me in.

Through his eyes, I saw the sea: great blue-green waves rolling onto a golden shore, their low and steady rumble like the breathing of the earth itself.

I saw Norrie, ever loyal, standing before me, and behind her the friends I'd come to trust in London: Penebrygg and Nat himself.

And then, even more miraculous, I saw myself as Nat saw me: arguing with him by candlelight; facing the Invisible College; mastering song after song. Behind every image, I felt an astonishing blend of emotions: desperation, frustration, admiration, respect, tenderness, desire. And weaving through them all, something more—a faith in me that went beyond anything I'd ever dreamed.

Nothing could have startled me more, or comforted me so deeply. Courage and strength streamed into me.

Still clasping Nat's hand, I heard the magic of the Chamber door call out to me. In triumph I sang it open.

A cool blue light poured in, illuminating the part of the Pit nearest us. Nat had been right: There was a grille between us and the ravens. But I had been right too: Behind the iron rods were hundreds of Shadowgrim hatchlings, their savage mouths red as blood.

We slammed the door shut behind us, and the hatchlings vanished from sight.

CHAPTER THIRTY-SEVEN
THE TRUTH

As we pressed our backs to the door, catching our breath, I offered up a silent prayer of thankfulness. The heavy door, encased in iron, was so thick that I could not hear the Shadowgrim hatchlings through it.

But my thankfulness splintered into desolation as I slung the ruby's chain back over my head. My mind cleared, and the truth of what I'd done came home to me. I had sung the moonbriar song. I had read Nat's mind. I had worked Wild Magic.

How could I have been so careless?

Suddenly weary beyond bearing, I forced myself to look down at the ruby. The faint light revealed what I had sensed from the moment I'd put it back on. A crack now crossed the stone's glinting surface.

Not a fatal flaw. Not this time. But there was a fragility to the whole stone, a trembling at its core, that frightened me.

"I shouldn't have read your mind," I said to Nat.

"No need to apologize," he said, misunderstanding me. "Not when I'm the one who pulled you in. It was the only way I could think of to save you."

To my surprise, he blushed—a reminder to me that whatever the mind-reading had cost me, Nat had paid a price too. The most private of persons, he had let me see straight into his soul. All he felt for me had been laid bare.

But that, at least, I could put right. I could tell him what he meant to me. . . .

"Nat," I began. My weariness was abating; my strength returning.

Something to my left clicked and moved.

Nat pointed in alarm. "The clock!"

On the wall, a golden disk shimmered in the hazy blue light. Ringed with stars and planets and signs of the zodiac, its stark black hands marked the time.

Nat knew what it meant. "Seven minutes till sunset!"

"So close?" I gasped.

"Yes. We'll have to move fast. Where is the grimoire?"

There was no more time to reflect on the immensity of what had passed between us, or on the price we both had paid for it. Instead, I scanned the long room. Though it had no windows, it did have another door, much larger than the one we had come through. It was evidently the main entrance to the room, and it was fitted with many locks. I had no doubt whatsoever that there were guards standing outside it.

But what about the grimoire?

As Nat ran to bar the door from the inside, I turned toward the other half of the room. With a strange mixture of excitement and revulsion, I recognized it as the place I'd seen through Scargrave's eyes. There was the section of glowing blue wall. There was the ledge that tilted out almost like a table. And there, at its center, was the source of the light: a mottled ivory book, bound fast to the stone.

"There it is," Nat said softly. "The grimoire."

A tremor shook my body. I remembered the sick feeling of being in Scargrave's mind, touching that book with Scargrave's hands, of . . .

No, this would not do. I must not go there again. I must concentrate on the present. I was seeing the grimoire with my own eyes now. And this time it was not Scargrave's will but my own that counted.

I strode toward the grimoire.

"Six minutes," Nat warned.

I must sing. But as I lifted my hand to the grimoire, I stopped short. Once I claimed it, who would I be?

Nat must have noticed my hesitation. He came up to me. "You haven't forgotten the song, have you?"

I shook my head but couldn't speak.

"Then what's wrong?" he asked. "Is it what comes after? You won't be alone then, you know. We'll fight them together. We'll fight them with everything we've got."

How had I ever thought those eyes hard to read? His loyalty, his passion, his faith in me—all were in plain sight as he stood beside me. He was hiding nothing now.

I knew then that I owed him the truth.

"It's the wrong song," I said, looking straight at him. "It won't destroy the grimoire. It will only let me claim it."

"What?" His eyes changed, and I saw his shock and his anger. "You meant to betray us. All this time—"

"No! I didn't know, not till today. My godmother only told me after you left. That's why we argued."

"So she knew all this time? She plotted against us?"

Remembering her death, I tried to do justice to her. "She wanted me to be safe."

"And what else did she want you to do?"

"It doesn't matter what she wanted. What matters now is what I want. And that's to defeat Scargrave. This song is all I have. If I don't use it, Scargrave wins."

"But there must be something else you can do. Your Wild Magic—"

"No!" I forced myself to explain calmly what had happened to my ruby when I'd read his mind. "I can't afford to do any more Wild Magic, especially not with the grimoire. It was risky enough with the moonbriar, but with something as powerful and strange as the grimoire, it's a hundred times more dangerous. It could shatter my stone—or make me sing music that sets every spell in the book loose, or that gives new powers to Scargrave. We can't take that chance, not with so much at stake."

The clock whirred again. Four minutes.

Nat's eyes had a shuttered look, and I could no longer read them. "So you'll claim the book. And then what?"

"Trust me," I told him. "I'll do my best to put an end to the Shadowgrims. I'll do what is right."

Nat shook his head. "You all say that."

I looked up at the clock. "Nat, there isn't time—"

"Open! Open in the name of the Protector and the King!" A tremendous shout went up on the other side of the great door. "Open, or we use the battering ram!"

The door quaked in its frame as they pounded against it. With a gasp, I turned back toward the grimoire.

"Another few blows, and we'll have her!" It was Scargrave himself, urging his men on. "Your Majesty, you must go back! Only the Ravens' Own should enter."

At the sound of his voice, my doubts vanished. I had to stop him.

Nat took half a step toward me—to protect me? to stop me?— but I was already singing.

The song poured through me and out of me, utterly foreign and yet somehow deep in my blood. And as I gave myself over to it, it began to reveal its meaning to me for the first time:

Before and after,

Again and now . . .

The great door cracked in two. With a howl, Scargrave's men burst through, with the Lord Protector himself among them. But before they reached me, I uttered the last notes of my song:

. . . I claim this book and its powers.

CHAPTER THIRTY-EIGHT
AT THE HEART OF FEAR

The book separated from its chains, its blue-white light flaring to a golden blaze. I felt only the most gentle warmth as it fell into my hands, but the air around me bent and curved, as if I were in the center of a great flame.

In that same instant, I saw the faces around me redden and freeze, as if a blast of raven heat had transfixed them. Every last person in the room stopped still: the King, hand on his sword; the Ravens' Own, rushing toward me; Scargrave, caught in mid-stride by the Raven Pit door. Even Nat stared at me and did not move.

I glanced at Scargrave again. Behind him, the Raven Pit door was no longer shut. Had Scargrave had time to open it? Or was it my own song, claiming the grimoire and the Shadowgrims, that was responsible? Either way, the door swung free. Behind it, the hatchlings' mewlings were now joined by a terrible croaking. The ravens were wakening. And then, with an ugly screech, the croaking twisted into a guttural whispering, vicious and foul: the language of the Shadowgrims.

As the sound stole over the room, a new terror came with it. I could see it in the sweating and petrified people before me. To my astonishment, however, I did not share their fear. I did not feel the ravens' fire.

Of course you do not. The Shadowgrims belong to you now; so do the Ravens' Own. They are yours to command; they cannot harm you. And the others are so transfixed with fear they cannot move or speak.

I arched back in shock. The strange, sibilant words came from the grimoire itself. "You can speak?"

Only to you, the grimoire said. *I have waited such a long time for you, Chantress. But now we belong to each other.*

As the singsong voice slithered into my head, I shuddered. This was not what I had expected. But there was one advantage to having the grimoire speak: I could ask it questions.

"Tell me," I said. "How do I destroy the Shadowgrims?"

You cannot.

"But I must!"

It is beyond my power. That clumsy Agnes and her incompetent songs damaged those pages past repair. The song to destroy the Shadowgrims is lost forever. Guardian, she called herself! She deserved what she got.

Frantically I flipped the grimoire's pages. If I could piece together whatever scraps remained . . .

But the more pages I examined, the more bewildered I became. "I . . . I can't read this. I don't understand the notation—"

My creator's own invention, the grimoire explained smugly. *There is none like it in the world. But if you turn to the end, you will find three scorched pages. That is where the song used to be.*

With trembling fingers, I touched the blackened stubs. "And there is no other way to destroy the Shadowgrims?"

None that I know, the grimoire said blithely. *And if I do not know, then no one does. But do not fret. It is no great loss. You will find the Shadowgrims quite useful, once I teach you how to understand them.*

Half blinded by the grimoire's blazing light, I could see the room only as if through the wavering heat of a fire. But even so, the agony on Nat's face made my stomach wrench.

"But they are hurting Nat!"

The grimoire rejected this. *The boy does not suffer, not in any permanent way. At this moment, he feels the power of the Shadowgrims. But it is only at your command that the Shadowgrims will attack. If you spare him that, he will be sound of mind once he leaves here.*

"Of course I will spare him," I said, horrified.

There is no "of course" about it, the grimoire snapped. *You call him your friend, but can you truly trust him?*

"He helped me," I said. "I would never have reached this room without him."

And he did this selflessly, without hope of gain? Or did he want something from you?

"He only wanted me to destroy the Shadowgrims."

And very good that would have been for him. But what good would it have done you?

"It is what I came here to do," I told the grimoire.

No. You came here to claim your old power. The grimoire sounded very sure of itself. *And it is well and good that you did so. The Ravens' Own would die to protect you now; they will do your bidding, no matter what you ask of them. But how long do you think that would last if you did not have the Shadowgrims? They would turn on you in an instant. Everyone in this room would.*

"Not Nat," I said.

Look into his heart if you do not believe me, the grimoire urged. *Use the Shadowgrims.*

The raven clamor rose in my head, swirling with anger, revulsion, and hatred. They had things to tell me, wicked things . . .

"No!" I shouted. "I will not use the Shadowgrims."

The clamor in my head died away. But everyone around me remained motionless, and I still saw terror in their faces.

The grimoire was silent for a moment. *Very well, then. If you will not use the full powers of the Shadowgrims—at least not yet—there are other paths we can take. The Shadowgrims are the easiest, it is true, for they were sung into being long ago. But there are other powers that need only the merest word from you to live again: songs for plague and famine, songs of pestilence. Songs to conjure up creatures who will control others' thoughts, and—*

"I will not sing such songs. Not ever."

Not even if you are afraid? the grimoire asked softly.

Fear slammed into me—a deep, sickening fear that made my

heart lurch and my knees buckle. The flame of the grimoire leaped and whirled around me as I fought to stay standing, to breathe. . . .

A ripple of pleasure, almost like laughter, radiated from the grimoire. *There. I think that makes my point.*

As it spoke, the fear slackened. I unclenched my body and gulped at the sweet air.

A very effective means of control, fear, the grimoire mused. *It worked well with Scargrave, too.*

For the first time ever, I felt a flash of compassion for the Lord Protector. Had the grimoire tortured him like this too?

I could not reach him as well as I can reach you, however. And, of course, you have much more power. We will make good partners, you and I.

"No." I did not want the kind of partnership the grimoire had in mind.

You have no choice.

I clamped my hands on its pages. "I am your mistress."

Are you?

Terror battered me again, bending my body like a bow. Everything in the room seemed to writhe. Pleading, screaming, sobbing, weeping—the sound of fear came at me from every direction, even from the grimoire itself.

Yes, even the grimoire.

Suddenly my own fear diminished. "You are frightened," I gasped.

No. I am never afraid.

But I was listening now with sudden hope. And in the

undertow of the throb of fear that racked the room, I heard at last what the grimoire wanted to obscure: a fleeting hint of a melody that would lead to its own destruction. And trilling high above it, the grimoire's great fear: that I would find this Wild Magic and use it.

Could I? Would I? Merely taking off my ruby to hear the song properly would be a terrible risk. And there was no guarantee that the song was the right one, or that it would work.

You wouldn't dare, the grimoire said quickly.

As it spoke, my fear of Wild Magic flared. How could I even be thinking of this? My ruby was my key to safety: What if I lost it forever?

But if fear almost stopped me, it also showed me the way forward: For why would the grimoire be so frightened unless it thought I could succeed?

Wrenching a hand free from the grimoire, I pulled off the ruby. As it fell onto the open pages of the grimoire, a fearful music enveloped me like a great wind. A thousand perverse melodies howled in my ear, desperate for me to sing them. But I plunged down and found the song I was looking for, tolling like a dirge beneath the others: the song that would destroy the grimoire.

As I let it sink into my mind, the full force of the grimoire's rage came barreling at me.

If you destroy me, you destroy yourself. The people in this room hate you. They will cut you down when I am gone.

I closed my eyes, wanting not to believe this, but achingly afraid it was true.

They are your enemies, all of them. The King—

"He has a good heart," I said weakly. "I could feel it when I was in his mind. He does not want to rule by fear."

He was raised to hate Chantresses. He was raised to hunt and kill them. If you do not have my powers, he will hunt and kill you.

A tremor ran through me. Was the grimoire right?

And those men who helped you, that so-called college—do you think they trust you? Do you think they admire you? Oh no. If they could, they would dissect you like an insect and take your magic from you. Even the boy Nat. He hates magic; he told you so. Which means he hates you. They are clever men, he and his companions. To control them will require all our power.

The world seemed to spin before me. Was the grimoire crazy for suspecting Nat and his friends? Or was I the crazy one, for trusting them?

Nothing is safe.

No one can be trusted.

Destroy me, and you will die.

Overcome by fear, I sank to my knees, clutching the grimoire. Dimly I remembered that I had found a song that would destroy it. But that made no sense. Why would I destroy the one thing in all the world that could keep me safe?

And then, beyond the fire of the grimoire, I caught a glimpse of Nat's hands. The hands that had brought me through the Raven Pit. The hands that had saved me. The hands that had pulled me into his mind and sheltered me there and given me strength . . .

My head cleared.

Nat did not hate me.

Which meant the grimoire was telling lies to save itself. While my mind was still clear, I must try to put an end to it in the only way I knew how.

Destroy me, and you destroy your own stone, the grimoire hissed. *You will never be safe again.*

My breath caught. Was this the truth? Perhaps. But there was another truth the grimoire was trying to hide from me: that some kinds of safety were not worth having.

Without waiting any longer, I plunged into song.

It was like diving down to the ocean depths. I clung to the notes, following the cool, dark line of the magic. And as I sang, I could feel the white heat of the grimoire fighting me.

Do not destroy me. Do not destroy us both.

The song drew on everything inside me—my hopes, my strength, my full self. Alongside my fear and my desperation, I felt a rising exhilaration. Whatever it might cost me, this kind of wild singing felt powerful and true and right. It was what I was born to do.

No, the grimoire wailed.

I sang on, and after a time, the wail died away. The grimoire was weakening. Colder and colder it became, till I felt as if I were holding not a book but a block of ice.

Only when the song curved toward its end did the grimoire speak again, this time in a whisper:

Do not sing me into darkness.

As I sang out the very last note, long and deep, the book turned clear and brittle; my stone slid from its pages, glowing like pure fire. The Shadowgrims quieted, their power ebbing. To my shock, one man was strong enough to break free of them: Scargrave.

He lunged—not at me but at the grimoire. Was it fear that drove him? Greed? Perhaps even grief? Whatever it was, it was his undoing. When he touched the grimoire, it shattered like ice, taking him with it. For an instant, tiny, glittering shards hung in the air like silver stars, before vanishing like snowflakes in summer.

The ravens' whispers ceased.

CHAPTER THIRTY-NINE

THE RECKONING

Dazed, I saw Nat look at me, the dreadful agony on his face replaced by confused joy. Behind him, the Ravens' Own dropped their swords and blinked their eyes as if seeing the world anew. But it was the King who appeared most transformed. His air of anxiety and fretfulness vanished, leaving him looking amiable, bewildered, and a little bit shy.

The grimoire had said that the King hated Chantresses, but he did not appear—I thought—as if he hated me. I scooped up my stone. Its chain was mangled, but the stone itself seemed intact. Had the grimoire lied about this, too? Another tiny crack was all I could see, surely not a fatal flaw. Rejoicing, I set the ruby back into its place over my heart.

"Come and see, Your Majesty!" One of the Ravens' Own, standing at the Raven Pit door, waved jubilantly. "They're ravens now— just ravens."

King Henry blinked and turned to me for confirmation. "The Shadowgrims are gone?"

"Yes," I told him. "Gone for good."

"And Lord Scargrave? He is gone too?"

"I believe so."

Sorrow and relief warred in his face. And then, hesitantly, he asked me, "Am I still King?"

From his look of awe, I ought to have known immediately what he was thinking, but it took me a moment to piece it together.

"Yes, Your Majesty," I said gently. "You are King. I have no desire to rule. I wish only to live in peace."

He received this in silence. Did he understand that I was not a threat?

As I stood there, wondering how to reassure him, two soldiers ran in, boots and armor clattering. When they saw me, they drew their swords. "The Chantress!"

Henry's own sword flashed. "Touch one hair of her head, and I shall have your own heads for it."

The soldiers dropped their weapons.

"She is beyond reproach," the King told them. "She has done what no one else could do: She has freed us from the Shadow-grims." To me, he added, "My father used to say that if anyone is to be trusted, it is not the person who seizes power. It is the person who turns it down."

I drew a breath of relief. It seemed I had been right to trust in his good intentions.

Raising his voice in full regal formality, the King announced,

"This lady has our gratitude—and be assured that she enjoys our royal favor and protection." Less certainly, he added to me, "If you have need of it, that is."

Behind the King, Nat stirred. I knew what was on his mind, for it was also on mine. "Your Majesty, what I most need right now is help for a friend who lies injured in the Feeding Room—"

"Guardsmen, see to it that the Chantress has every form of aid she desires," King Henry commanded. "Food, drink, surgeons: whatever she requires."

With Nat at my side, I went to the Raven Pit door. The ravens were clicking and cawing, a softer sound than I had ever heard from them, a sound without malice.

They are only birds, Nat had said. Only birds. And now it was true.

I walked past their beating wings without fear.

† † †

The next hour was a busy one. Never had anyone had so many doctors at his bedside as Penebrygg did. The guards carried him by stretcher to a luxurious chamber upstairs, where he quickly regained consciousness, to my great relief. Even so, the doctors kept taking his pulse and checking his eyes and examining the purple lump on his head. At last, however, the Royal Physician pronounced himself optimistic. "Your man has a broken ankle as well as a broken head," he cautioned us, "and he'll need rest and care. But in the end, there's no reason why he shouldn't make a full recovery."

A page careered into the room and planted himself in front of me. "The King salutes the Lady Chantress, and would she please join him in the Great Hall, on a matter of urgency."

What could it be? Fearful of renewed trouble, I excused myself and followed the page to a grand room, where I found the King in conversation with Sir Barnaby.

"A proclamation has already gone out, announcing the end of the Shadowgrims and the Protectorate," the King was saying. "And we'll want to restore Parliament as soon as possible."

"Wonderful!" Sir Barnaby looked as if he were about to dance a jig, cane and all.

"Lucy!" From the other side of the room, Norrie rushed forward and enveloped me in a terrific hug. "My lamb. You're safe. Oh, thank Providence, you're safe."

"More than safe, madam," a deep voice behind us said. "Indeed, Miss Marlowe has saved us all."

I looked up and saw Oldville regarding me with warm approval for the first time. At his side, Samuel Deeps bobbed up and down in fine array, a huge grin on his face. He started a chorus of loud huzzahs, backed by Christopher Linnet and others of the Invisible College, all of them jubilant.

"Come up to the roof," the King urged me.

"Oh yes," Norrie said. "Oh, Lucy, you must see."

"See what?" I asked.

She wouldn't tell me, nor would the King or any of the others. Mystified, I followed them up to the top of the White Tower, and only when I gazed down from the parapet did I understand.

"Lights!" I whispered. "Oh, look at them."

It was night, and yet all across London the lights blazed: lights in churches, lights in taverns, lights in homes. I saw what looked to be great bonfires in the parks, and yet more blazes on the hills above and beyond the city walls. Even on the River Thames, hundreds of small lanterns glowed and bobbed, illuminating the ferries and barges and boats that carried them.

"They're celebrating," Norrie told me. "We came through the streets on the way here, Lucy, and you should have seen it. They're all out celebrating the end of the Shadowgrims."

I clutched at her hand. "Norrie, Lady Helaine—"

I couldn't say the rest: how she'd died, how I'd held her cold hand, how my kerchief had floated down over her face before the guards had carried her out.

"I know," Norrie said. "I'm so sorry—for you and for her. But look out there, Lucy: Look at what you've done. You've freed a kingdom. She would be so proud of you."

Maybe not, I thought. Yet as I gazed out over the shining city, I was comforted all the same.

"Listen," Norrie called out to everyone.

The crowd on the roof went quiet. And then I heard it, out there in the city: music drifting up to the stars.

"They're *singing*," I said.

"Singing for joy." Norrie hugged me. "There, now, aren't you proud?"

† † †

I spent the next few days in the Tower—not as a prisoner, this time, but as the King's most favored guest. A fortunate post, I knew, and yet it turned out to be a burdensome one too, for he wanted me at hand as he set the kingdom to rights. When I wasn't with him, I spent most of my time besieged by courtiers. I hardly saw Nat. But finally, on the fourth night, we had a moment alone, as we kept vigil together in Penebrygg's room.

"How was he today?" I asked.

"The physicians say he's out of danger." Nat watched Penebrygg's face, now slack with sleep. "Of course, his head still aches, and the ankle will take weeks to knit together. But he talked like his old self for much of the afternoon."

"Thank heaven," I said.

"And your godmother?" he asked.

"Her funeral is tomorrow." It hurt me to think of it, not only because Lady Helaine was gone but also because I was still shaken by how she had lied to me. Yet I wanted to honor her anyway. For better or worse, she had helped shape me, and she had been right about more things than I cared to admit. "We've kept it very quiet. I'm not expecting many mourners."

"If you want me there, I'll come," Nat said.

I looked at him in surprise.

"You shouldn't be alone," he said.

"You're very kind," I said slowly. "But I think I need to go by myself." I was struggling with so much that I felt too shaky for company, even—or was that especially?—if it came from Nat.

"I understand," Nat said, though his eyes said he didn't quite.

The silence between us was becoming fraught. I stood up to go, then leaned over to smooth Penebrygg's blankets.

Nat looked at me, startled. "Your stone!"

The necklace had escaped my bodice, and the ruby was dangling free. I flushed in mortification. I hadn't wanted anyone to see it so close, especially Nat, who was too keen-eyed for comfort.

"It doesn't shine anymore," he said.

"Please don't speak of it," I begged as I slipped it out of sight. "Not to anyone."

"But why—?" I saw the truth dawn on him. "It's broken?"

"Shhhhh!!! No one must know."

My enemies were not so numerous as Lady Helaine had feared, or as powerful, but over the past few days, I had learned they did indeed exist. Some noblemen were unhappy with the King's plan to restore Parliament and other longstanding freedoms, and they blamed his liberality on me. Other courtiers simply disliked magic workers on principle. Believing me to be powerful, they did not attack me openly. But that would change if they learned how weak I really was.

I'd been so sure that the grimoire had lied about destroying my ruby. One small crack—that's all I'd noticed at first. But later that night, as exultation ebbed into exhaustion, I'd realized the weight felt wrong; somehow the stone had become as light as a shell. Taking it out for closer inspection, I'd seen to my horror that the grimoire had told me the truth: The crack, though small, went straight to the ruby's heart. The stone's magic had leaked away, and its light was gone. Now it was as clouded and opaque as Lady Helaine's stone had been.

To forestall awkward questions, perhaps I should have accepted the jewels the King had offered me, and worn one of his rubies on my chain instead; there had been one of about the right size. But no doubt Nat would have seen through the subterfuge anyway. And cracked or not, my own stone was still all I had left from my mother. Though it no longer had any power, I could not bear to set it aside. The best I could do was try to keep it hidden—a strategy that had worked until now.

Nat lowered his voice but did not drop the subject. "Are you saying you can't do Proven Magic anymore?"

"It's worse than that." I hadn't meant to say anything, but something in me needed to tell him the truth. "I can't even do Wild Magic."

"What?"

"Ever since I destroyed the grimoire, I can't hear a single note."

Whether I had the stone off or on, it was the same: utter silence. After four days without music, I was terrified that it was gone forever.

And the worst of it was that I didn't even understand why. Both Lady Helaine and the grimoire had warned me about losing my stone, and with it my ability to work Proven Magic. But no one had ever said that I might lose my ear for Wild Magic, too. And yet that's what had happened.

Wild Magic will betray you when you least expect it. Wasn't that what Lady Helaine had told me?

"You can't hear anything?" Nat asked.

"Not even from the moonbriar."

I saw consternation cross Nat's face, and then relief. "You mean, you're just like the rest of us now?"

Was he *glad* I had lost my magic?

I stared at him in dismay. "Nat, I've lost everything. My birthright, my craft, everything I've worked toward, every way of protecting myself—"

"I'll protect you," he interrupted.

"I want to protect myself."

In the silence that followed, I stared at him, suddenly and shatteringly aware of the gulf that lay between us. I had thought myself closer to him than to any other human being. Yet he could not understand me, nor could he accept who I truly was. I felt broken, but to him I was better with my magic gone.

The blow left me almost breathless. "I need to go," I said thickly. *I will not cry in front of him.* I rose and backed toward the door. "Swear to me you will tell no one about this."

"I swear. Lucy—"

"No." I could barely get the words out. "We will say nothing more. No good can come of it."

Before he could stop me, I slipped from the room, too upset to say good-bye.

CHAPTER FORTY
NEW SONGS

Three months later, I sat by the sea, cross-legged and single-minded, watching the tide come in.

It was a lonely stretch of coast, this place that the King had granted me. He had wanted to give me something much grander: a London palace, or a magnificent country estate. But what I had wanted was a refuge. Aside from the King, very few people knew that we were still in England, let alone exactly where we had settled. Norrie and I lived here in seclusion; we had not seen another soul for weeks.

"Lucy! Where are you?" Norrie called out.

I turned and saw her scuffling across the sand. I waved, and she headed toward me.

Our time by the sea had done Norrie good. After many weeks in the fresh air and clear light, she was almost back to her old self. Which was mostly good news, except that she had taken to watching over me like a hen with a single woebegone chick.

Her one distraction was her garden, where she had been digging when I slipped away.

"Lucy, dear, have you been here the whole morning?" She stood before me, her face ruddy with sun. "You're driving yourself too hard, really you are."

"I have to keep trying," I said. "And this is where I hear it best."

"But—"

I put my finger to my lips. "Shh! There it is again."

Norrie went quiet as I leaned into the wind. I almost had it, almost . . .

No.

"Did you get it?" Norrie asked.

"Not quite." I did my best to keep my voice even and bright. Norrie worried about me enough as it was; it wasn't fair to make her worry even more.

"Well, there's always tomorrow," Norrie said. "You don't want to go too far, too fast, do you?"

I winced. She meant well, but it was like salt water in a wound. "No danger of that."

Two songs. That was all I had. Two songs in three months. And both of them quite paltry, one for making tidal pools ripple and another for draining them away.

You should be thankful even for that, I told myself. We had been here a full six weeks before I'd heard the first delicate notes on the air. My initial reaction had been disbelief. After that, fear. Would Wild Magic lead me to my death, as Lady Helaine had predicted?

But then I remembered my mother. Wild Magic had kept

her safe for many years. Wild Magic had helped her protect me. Yes, there were dangers in it, as I knew only too well. But it had unquestionable power, and it had saved me from the grimoire. And with my stone destroyed, it was the only way open to me.

So I let myself listen, and then, once I was sure of myself, to sing. A fortnight ago, I had unraveled my first song-spell. The second had come to me yesterday. I was here today hoping for a third.

But my progress was achingly slow.

I wished that I had my mother to advise me. Instead, I only had Norrie, who tolerated my magic but did not understand it. For all intents and purposes, I was on my own.

"Lucy, did you hear me?"

"Sorry, Norrie. What did you say?"

Norrie looked down at me, concern in her eyes. "I said you should come back to the cottage with me—"

"Not yet, Norrie." I turned back to the sea. If I concentrated with my whole might, I could hear the faintest of melodies coming from the whitecaps, a melody quite distinct from the occasional murky notes coming from the depths.

"But we have a visitor," Norrie said with suppressed excitement.

I swerved around in dismay. "No one's supposed to know where we are."

"This one knows," Norrie said, unruffled. "He had it from the King himself. Young Nat." She smiled. Ever since Nat had guided her through the tunnel, he could do no wrong in her eyes. The fact that he had helped save me had only confirmed his worthiness. A lad in a thousand, she called him. A treasure. And she had worried when we hadn't heard from him.

"Nat?" I scrambled up from the rock. "He's here?"

"I thought that you'd be pleased," Norrie said, taking my arm as we took the path to the cottage.

I nodded, but what I felt was far more complicated than pleasure. I had not seen Nat since that last night in the Tower. Penebrygg had soon recovered enough to return home, and I had visited him there during my last days in London. But Nat was always out when I called. I guessed he was deliberately keeping away.

We would never be able to bridge the differences between us. That was the problem. If I hadn't cared so much about my magic—and if he hadn't hated magic so much—then perhaps we would still be close. But we were who we were, and that was the end of it. His very avoidance of me confirmed it.

I told myself it was his loss. But it felt like mine. Not a day went by that I didn't think of him, of the rapport we'd once shared, of the revelation of seeing myself through his eyes.

And now he was here. Why? What did it mean?

Apprehensive, I approached the cottage. As we came close, I saw Nat standing in the garden, by the stone bench built into the wall. He looked older than I remembered, and taller, and he greeted us with a courtly courtesy that took me aback.

"I know you said you weren't hungry, Nat," Norrie said. "But you must be famished after that journey. I'll fetch you something from the kitchen."

"No need," he said, but she was already gone, leaving the two of us alone in the garden.

"Did the King send you here?" I asked. Henry had said he would send a messenger if he thought I was in danger, or if he had need of me.

"The King? No. I came on my own, as soon as I could."

As soon as he could? It had been three months. "You've been very busy, then?"

"That's one way of putting it," Nat said. "I've spent the past fourteen weeks shut up in Ravendon House."

So he hadn't been trying to avoid me, after all. "Why on earth—?"

"Scargrave's papers," he said. "Room upon room of them. The King thought they might involve the defense of the realm, so he wanted them investigated speedily and in secret—and he put me on the committee to help."

"Why you?" I asked, before thinking how it would sound. Flustered, I added, "I mean, I'm sure there's none better—"

"Oh, hundreds better, I'm sure." He grinned. "But it was Sir Barnaby who recommended me. You know he's the Lord Chancellor now?"

I nodded. The appointment had been made while I was still a guest in the Tower.

"He suggested to the King that I could help, and I agreed before I quite understood the conditions. It turned out we had to live there under guard, and we couldn't communicate with a soul while we were there. I couldn't even tell Penebrygg where I was going."

"How awful."

"Well, it's good to be free again, I can tell you. And I could live without seeing another file."

"What did you find in them?" I asked.

"Confessions, mostly," Nat said somberly. "Drawn from his victims. Thousands and thousands of them down in the crypt."

"You read them all?" I asked.

"Enough to know what they were."

"And where are they now?"

Nat looked up at the clouds. "Funny you should ask that. Some of the King's advisers wanted to keep them on file, in case of future unrest. But someone broke into the crypt and set fire to the place. Nothing else burned—the crypt is stone, and quite separate from the rest of the house—but every single one of those confessions is gone."

I gave Nat the ghost of a smile. "And they have no idea who did it?"

"None," Nat said with an answering smile. "Luckily, the King didn't seem overly dismayed to have lost the papers, and he wasn't inclined to make further investigations, so we were allowed to leave last week. I've been on the road ever since."

"You mean, you came straight here?" I said, amazed.

"Well, I went back to check on Penebrygg first. He's doing well; his head hardly ever pains him now. And after that, I was off. I thought it would take five days, but I made it in four."

"If you've been on the road for four days, you *must* be famished." I glanced back at the cottage. Norrie was taking a very long time about the food.

"I'm fine. But I'm tired of talking about me," Nat said. "What I want to know about is you."

"What exactly do you want to know?"

"Everything."

"I'm well enough, thank you," I said warily. "It's good to be by the sea again."

"And your magic?"

"Why do you ask?" The question was too sharp, my voice too defensive.

"Is *that* what's wrong?"

I looked away. "What makes you think something is wrong?"

"The look on your face," he said. "The way you stand. Everything about you."

It seemed Nat didn't need magic to read me. I couldn't speak.

"Lucy, what is it? Can you still not hear any music?" His voice was tense, as if too much hung on my answer. Was he hoping, then, that my magic was gone for good?

If he was, then I would have to disappoint him. "I can hear enough to do a bit of magic. In time I hope to do more. But it's a start."

"I'm glad," he said.

His polite rejoinder was the last straw. Surely, after all we'd been through, we owed each other a little more honesty.

I turned away from him. "Don't say that. Not when you don't mean it. You never liked my magic; you've been clear enough about that. You'd probably be glad if every scrap of it went."

"No," he said. "No more than you'd celebrate if I could no longer do science."

I looked back at him, not sure I'd heard right. "But you hate magic—"

"I can change my mind, can't I?" he said. "I used to hate magic, yes. I thought no one with magic could be trusted. But when you destroyed that grimoire, you proved yourself as steadfast as anyone alive. I'd trust you anywhere, with or without magic. Though I hope for your sake it's *with*."

I stared at him, astonished.

"What you said about having a gift, a craft, and being allowed to explore it: That struck home," he said. "That's what I want for myself. Why shouldn't I want it for you?"

I stood very still.

"I really mean it." He reached inside his coat and pulled out a parchment packet. "Here's proof."

Mystified, I took the packet. Inside I found sheets of paper with familiar handwriting:

For my daughter, Lucy . . .

"My mother's letter," I whispered. "Where did you find it?"

"In the secret passage at Ravendon House. I didn't say anything about it to the King's advisers. I was afraid they'd lock it away if I did. And I thought you ought to have it."

I sat down on the stone bench and studied the letter. Even in bright sunlight, the water-splotched pages were impossible to read. But when I held them close, I heard a fragile thread of melody spiral out from them, a tune sung in my mother's own sweet voice, every note soft but clear. As I joined in, the handwriting began to darken, and I could read passages that had eluded me before:

My daughter, you are very dear to me—and would be even if you had no magic at all. But since I must leave you here, perhaps for a very long time, it is a comfort that you have the gift of Wild Magic. I can hear it in you already, even though you are so small, and I believe it to be even stronger than my own. . . .

Do not be afraid. There is much said about Wild Magic that is not true, and there are more ways of protecting yourself than anyone guesses. . . .

I could hear my mother's voice clearly, almost feel her arms embracing me. The pages trembled in my hand.

There will be times when your ability to do Wild Magic is compromised; this happens sometimes after illness or turmoil. Indeed, after you have worked a very great feat of magic, your gift may even appear to vanish altogether. I know myself how distressing this can be, but do not fear: The magic is inside you still, dearest daughter, and with time and rest, it will return. . . .

There was more, but my eyes were too blurred with tears to continue. I folded the letter and held it close, yearning for the mother who had reached across time to comfort me.

"Thank you," I said, looking up at Nat. "Thank you with all my heart. You don't know what this means to me."

"I can guess."

I rose from the bench. The bond between us was so strong I could almost hear it humming in the air.

"Nat?"

He looked at me then, his gaze quiet and clear. He looked at me with liking and respect and kindness, and perhaps something more. . . .

Oh! What wouldn't I give to be able to read his mind again, just long enough to know what he truly thought of me now?

But that was beyond me, at least for the time being. And perhaps that was just as well. Some secrets shouldn't be forced. I needed to be patient, letting the future unfold in its own time and its own way.

I began to pull back, but Nat leaned forward. With the fiercest look I'd seen from him yet, he curved his hand against my cheek and gently kissed me.

The humming in my head burst into full song.

As I stepped back from him, Norrie called to us from the cottage door. "Nat? Lucy? Are you still out there? I've set us a table in here. You need a proper meal, Nat. And you could do with one too, Lucy."

Nat offered me his hand. I took it.

"We're coming," I called. We walked up to the house together, and my heart sang all the way.

AUTHOR'S NOTE

How much history is in this historical fantasy?

A fair amount, as it happens.

Chantress, for example, is a real word, and you really can find it in the *Oxford English Dictionary*. Penebrygg's statements about its derivation are correct.

Although the story takes place in 1667–1668, London's geography is more or less as it would have been before the Great Fire of 1666 (which hasn't happened in *Chantress*'s world). Furnishings, clothing, and food are in keeping with what was available in the period, depending on the various characters' positions and circumstances.

The Great Devastation owes something to Guy Fawkes's failed Gunpowder Plot (1605).

In real life, King Charles I was much like the "tyrant" Nat describes. In our world, he lost both his crown and his head in the English Civil War and its aftermath. In *Chantress*, he manages to subdue his enemies before war breaks out, only to be killed along with his court in the Great Devastation. His successor is King Henry IX, Henry Seymour. In the real world, an older Henry Seymour was, in fact, a distant claimant to the throne, a descendant of the Tudor line.

Nat's microscope would have been a new, unusual, and very high-tech device at the time. The remark about fleas looking as big as lambs comes from a comment by Galileo, who built some of the earliest microscopes.

There really was an Invisible College, a loose association of mathematicians, alchemists, and natural philosophers who were active in the 1640s and 1650s; historians debate the exact nature of the organization and its membership. In 1660, under Charles II, some Invisible College members were involved in founding the Royal Society of London for Improving Natural Knowledge, now known simply as the Royal Society. My Invisible College engages in many of the same activities as its prototype, but with an extra helping of danger, intrigue, and magic. The astute observer may notice a certain uncanny resemblance of characters in my IC to those who belonged to the real-life IC and Royal Society.

The alchemy and firebox experiments that Nat mentions to Lucy are very much in line with the kind of phenomena the Invisible College and Royal Society liked to investigate. Nat's firebox would have been one of the earliest cast-iron stoves, which only became common in the eighteenth century.

The Tower of London is essentially like its real-life counterpart, although there have been certain alterations made to it under Scargrave, in part because of the Shadowgrims.

Legend has it that there have been ravens at the Tower for centuries, though hard evidence suggests they may date only to the nineteenth century. The legend, however, has stolen the show, maybe because of the birds' sheer presence. Enormous, clever, and bold, they strut on Tower Green as if they owned it. I first encountered them years ago, and they've haunted me ever since.

ACKNOWLEDGMENTS

I began this book in 2006 in a Massachusetts coffee shop. Almost six years later, I finished the last draft in my new home in England. During that time, I moved countries, had a child, nearly died, inched back to life—and somehow held on to this story, even if sometimes by a thread. In truth, it often seemed as if the story were holding on to me. Without the help of others, however, I'm not sure I could have seen it through.

I owe an especially great debt to Kit Sturtevant and Nancy Werlin, two remarkable writers who sustained me through the whole journey, encouraging me in the doldrums and offering helpful comments when I finally dared show them the manuscript. I am hugely grateful, too, to the other wonderful writers who critiqued the manuscript in full—Kristina Cliff-Evans, Amanda Jenkins, Teri Terry, and Jo Wyton—and to those who read draft chapters: Nick Cross, Paula Harrison, Tina Lemon, Penny Schenk, Nicki Thornton, Jan Carr, Philippa Francis, George Kirk, Lois Peterson, Joyce Taylor, Stephanie Burgis, and the SCBWI-BI 11+ Fantasy E-group.

My thanks to many others who cheered me along the way, among them Cathy Atkins, Jeannine Atkins, Kathi Fisler, Shirley Harazin, Lisa Harkrader, Cynthia Lord, Kirsty Luff, Amy McAuley, Mary Novack, Mary Pearson, Marlene Perez, Samantha Scolamiero, Jenny Turner, Laura Weiss,

Sue Williams, Melissa Wyatt, and the generous LiveJournal, YAWriter, and SCBWI communities. I am deeply grateful to Ada Jiménez and Kathy MacGregor, who took loving care of my daughter, allowing me some hours to write. I also extend profound thanks to the health professionals who helped me in dark times and to blood donors everywhere.

It's my good fortune to have the smart and thoughtful Julie Just of Janklow & Nesbit as my agent; it's a delight to work with her. My thanks as well to the rest of "Team Chantress," marvelous women all: Tina Bennett, Svetlana Katz, and Stephanie Koven.

My editor, Karen Wojtyla, sees to the heart of things; it's an honor, a challenge, and a pleasure to be edited by her. At Simon & Schuster, I'm also grateful for the help of Justin Chanda, Paul Crichton, Michael McCartney, Emily Fabre, Annie Nybo, Bridget Madsen, and everyone who has looked after *Chantress* so well. I appreciate Jen Strada's careful copyediting too.

I send loving thanks to my family, who've helped in ways large and small: Barbara and Crispin Butler; Pat and Bert Greenfield; Steve and Sabine; Jon, Valerie, Sofia, Carlo, and Vivian; Stephen, Sarah, Ruth, and Grace.

Above all, I want to thank my husband, David—co-conspirator, reader extraordinaire, and steadfast friend—and my beautiful, brave daughter. You bring music and magic to all my days.

CONTINUE LUCY'S STORY IN
CHANTRESS ALCHEMY.

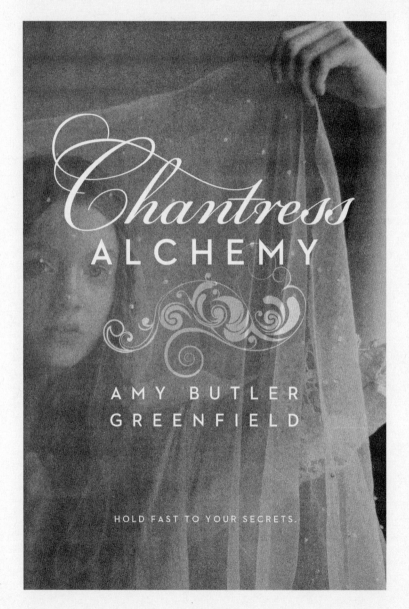

Chantress
ALCHEMY

AMY BUTLER
GREENFIELD

HOLD FAST TO YOUR SECRETS.

CHAPTER ONE
A SONG FROM THE SEA

One more spell, that's all I meant to sing. One more song-spell, and then I'd go home.

I blew on my icy fingers and faced the wintery sea. I'd been out for hours, honing my magic, and the sun had long since vanished behind sullen clouds. My boots were damp from the froth of the ocean, my cheeks wet with its salty spray. The wind sawed along my very bones. I thought with longing of the snug cottage I shared with Norrie and the soup that would no doubt be simmering on the fire.

Something easy to finish on, I promised myself. *Something that won't go wrong.*

Clutching my woolen cape, I tilted my ear toward the ocean and its tangle of watery music. A simple song-spell, that's all I needed. . . .

But what was that sound? That distant humming?

Forgetting my frozen hands and feet, I listened, perplexed.

No one knew better than I that the ocean could sing a thousand songs: music to cradle me, music to drown me, music to call up waves and tides and storms. I was a Chantress, after all. Yet this wasn't a tune I had heard before. Indeed, its faint thrum was quite unlike any melody I knew. That alone was disturbing.

"Lucy!"

A woolen bundle clumped toward me: Norrie in her winter wraps. The wind snatched at her hood and cap, and her silver hair stood out like dandelion fluff around her wrinkled face.

"You've been out here too long," she called. "You'll catch your death of cold."

I was about to reply when I heard it again: a disquieting drone in the midst of the sea's other songs.

Norrie marched up to my side, her gait uneven. "Lucy, are you listening to me?"

"Yes," I said quickly. "Of course I am." But I was listening to the humming, too. If I concentrated hard enough, I usually could make out at least the gist of the sea's songs. Of all elements, water was the easiest for me to understand. Yet these notes held fast to their secrets.

"There's no *of course* about it." Norrie scrutinized my face. "Is something wrong?"

"No." Norrie might be my guardian, but I hated to worry her, especially when I had no clear idea what the trouble was. She wouldn't be able to hear the song anyway; only a Chantress could do that. "You shouldn't be out here, Norrie. Not on such a bitter day."

"Maybe not, but what else can I do when you won't come home?" Norrie said.

The elusive drone was fading now. I swung back toward the sea, trying to catch its last echoes.

Norrie kept after me. "You've been out here since dawn, Lucy. You need to come home now."

The drone was gone. What did it mean? "Just one more song, Norrie—"

"That's what you always say. And then you stay out, working till all hours, in all weathers—"

"But that's why we're here," I reminded her. "So I can work."

Nine months ago, I had freed England from a terrible enchantment, and as a reward King Henry the Ninth had offered me any gift in his possession. To my alarm, he'd talked of building me a palace. What I'd asked for instead was a secret refuge by the sea.

The King, bless him, had abandoned his palace scheme. Norrie and I now lived on a remote part of his estates in Norfolk, in a cottage just big enough for two. Almost no one in the kingdom knew where we were, and the King made sure we were left alone. Although his gamekeepers patrolled the outer limits of the estate, we never saw them. Every month we had supplies of food and fuel delivered to us, and occasionally the King's messenger came by. But that was all.

"Working's one thing. Toiling till you're skin and bone is another." The wind chafed Norrie's cheeks, turning them red. "You're seventeen and nearly grown, so I've tried to bite my tongue. But you're getting worse and worse, Lucy. We came here so you could rest, too. You've forgotten that part."

"I can't rest yet. Not until I've learned more magic."

"But you already know so much," Norrie protested.

"I know hardly anything."

"You knew enough to put an end to Scargrave and those horrible Shadowgrims," Norrie countered.

"At a cost. Don't you remember how bad it was when we came here? I had nothing. Not one single song." My hand went to my heart, where a bloodred stone nestled underneath my woolen scarves. The stone had once allowed me to work the safe song-spells of Proven Magic, but in battling against Scargrave and the Shadowgrims I had shattered its powers. Now the only enchantments open to me were the dangerous ones of Wild Magic.

A fraught path—and I had no one to teach me the way. Among Chantresses, Wild Magic was almost a lost art. Even before Scargrave had worked to destroy my kind, very few could have instructed me in it. Now there was no one. I was the only Chantress still living.

To guide me, I had only a letter my mother had written before her death years ago. Although it was replete with wise advice, it was not nearly as long or as detailed as I needed. Most of the time, I had to rely on my own instincts.

"Yes, that was a bad time," Norrie agreed. "But look at all you've learned since then. You can make the waves come when you call. You can sing water up from the ground. Heavens, child, you can even make it rain when you want to."

"Only for a minute or two, and only—"

Norrie rolled on, ignoring me. "That's more magic than most of us can dream of."

"It's not enough."

Norrie looked unconvinced.

How could I explain matters more clearly? My magic made Norrie nervous, so we rarely talked about it, but I could see I'd have to spell things out now.

"I'm good with water, yes—but not with anything else. I can kindle a flame, but I can't keep it burning. I almost never hear music from stones or earth or wind. I'm no good at making plants grow. Even the sea's songs don't always make sense to me. And when they don't make sense, they're dangerous. If I sing them, I could do harm to others. I could harm myself."

My cape snapped in the wind, and I stopped.

Norrie laid a mittened hand on mine. "Child, I know there are dangers, and of course I'm concerned about you. But I'm not sure you make yourself any safer by practicing till you're worn to a thread." She gripped my fingers through the wool. "Scargrave's gone now, Lucy. You've won the war. Yet you're still driving yourself as hard as you did when he was alive. Why not take things a bit easier?"

"And what if I have to defend myself? What do I do then?"

"Why should you need to defend yourself?" Norrie said. "The King would have the head of anyone who hurt you."

It was true: King Henry had sworn that the old days of Chantress hunting were over. Nevertheless I lived in terror that those days would begin again—and that I would not be ready. Night after night I dreamed hunters were coming after me, only to wake up alone in the dark loft, heart shuddering.

I was pushing myself too hard, that's what Norrie would say. But she was wrong. My nightmares didn't come from working too hard, but from the terrible truth of my situation. *The Chantress line is almost dead. We are hunted; we are prey.* So my godmother Lady Helaine had warned me before her own untimely end. To be a Chantress was to face enemies, for the world feared women with power.

"I'm glad the King wants to protect me," I told Norrie, "but I need to know I can protect myself. And my magic is too weak for that. It has too many holes. So I need to keep working. I need to make myself strong."

Norrie looked at me with a compassion that tightened my throat. "Oh, Lucy. You're strong already. Much stronger than you think. Can't you see?"

"But—"

She waved me away. "Let's not argue about it now. You're turning blue, and I'm not much better. Come home, and we'll talk about it in front of the fire."

I'm not cold, I wanted to say. But it wasn't true. And Norrie's lips were pinched as if she were in pain. *She's been out here too long*, I thought with concern. Her back and hips had been bothering her lately, especially on cold, damp days like this one.

"All right." I pulled up my hood. "We'll go home."

We had only just started trudging up the shore when a sharp

gust of wind swirled around us. It blew my hood back, and I heard the ocean humming again in its troubling new way. Had it been quiet all this time? Or had I just been too wrapped up in my wrangle with Norrie to hear it?

Hoping she wouldn't notice, I trained my attention on the drone, trying to understand it. With patience, I could usually unravel the basic meaning of a song, even if I couldn't fathom all its subtleties.

This time, though, the tune wouldn't yield. *More*, I pleaded.

As if to deny me, the strange song twisted in on itself and coiled into nothingness. But just before it vanished, I heard the meaning at the heart of it:

Danger.

The word slipped into my head as if the song itself had placed it there. I felt my unease grow.

"Wait here," I said to Norrie. "I'm just going up to the bluff to have a look around."

Before she could object, I ran up the steep bank that rose directly behind us. Reaching the crest, I looked up and down the coast, then out to the watery horizon. I saw no warships, no fishing boats, no vessels of any kind. Nothing met my eye but the endless wind-churned waves of the sea.

I turned my head in the other direction, to the rolling hills that sheltered our cottage, and the stretch of the King's wood beyond them. All was well.

And then, out by the wood, something moved.

A deer? No. A rider. And more behind him.

I sank behind the bluff's waving grasses and watched them emerge from the wood, one after the other. Half a regiment of mounted men, clad in armor and bearing spears.

Armed men, coming here in such great company?

Holding my breath, I shielded my eyes with a rigid hand as I looked out. They were riding straight for our cottage, the tips of their spears sharp against the gray sky.

Danger, the sea had said. Was this what it meant?

I skidded back down the bluff. "Norrie, quick! We need to run."

CASSANDRA CLARE'S

#1 *New York Times* Bestselling Series

THE MORTAL INSTRUMENTS & THE INFERNAL DEVICES

A thousand years ago, the Angel Raziel mixed his blood with the blood of men and created the race of the Nephilim. Human-angel hybrids, they walk among us, unseen but ever present, our invisible protectors.

They call themselves Shadowhunters.

Don't miss The Mortal Instruments: *City of Bones,* soon to be a major motion picture in theaters August 2013.

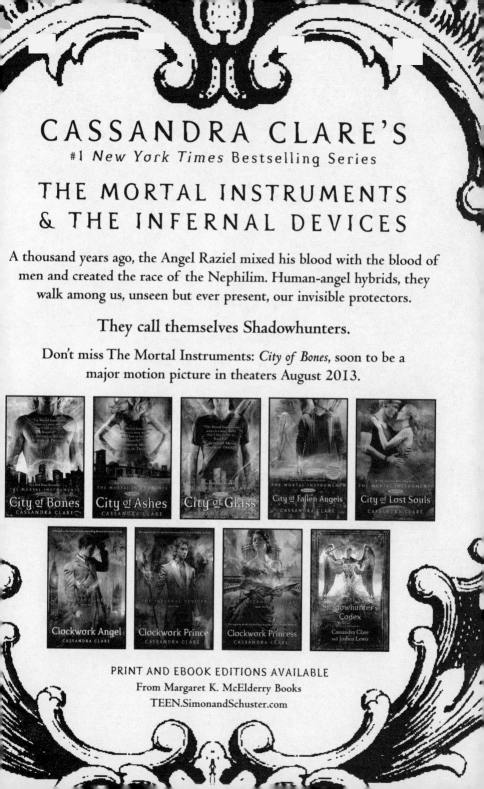

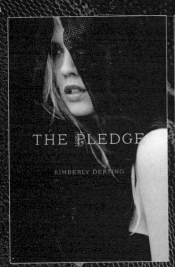

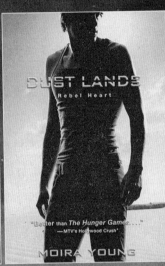